KU-327-456

S/10/20
Leabharlann na Cabraí
Cabra Library
Tel: 8691414

Withdrawn from Stock
Dublin City Public Libraries

Praise for *The Short Knife*

'A distinctive and engrossing tale'
David Almond

'A gorgeously written tale with a sublime lyricism to
it . . . the story resonates across the ages, holding a
mirror up to contemporary Britain'
Catherine Bruton

'This is an important and inspiring novel. Here is some
of the best contemporary UK YA that I've read for a
very, very long time. Elen is an exceptional voice and
talent in writing for young people'
Lucy Christopher

'I just loved *The Short Knife*. Beautifully written, lyrical
and powerful – it's a fascinating insight into dark and
desperate times which I found utterly absorbing. Grim
and gritty but ultimately uplifting – it's a beautiful
tribute to the courage and ingenuity of sisters'
Tanya Landman

'Elen Caldecott presents the sensory world of Late
Antique Britain – clothes, artefacts and precarious
lives – with compelling originality'
Caroline Lawrence

'As bright and real as the midsummer sunlight, and as
powerfully drawn as a sharp, short knife'
Hilary McKay

Young
Adult

THE
SHORT
KNIFE

ELEN CALDECOTT

ANDERSEN PRESS
LONDON

First published in 2020 by
Andersen Press Limited
20 Vauxhall Bridge Road
London SW1V 2SA
www.andersenpress.co.uk

2 4 6 8 10 9 7 5 3 1

All rights reserved. No part of this publication may be reproduced,
stored in a retrieval system or transmitted in any form, or by any
means, electronic, mechanical, photocopying, recording or
otherwise, without the written permission of the publisher.

The right of Elen Caldecott to be identified as the author of this
work has been asserted by her in accordance with the Copyright,
Designs and Patents Act, 1988.

Copyright © Elen Caldecott, 2020

British Library Cataloguing in Publication Data available.

ISBN 978 1 78344 979 8

Printed and bound in Great Britain by Clays Ltd, Elcograf S.p.A.

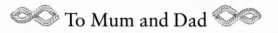 To Mum and Dad

Historical Note

For nearly 400 years, the Romans had ruled the people of Britain, making them part of the Empire that stretched from Syria to Scotland. But in 410AD, the army was recalled to defend Rome against the Visigoths. Without the army, civic life in Britain fell apart, towns were abandoned, trade was disrupted, coins lost their value. Saxons from northern Europe saw Britain in chaos, seized their opportunity, and sailed west.

1

SUMMER SOLSTICE, AD455,
WELL BEFORE DAWN.

I WALK BACK down the rabbit path alone. The stars
and pale moon show the way. And there is bonfire light
from the village. I don't think about what's burning.
My feet are grey on the rocks. I might be the only
person left in the whole world. It might belong to me.
Foolish thoughts. Childish thoughts. The hills are full
of hunters, even if I can't see them in the dark. My walk
quickens.

The village at the bottom is nearing empty. Still, as I
get closer to our barn, and hear moans, I wish my sister
would suffer with less noise. She is too loud. I want to
gag her mouth and push the sounds back down where
they come from. Safer that way. Safe is all that matters.

As I pull open the flapping leather door, I stop and
look back at the hill. The path is bone white in the
black before dawn. I see no people, no movement.
I stand on the threshold. It isn't too late to turn back.
To follow the path, if that's what I choose.

'Close that, Mai!' Sara snaps. 'Where have you been?
Get in here and help.'

Leabharlanna Poiblí Chathair Baile Átha Cliath
Dublin City Public Libraries

I drop the leather as though it burns. Sara has the fire banked low, but still she's right, the light might be seen from the path.

She is busy looking through pots and jars and baskets, things that don't belong to us, looking for anything that might help my sister. I hear her moan again.

If the men hear the sounds of labour, they'll know we are in here, light or not. It's dangerous to be in the midst of their notice.

'How much longer?' I ask Sara, who has seen babies born before. I've only seen Rat-cat have kittens, and they slid into the world easy.

She tuts at me: *soup-stupid girl,* the sound says. 'We're not ready for it, no hot water, no swaddling. Don't wish it to come any sooner.'

But I do wish it. I do.

The faster the baby comes, the safer we will be.

And if it comes too early to live, then maybe all the better.

The Welsh barn is dark and I hope Sara hasn't seen the thought on my face. I ask Iesu Grist the baby, his Father and the Ghost for forgiveness. This baby can't help being wild-chick born. I feel my cheeks pink in the dark.

My sister cries out. I can't see her from the doorway. She labours behind the sack curtain that Sara has

2

hung to hide her shame in case any of our people come back. Sara and I wait on the other side in blackness that drips from the roof like something living. The shapes of the barn, so familiar in daytime, are clob-clumsy shadows.

I'm glad, for the moment, that my sister can't see me. She would have seen the hate-filled thought written clear on me. She knows me better than she knows our own hearth.

'What can I do?' I ask Sara. 'I want to help.'

'The baby comes in its own time.' Sara presses her palms into the base of her back. The night has been hard on her bones. 'Sit still, Mai, stay shushed. Wait.'

I come away from the door and drop onto one of the stump-stools that circle the fire. Even with the leather pulled across and the thin smoke of the embers, I can smell the village. The sweet smell of burning meat that makes my teeth draw water and sickness rise in my throat.

'Don't think about what's happening out there,' Sara tells me. 'Or what's happening in here, either, truth be told.'

I sit and stare as the red and gold flames lick hot-tongued over charcoal, imagining what lies beyond the barn.

How can I not think about what I've seen? I can feel my heart, bird-trapped in my chest. Its wings desperate

to escape. The longer I sit, the worse it gets. The wait blisters my skin. What if I lose my sister tonight? After all I've lost? If that happens then I will welcome my own death. I would open my arms to it.

'Sit still,' Sara chides me.

I'm listening to her for now. But my obedience won't last.

My sister dog-pants in the dark.

Sara goes back beyond the sack curtain. I'm alone. Heart beat-beat-beating so there's no room for breath in my chest. No place in my bones not pulled bandage-tight. I press my fingers to my eyelids until I see green and red flashes.

In the smoking dark, I feel rage course through me suddenly. Anger at the panting and moaning and the awful, awful way this baby has come to be. Anger at the people free to flee into the hills. Anger at all the world and everyone in it. I want to open my mouth and let the fire out, burn it all into blackness.

But I'm not the child I was. I can't sit and wail in the dark. My anger is gone as quick as it came, burned to nothing, leaving me clean tired.

My sister needs me.

While she is as tethered as cows to their posts, so I'm tethered too.

I hear Sara making soothing noises. As if the baby were already here and loo-loo-listening to her song.

'Hush, child,' she whispers. 'Hush. There's work coming and you need your strength.'

It would be easy to run. I know that. I've done it before. But this time, I have chosen to stay. The baby will be here before the sun arcs the morning sky. If it lives, it will be my kin.

I've duty here.

I have to stay. I owe that to my sister, and all the mothers and sisters and aunts who came before me and made sure I was kept breathing. I'll try to keep it breathing. I will tell it the tales my tad told me. As much as I remember, anyway.

I wrap my arms about my knees in the darkness. And I plan the tale I will tell the infant, if it lives. If any of us live.

2

THE PREVIOUS AUTUMN, AD454

TROUBLE CAME WITH the frosts of dying autumn. Our farm lay too close to the road, Haf said, it brought nought but worry. Our father was different, Tad had been born in better times, when this land was ruled by far-off emperors. He remembered the tramping march of men, the Roman army plumed under eagles. He was full of stories of adventure and glory and great men, and gods born in stables.

Tad was up in the top field when the danger arrived. Three men. Only me and Rat-cat were there to watch them walk. I don't know where Haf had got to that day. Outside the hall, in the farmyard, me and the cat stood and I saw.

'Who's that, cat?' I whispered. The men made raucous calls as they strolled ling-di-long farmwards, swinging their walking sticks. 'Are they friend or foe?' I asked cat.

As they got close, I saw there was no real need of the question. No travellers who walked with such rolling ease could be friendly.

The beat of my blood quickened as they came closer.

Should I leave the farm empty while I ran up the hill to fetch Tad? Or stay, but let Tad delay untold? I was caught between the devil and his sty.

They were near our yard now. They wore flapping layers of brown, like corpse-bird feathers. Brown hair knotted and tangled atop nut-tanned skin. Mud men, I thought. Spawned in road ditches.

'*Boré da, bach!*' The man who led them spoke the correct greeting, but accented strangely; the sound that should have rolled was flat as floodplains. He had clearly learned the phrase in thick-tongued adulthood. Saxon.

I said nothing. The cat stalked away. I never saw her again.

'Have you food for strangers passing? Somewhere we will rest until the morning break?' He was bird-speckled with freckles. His smile too eager, his accent hard to grasp.

I've the wisdom of tomorrow now, and know that I shouldn't have said another word. I should have put my feet to the earth and run.

But in that moment, I did nothing.

They crossed the yard, coming closer. I had my back to the hall door. Behind the hall was the storage barn. To my right, the old byre, long since empty of cows, though still standing, built as it was with sweat and good Roman nails reused. I stood alone to guard it all, with only the useless short knife at my waist; it was meant for eating, cutting cheese and bread, no more.

Then, I heard my sister speak. *'Bore da, syr,'* Haf said. The 'syr' wholly ill, in my own opinion.

She'd come from the byre. I scowled at her. She hid sometimes, up there in the rafters, to get away from me, she said. But I knew it was to get away from the wife-work of the farm. She smiled as though she were five years older than me, not two, and was the woman of the house. Haf eased me aside as if I were planked wood. 'Don't mind Mai,' she said. 'The little mouse has no manners.'

Haf opened the door to the hall and let them, all three, step inside. Then, she poked me keenly. 'Check the barn is sealed. Then go fetch Tad.' Her voice was hare soft, 'I'll feed them what I can from what there is in the hall.'

My thoughts flew to the barn. It was the end of autumn and Tad had worked arm-and-shoulder to fill it for winter. There were dry roots in baskets and barley grains wrapped tight in their chaff to keep the damp out. There was smoked meat from whatever animals Tad had hunted. We'd eaten the purple patches of fresh leaves and there would be no more of that until late spring. Everything was packed tight to carry us through winter. It was ours. Our food. And Haf had smiled at these men and welcomed them in like Bathsheba did King David in the tall tales Tad told. But these men were no kings of the east. They were drain-ditch dunmen.

We should have run at them with swords.

8

There were no swords.

So I went to the barn. The bar was lowered and bolted. I shook it hard to check. If their eyes went prying, they could open it quick enough. But it wasn't flung open in invitation at least.

I galloped on wild hooves to the top field, my breath coming in white clouds. Tad was digging the earth over, ready for seeding. The thin copse of trees and the hill would hide the tall stalks, when the time came. But, for now, the black earth was bare. I was out of wind by the time I reached his side. 'Men,' I said, through gasps. 'Three men. At the hall.'

'What men?' Tad raised his eyes from the spade beneath his foot, his forehead as furrowed as the land.

'Saxons.' What else was there to say? Men where they shouldn't be.

I willed him hard to stop work and come. We needed him. Haf couldn't be left in charge.

He let go the spade. He was coming. He saw the threat was real.

We walked back, me behind. I could see sweat beading wetly at the base of his trimmed hair, turning the grey black. Did his own heart beat fast like mine?

'Mai,' Tad said, 'guests are always honoured, be they Saxon or Briton, or even wild scare-bods from the heath.'

'Be kind like the Samaritan,' I whispered.

'That's right. But it's more than that. Guests in your home should be protected and cared for, wherever they come from.'

I thought about the thick sticks I'd seen. 'What if they aren't guests, Tad?'

'Do you think they might be wise men disguised as travellers? Elias or Job or one of the old prophets from the desert kingdoms come to test us. Hmm? Is that what you're thinking?' I could hear the smile in his voice.

That was not what I was thinking. 'They aren't prophets, sure certain.'

'Well, we won't know what they are until they tell us. Come on.'

As we dropped down from the hill, the stone footings of the hall looked cave-damp and cold. The wooden slats that rose from the low walls were shadowed under the eaves. The byre and barn were silent. Only smoke curling from the thatch-hole in the hall roof showed that there was anyone inside alive.

Tad didn't speak, so neither did I.

Soon, we heard them from the hall, voices crackling like fire. They spoke their own tongue together. Saxon. To my ears it sounded like half-swallowed song, with nothing to mark the edges of words.

'*Dasmädchen – ja – istschön.*'

'*Ja!*'

'*Derhof – ja – iswunderschön.*'

I tried out the sounds: *Wunderschoen. Wun derschoen. Wunders choen.*

I wondered what it meant.

The sounds were spells, making me see scented

Woods, dew-wet, where Woden walked.

Thick-pelted boar, blind hunted,

By men like these.

Tad held me back. 'It might be best if you stay out of sight. Just for now. While I go and find out if they really are prophets.' He winked, and squeezed my shoulder.

They had already seen me, with Haf, but I was grateful for his wish to keep me safe. He paused at the threshold, his hand on the wooden latch. Then, he pulled it open and headed into our hall alone.

I stood staring at the door, stupid as brushwood.

Moments later, it opened again and Haf came out. When it closed, she leaned to listen, ear close to the knots in the wood.

'What's happening?' I asked. 'Is Tad making them leave?'

'*Isht*, Mai.' She stepped away from the door, grabbed my wrist and dragged me. I was going to yell at her, for the pain and the cheek of it. She wasn't my mam and shouldn't tell me what to do, though she did all the time. But there was something about the tilt of her head, the whiteness of her knuckles, that kept me quiet. She stopped under the window. It being autumn, the wooden shutters were closed. But part of the wood was cracked and sound escaped the hall as much as the heat.

Haf crouched beneath it, with me at her side.

I wanted to ask her what had been said, where were the men from, what were their names. I wanted the whole tale. But I crouched too, copying my big sister.

Listening, I heard the leader thank Tad, in British, for the feast.

The man said something to Tad about his daughters.

Haf gripped my shoulder, forcing me down lower.

But there was no danger of being seen, the window was shut tight. I nudged her, harder than was kind.

The man inside switched back to Saxon. His words were again like the Wild Woods and the Midnight Hunt, myths of old. The sound was of the dark places of the earth that Tad told us about, the cracks in the rocks where devils lived.

'Haf.' I heard him say *Haf*.

Was he talking about my sister? I looked leftwise at her.

She was pretty as morning. Even I, her little sister, who'd seen her wipe snot on her sleeve when she thought no one was looking, knew that. Her hair was long and wild as wolves. It spun out, dark from her head. That wasn't sudden-strange – we all had dark hair. But her eyes were blue, striking as the summer sky. Her skin promised health and honeyed life. Even when her lips were snow-burned in winter, she looked well. And she could be quick-witted too, when she tried hard.

We heard the door slam open, it shook the front wall. 'Haf!' the man shouted.

He knew her name, sure certain.

She must have told him. She was stupid as soup.

'Haf!' He stepped away from the hall, spun around in the yard. We shrank back, but he saw us. He spread his arms and smiled. 'You are here. You quickly left.' He looked all at Haf, as if I wasn't taking breaths. 'Come sit. Eat. We're not bad men. And you are Freya herself.'

At the name of one of their heathen gods, I felt my spine stiffen. My sister was no pagan. Though it was sure she was no angel either.

Haf dropped her knee towards the ground in curtsy. 'Syr, my tad sent me to do the work he's been called away from. I can't disobey my father.'

The man stepped closer, his hands in fists, his kindness hanging by the thinnest thread. He looked goat-eyed at Haf. 'Why not? You want not to sit with Saxons?'

I was shocked to see her blush to her crown.

'No, syr,' she said, 'of course not! But when there's guests, there's work. My sister and I must see to the farm and the fields.'

She gave another curtsy for good measure. She was being too sweet. Like glutting honey that sticks teeth shut. I kept my eyes to the ground and sensed that Haf was doing the same. The man was close enough to smell now. Mostly sweat and days spent walking, but also lakes and rivers, otter-scented. He smelled of free things, wild creatures. With his strange British, he was like no man we'd seen before.

I felt my blood beat again, my heart in my throat. This is how deer must feel, I thought, when they know there are arrows flying. I willed him to step back, to leave us be.

But Haf lifted her head and smiled like the lollin that she was. 'Syr, we can't come inside,' Haf said, 'but when our chores are done, we eat together in the evening. You will still be with us?'

The Saxon smiled, idle-mawed. 'It's certain,' he said. 'Keep your word. Yes? Yes.'

I looked up from under my scowl at Haf as the man turned and re-entered the hall.

'Why did you say that?' I muttered. 'I don't want to eat with them.'

She shrugged. 'Neither do I.'

'Then why did you say we would?'

'To keep the dish steady. He went in happy, didn't he? And we're out here safe.'

'But you said we'd go inside.'

'I said we'd go inside late or later. Those men will sleep and scratch the day away and will have long forgotten about us by the time the next meal rolls around. You'll see.'

I hoped she was right. It was Haf who had all the ideas for our games, who thought of things to cheer Tad. She seemed to know, often, what was for the best. So, I let her pull me away from the hall to the byre.

Haf could remember the last beast that lived here. I had only flashes of memory, brown, coarse hair, her black nose bigger than my head. She had got too old for milking and Tad had hoped to make Mam better with strong stew, Haf said. But it hadn't worked. I was three when we lost the cow and Mam.

Haf climbed to the top of the low wooden wall that marked the stall, then pulled herself into the roof rafters. It was her favourite spot to hide from chores. She'd fold herself, igam-ogam into the space and stay quiet, unnoticed. I followed her up, grasping the rough wood beneath my fingertips.

'Don't fret, Mai,' she told me. 'They won't be taking everything. See?' Haf reached for the pouch that hung at her belt next to her eating knife, and pulled out something small. Something the colour of water droplets or moonlight. I recognised it. The silver cross that Mam had worn, when she was with us. It was meant to be pinned to draped tunics, to hold them in place. It had belonged to her mam before her, Haf said.

I had no memory of Mam wearing it. My few memories

of her were fleeting. But I did have memories of Haf, curled up close in the bed we shared as infants, holding it up to the light and telling me about Moses on the mountain and Iesu in his crib and all the power he had to make the sick well. Magic tales she'd heard from Tad, when he had time, in the late sun of summer.

She'd taken the cross from her wooden cist in the hall, without the men seeing.

Haf reached up into the thatch of the roof and pressed the cross into the hollow she kept there for her secrets.

It made me feel better to know that they couldn't take that little bit of Mam away, even if they took everything else.

Slow as ivy grows, the spine of the day bent into evening, with no sign of Tad or the men. We brought the three hens into the byre. Then we just waited.

'You told them we'd go in when it got late,' I said.

'I know.'

'It's late now.'

'I know, Mai.'

I crossed my arms tight as though I were holding Rat-cat. 'We shouldn't go in. Tad wouldn't want us to.'

'It's up to me,' she said, almost to the wind. 'It's up to me what I do.'

It wasn't true. We both knew it. Tad was in charge. Then Haf. And she only had me and Rat-cat at her feet.

'Tad hasn't given me orders,' she said. 'He didn't say I

wasn't to go in, did he? You just think that's what he wants.'

'He'd want us to stay away.'

But she had found narrow council for herself, thin enough for doubt to slip through at any rate. I could see it in the way she pulled her spine straight. She wasn't going against his wishes, because she hadn't heard those wishes. The tale was untidy, but she could ignore that in the telling.

'What will you do?' I asked. I walked to her side, both of us jammed into the open doorway. She was only two summers older, but she was taller than I was and I had to look up to see her face. Now shadows swaddled the roundness of her cheeks, making her look much older still.

She pressed her nails into the wood of the doorframe, picking splinters free. 'Tad needs us.'

'You can't know that.'

'We haven't seen him come in or out. They might have—' Whatever it was she was going to say she bit back behind her teeth.

'What?' I asked. 'What might they have done?'

'Nothing. They're just guests. Just boring old men. But Tad might be tired of looking after them alone.'

I thought of the walking sticks the men carried.

'Right,' she said. 'I'll go inside, with cider. I'll pour the bottle until stupor takes them.'

17

This was nonsense that passed for planning. Three men full of drink was worse than three men without. It was obvious.

'The plan is lollin,' I said with scorn.

'Noah drank after the flood and fell straight to sleep,' she said.

'They aren't prophets, we already decided that. We should fight them with crosses painted on our shields and fire in our hearts, like the Emperor Constantine.'

Her only answer was to stare at me.

She was right. If we ran in, would we two fight three grown men? With what, the knives we used for eating and stones found on the farmyard floor?

My plan was as weak as hers. 'But you can't go in there, you can't.' I hated the whine that found its way into my voice.

'We have to do something. It's been too long since we've seen Tad,' Haf said.

'You think they've hurt him,' I accused.

'No! But I want to see him, just in case.'

'But they're more dangerous drunk,' I whispered.

She stepped so close we were sharing the same breath. 'Don't fret, Mai, please. I've seen drunk men at the market. The Noah story is right. They sing, then they sleep. We can slip out as soon as their eyes close, with Tad too.'

Was she right?

She stepped past me and back into the yard. Headed to the shut barn.

I followed. She was the cow to my wet calf as I bleated behind.

'Go back, Mai,' she said. 'Go and sing somewhere else! It's best I do this by myself.'

'If they aren't dangerous, then there's nothing to stop me coming too.'

She tutted. I had her cornered. 'Fine.'

Her skirt trailed in the dust behind her. Her arms swung with her stride as she crossed the farmyard. She reached the barn and lifted the heavy wooden bar. We both went inside. It was cool as lake water and the smell of old onions and turnips made soup of the air. Wooden tubs lined one wall. Most full; not all. Beside them were old sacks. Haf clambered around them, sending apples drumming to the ground in her impatience. Then she sighed grimly as she found what she was looking for – the cider.

It was kept in one of the few clay jars we had left. It was black earthenware with faces pinched into it by the ancient potter. Tad said it had once been used for wine, back when the Roman army had tramped the road and merchants and traders had followed behind. In those days, Tad said, every fine table would have had one. I'd never tasted wine, though I imagined it was sweet like hedge brambles. The cider was not. That I had tried, once, when

I fell into the swampy waters by the river, and had to be pulled out gasping. Tad had poured it down my throat and I coughed up the murky weeds as it burned its way down.

Now wine was gone, Tad bought the strong cider from the dunmen of the woods. It never sat on our table, but he drank it alone sometimes, late at night when the embers glowed. He never sang.

Haf tucked the jar under her arm, then grabbed the bruised apples from the floor. Armed with weapons that seemed worse than useless to me, she left the barn. I followed and lifted the heavy bar back into its sockets.

We marched, me still the calf, back to the farmyard. She stopped beside the shuttered window. She pressed her eye against the crack and watched.

'What can you see?'

'Nothing,' she said.

'True as true?'

She stepped back and blocked me from looking too. 'Go to the byre.'

I shook my head. 'If you're going in, so am I.'

'No, you're not. Go, now.'

I didn't move.

Haf leaned forward, her eyes so close to mine I could see my own shape reflected, despite the dark. 'You have nothing between your two ears. Don't you know I'm doing this to keep you and Tad safe?' she hissed, cat-angry. 'You need to stay out of the way.'

I folded my arms across my chest, but didn't reply.

Haf held my glare with her own. Then, seeing that she was ploughing sand, she gave up. Huffing, she headed to the door and went inside.

3

I ALMOST LET the door close behind Haf, leaving me behind on the worn patch of earth by the threshold of the hall. Cold starlight threw shadows across the farmyard. For one moment, I was alone with worry about my head.

No.

I needed Haf. And Tad. I couldn't get through this night without them.

So I pushed on the door and followed her inside.

It didn't feel like our hall any more. It smelled wrong. The men had stained it with their breathing bodies. Not the sweet sweat that came with hard toil and effort. This was sour with long-laid grime.

I looked around, cautious. No one watched me come in.

Haf was the centre of their notice, standing near the fire, in the middle of the hall, smiling and shield-holding the jar before her. The firepit was big, with rocks all around to catch stray sparks or hold warming flatbreads. Instead of good food, the embers warmed the feet of the three men. One sat upright on the floor. Another looked half-asleep, rolling on his own roadpack. The last, the one who had spoken earlier, had dragged the settle from the long wall – the settle our own grandfather had made lifetimes ago – and pushed it right next to the heat. He sat on it as if it were his throne. He barked harsh laughter as Haf swirled the cider jar.

Where was Tad?

My eyes searched for him.

And found him at the back of the hall. Was he hurt? Did he need us? The wicker hurdle that shielded his bed space from the main room had fallen, somehow, to the ground. The ladder that led up to the wide shelf where Haf and I slept was on the ground too. Tad sat on his low box-bed, wide enough for two, with his head in his hands, his hair in cockscombs between his fingers. His eyes were on Haf. I was too far away to guess his thoughts. I could see no bruises or blood, though.

He hadn't been hurt. Haf had told the truth, they were just wild guests. Relief flowed through me like floodwater. Still, I wanted to feel the weight of his arms about me, all the same.

I edged around the wall, eyes down, heading for Tad.

The man on the settle noticed me.

'The second girl!' he yelled in British. Louder than was right for our quiet home. I didn't think the other two understood what he said. They didn't react.

Tad, though, shifted his eyes. He saw me. His cheeks

wan-white as winter outside, his eyes grey-shaded. I saw his face change to horror that I had come.

His look said everything I had feared. The men were dangerous. We should have stayed hidden in the byre, or run to the woods, and waited until the locusts ate their way onward.

But it was too late.

'New girl. What are you called?' the nut-tanned man on the settle asked. 'Hey, girl. Answer me.'

'Mai.'

'Mai. Fresh as spring! Mai, I'm named Algar. That one's named Nyle. The sleeping one is named Ware the Tall.' He pointed to his road companions as he spoke.

My breath was shallow and quick. The beat of my blood fluttered too fast.

'Come join us!' Algar said.

I was too scared to do anything but step nearer to him. Up close, I saw that all the men were thin as winter hens. The folds of their clothes hid the worst ravages of hunger, but their cheeks were bruised pools, their eyes lost in shadow. Their hair was lank, tied back in loose tails.

I reddened. Under his eyes I felt the comfortable flesh on my bones, filling the fabric of my tunic. I could feel the roundness of my cheeks, apple-rosy. We didn't eat well, but we ate. Tad made sure of it. We traded no longer, now that the road to market had become so dangerous.

So there were never any treats, no honey, or dried fruits or spices. But there were roots and fresh-grown herbs, there was clean water and our own grain. As long as there was no blight, or bad weather, we ate.

This man knew it, just by looking. I trembled like new chicks in the fist of the farmwife.

Haf held up the earthenware jar. 'I brought good spirits,' she said. 'To spread good spirits.' She laughed at her own weak joke. Her voice was one I barely recognised.

Algar grinned. 'We were right to walk up the path. The smoke from your roof was gods-sent. Praise Woden!'

Pagans. Worshippers of devils, sure certain.

The cork slid out of the jar with the most gentle pop.

Algar emptied his wooden beaker of water into the fire, sending steam hissing. Haf poured the cider, golden glinting, into the empty cup. Algar slammed it down the red road of his throat and reached for another. Haf poured again, smiling. Then, she moved around the fire, pouring and simpering at all the dirt-smeared wanderers.

'And Mai. Will Mai share the cup with us?' Algar was looking at me.

I felt like prey frozen to the ground. The arrow of his eyes pinned me still.

'Well?' He held his drink out towards me.

Haf looked out from under her scowl at me. I couldn't tell whether she was telling me to drink or forbidding me to move. I couldn't tell what she wanted and I couldn't decide for myself. So I stood post-dumb and mud-stuck.

Algar laughed and swilled back the drink himself. Then he grabbed my arm and pulled me onto the settle beside him. I gripped the edge of the seat, my nails sank into the wood, my arms were sapling-straight and clamped to my sides.

'How old are you?' he asked. Fumes from the cider spread like mist as he spoke.

'Thirteen,' I said. Grown, I was meant to be, but the day had made me feel infant-small again. I wanted to turn and look at Tad, ask for his help, hide my face in the crook of his knee like the babe I used to be. But some shocked piece of me knew that I had to keep Tad safe now, not the other way around. I could keep their attention off him.

'Thirteen summers,' Algar laughed. 'Thirteen summers with your nose near your own fire.' He paused and held his cup for more. Haf obeyed.

'Do you know what I was doing these past thirteen years?' Algar asked.

I shook my head.

'Keeping myself alive.' He took another slug, banging the lip of the cup against his front teeth. 'Have you seen the country outside your hall, Mai?'

I hadn't, not for eons. Tad had kept us close to the

farm, mostly. We went into the woods to gather and hunt, sometimes. But we hadn't seen the market in Cwmnant for three years. There was nothing to trade that made the dangerous journey worth it.

Algar leaned in. 'I came here,' he said. 'I came from over the sea. They said the land was empty.'

I had nothing to say, so was silent.

He pulled at my arm, dragging my ear close to his mouth. 'They said it was empty. But it wasn't. Saxons and Angles and Jutes fight for land. And the Britons, the bloody Britons, they look like rabbits, but they bite like . . .' he searched for the right word, spun the dregs in his cup, '. . . like weasels. They hide up on their hilltops and raid real men at night.'

I tried not to breathe in his breath. I didn't want to share my island with him, let alone my air.

'Pitiful. Pity full. Pity.' Algar was playing with his words, testing the taste of them on his tongue. I wondered if the cider had gone to his head. He bark-laughed and I jumped. 'I'd go home if I could,' he said.

'Why don't you?' I dared to whisper.

'We all answer to someone,' he said.

I crouched lower, wishing I'd never spoken. I wished I could sink into the wood of the bench and scuttle like his rabbits, away from the light. Was Haf all right? I tried to see, but Algar sat square in the way. I couldn't move without drawing his attention.

'You know the fields from here to London are grown-over with bramble. The loose pigs have gone back wild,' he said. He paused. His thought lost. He leered and his tongue was slug-wet in his mouth. 'I like pig meat when I can get it.'

I looked away. We needed to get out of here, Haf and Tad and me. We needed to get up and leave.

Getting them drunk was stone-stupid.

We should get up and run on our two legs.

My heart beat angry in my chest.

I lurched up. I reached for the short knife at my waist as though it were my sword.

Algar clamped his hand around my wrist. Laughed. 'What are you going to do with that, I wonder? What can that sorry little blade do? Core apples?'

He was right, the blade was no bigger than my thumb.

He let go of my wrist. It throbbed where he had held it.

His fingers trailed the blade he had at his side. Short and stocky in its scabbard. He gripped the hilt, but didn't draw it. 'Do you know why we're called Saxon?' he asked.

I shook my head.

'It's for the blades we carry – the sax. Blades used for cutting meat or cutting men. It makes no odds.'

'Fetch more wood, Mai,' Haf blurted. 'It's getting cold enough to straighten thorns.'

It wasn't. If anything, it was stuffy, fetid. But at her words, Algar moved his hand from his blade.

The short wall at the back of the hall was stacked with logs. Weeks and weeks of summer and autumn work by Tad had piled them high. I went and picked up my armful of logs slowly. Flakes of bark came away under my finger-touch. They were good, dry logs that would burn pine-scented.

'Tad, what should we do?' I hissed as I passed his bed.

'Don't worry,' Tad whispered. 'All will be well. The plague will pass as it passed over the Israelites. Iesu is watching. Amen.'

Praying. That's what he was doing.

I could do that too. I could follow his lead. I leaped to it, muttering over and over as I crossed the hall, sending prayers to Iesu the baby, the Father, the Ghost.

At the fire, amber tongues licked the dark bark as the first log caught light. Fresh waves of heat spread. I smelled sweat stewing wetly. Beads formed on brows, fresh stains spread over backs.

Before I could step out of the firelight, Algar reached for me and pulled me back to sitting. He lunged for Haf too. He wanted us both to sit, thigh to thigh, beside him. Haf pulled back as though burned. He growled and lunged again.

He gripped her arm. Red meat on honey. Bear paws on bare wrist.

Tad shouted then. 'Don't touch her!'

Algar laughed.

The sound struck my heart cold. There was pity in the

laugh. Algar knew that Tad was more thunder than strikes. He had lost already, and the fight not even begun. There were three men in his hall and he could do nothing to stop whatever storm was coming.

Algar laughed and laughed.

I couldn't breathe. The air was thick with smoke, the fire banked too high. My heart was full and fuller with each breath.

Haf tried to pull her arm free, but Algar stood and pulled her to him.

His mouth was on hers.

His arms around her staff-straight back.

I stood.

I heard Tad rise too, curses in his mouth.

I joined the cursing.

Haf pushed Algar.

He buckled, hit the settle. His knees folded and he landed hard on the wood. '*Scheisse*,' he spat. '*Hündin!*'

Shot through with anger, he lifted the earthenware cider jar from the floor, hurled it at Haf. It thudded into her arm, fell, and shattered against the hearthstones.

Black pieces broken blink quick,

Then blue burning flames biting,

Fire dancing in the rushes.

I gawped at the fire that spread beyond the stones.

'Put it out!' Haf acted first. The burning spirit spilled from the jar had set the floor straw aflame. Haf stamped on the red tongues. But as her leather soles squashed one . . . two more sparked alight.

I heard crackling. The stems of rushes curling and breaking. Smoke spread.

I jumped and stomped too. The one called Nyle shouted as burning embers floated in the air. He was up. Yelling. Saxon words. Cursing.

There was more smoke now. Thickening the air. I tasted it, felt it scratch at my throat. More than rushes burned. Roadpack sacking had caught. Butterflies of flame floated upwards to the roof.

'Water!' I heard Tad cry.

But the men didn't listen. I heard, felt, sensed them moving. Blue smoke filled the room. I ducked to find cleaner air. The hall door opened, fresh air fanned flames.

Then, I heard the terrible sound of thatch alight. With eyes closed it might be the sound of rain on leaves, or blown sand hitting rocks. But with eyes open, it was clear as the sun on the hill that the hall had caught fire.

Red,

    Yellow,

        Blue tongues dancing in and out of the rafters, tasting the beams and the boughs, devouring them. Smoke billowed now, like grey wool rolling in all directions.

Crash. Something heavy fell.

I heard screaming.

Get out, get out. My body struggled against the smoke.

Where was the door? Heat rolled in all directions.

Small hands grabbed mine. Haf. 'Help me find Tad?'

I nodded, throat too torn to speak. The fire had spread too fast. Animal fierce. Hunting.

Haf led. The heat was impossible, the air had become hot walls, stopping our movement. My eyes streamed. The crackling of fire gave way to thuds and bangs: thatch and thick twigs fell to the ground, burning rain.

Something huge fell then, roaring as it broke. The ribs of the roof snapping. I heard Tad cry out.

Haf gripped me, pulled hard.

I saw him first. Tad, lying still on the ground. His chest bloomed red poppies. The edges of his shirt smouldered.

'Tad! Tad!'

'Mai, help! Lift his legs. Lift, I said!'

I tried, I tried. He was so heavy.

'Do it!'

I screamed and pulled and got him up from the floor. Haf held his shoulders. We struggled, through ash and the very breath of Hell, with his weight borne between us.

4

THERE ARE FIRES burning at the edge of the village tonight. The smoke from them is gaggingly sweet. I couldn't look at the shapes burning between the logs as I ran down the rabbit path to this barn. Not even now, after all I've seen in all the months since Algar lit those first flames.

I shut my mind to what is happening beyond the leather door. I've chosen to stay here. Any chance I had to flee is long gone, leaving me as empty as the day after market.

'Sara,' I whisper at the sack curtain. 'Is the baby coming? Is anything happening?'

'Everything and nothing,' she says. 'That's the way it is.'

5

LATE AUTUMN, AD454

'LIFT HIS HEAD! Off the ground!' Haf yelled like murder to mind how I carried Tad. We staggered together, one beast with many limbs, into the yard. I saw the Saxons in the corner of my eye, staggering from the fire. I'd have sent them to their judgement in that instant if I could, but I had Tad to think about. The night was bright with the light of the flames. Our unnatural shadow stretched across the dirt. I could feel the heat on my back. The sound was worse, though. The fire was so loud, so angry. Its hunger roared as it ate, chewing through thick beams as though they were twigs and bark.

And Tad was so heavy.

'Get him to the byre,' Haf told me.

We laid him inside, glad that he moaned – dead men were silent.

'Fetch water. To cool the wound. I'll fetch willow bark. There's some in the barn, I think.'

I ran then. Once I knew what to do, I was eager to act. The well was beyond the byre, nearer to the road. The sight of Tad lying still with the red poppy bloom of his wound was branded on my eyes. I could see it as I let the bucket drop into the water. It was there as I drew it sloshing back. Was it too late? Had he come to the end of his song? I unhooked the bucket, waddled back with the water.

I washed away dirt and burned fabric from his chest. The skin beneath was bald pink in patches, deep red in others. Bubbles of yellow liquid had formed on his belly.

'Tad? Can you hear me?'

Slowly, his eyes opened. He saw me.

'Tad, can you speak?'

'Sore.' His voice was reed-thin. His throat must be as parched as mine. I soaked the rag I held and twisted it above his lips. His tongue licked them dry.

'Haf's gone to find something for the pain,' I told him.

His eyes closed again. We stayed like that, my hand in his, until he fell into restless sleep.

Haf was gone all that time.

Perhaps she wasn't coming back?

The thought struck lightning quick. Haf was gone and had left me on my own with Tad. Black, black thoughts twisted like snakes in my stomach. She wouldn't. She couldn't. She would never leave us. She'd never leave me. Something must have happened.

'Haf?' I whispered into the night. But the sound was too weak. 'Haf?' I let go of Tad and stood. Panic beat in my chest.

Where was she?

'I'm going to look for Haf,' I told Tad, urgent. 'I'll be back in moments. Moments. I promise.'

I raced towards the barn, arcing wide around our burning hall. My steps took me into far-flung shadows.

That's where I found her. I almost tripped over her before I saw her shape on the ground, lying still.

'Haf? Haf?' I fell to my knees, dirt and stones grazing my skin, but I hardly felt it. 'Haf! What's wrong?'

She pushed me away. Hard. With both hands.

'What's the matter?' I asked.

'Get back.' She held her hand up, to stop me from speaking. Her voice was flat and empty. No feeling at all.

As she turned her face towards me, moonlight and firelight showed up the dark mark of bruises, her swollen lip.

Someone had hit her.

'Algar?' I asked.

She flinched at the sound of his name.

Anger bloomed in me again. I stood and looked about for any sign of him or his men.

'They've gone,' she said in that same flat voice. 'They took what they wanted and ran to the road. The barn's empty.'

I had to see.

The cloven doorway was cave-dark. I went in. It was pitch black beyond the unnatural glow in the doorway.

Once I had taken three paces I had to grope my way forward. My stiffening fingers trailed through dry dirt, finding shallow pits where wooden buckets and barrels once stood. Now they were fallen, empty, rolled like game pins. The smell of newly uncovered earth rose, covering all else. I found dried apples, forgotten and fallen. One jar was still unopened. They hadn't had the time or the light to clear every last shred. But what was left was meagre. I scooped my finds into the front fold of my tunic and stood.

The store was gone. The house, going. And Tad was in more pain than I could bear.

6

SUMMER SOLSTICE, AD455, BEFORE DAWN

SARA PULLS BACK the sackcloth that hides my sister from me. She hasn't made any sound for far too long.

'Mai,' Sara snaps, 'I need you. Get up.'

I hare-spring to my feet, knocking the stump-stool to its side. I've been lost in my own tale. My face reddens. 'What can I do?'

'She's cramping but there's no sign of the baby. Raspberry leaves will help. Go and fetch some.'

'Outside?' I glance fearfully at the leather doorway.

'Well, I don't see anything growing in here but fools, do you?' Her tone is kinder than her words. Rough pity lines her brow. 'You don't have to go far. Rowan has some dried in her hall. Or you can get it fresh from the hide-acre. Fresh is better.'

I nod. I don't want to go into any of the big halls tonight. I want no Saxon staring at me, wondering where I've been or what I've done in the colours of the night. To see the guilt on my face.

'I'll go to the hide-acre.'

'Be quick,' she tells me.

I right the stool and stare at the low embers. There's more fire outside than I'm ready for.

'Mai,' Sara snaps. In the summer dark I can see her face plainly. Her mouth is drawn tight. Whatever she's thinking, she has no time to tell me even the dry bones of the tale. 'Hurry,' is all she says.

'I don't want to see what's happening out there.'

'I know. Still. You must go.'

I wrap my arms around Sara and hold her with fierce love, just for one heartbeat, then I do as she says.

I'm out. Leather flipping and flapping in the night air.

I taste burning.

The midnight, midsummer air is thick and wet. I feel ash slick against my skin. I breathe, fish-mouthed, once, twice. The village is quiet, no blessed being to be seen. They aren't sleeping, I know that. They are all in the woods, in hiding. Except the big men, the brave men, who are out there rounding up whoever they find. For one moment, my heart beats for those running like hares through heather to get away from the men. Please, Iesu, don't let them be caught.

I small-sly creep along the path, from the barn. The woods are behind me, and the stream. All I can hear is the crackle of fire at the head of the village. I keep low to the good earth. My tunic is mud brown, grey in the dark. I'm glad of it. The river sludge colour will make

it harder to be seen. I cover my nose to block the smell. I try not to think what I'm smelling.

It is like roasting boar.

My mind sees cloth burning, long bones, hair and beards lit like tinder.

I keep away. Take the long path. Stick to shadows.

The hide-acre is up the hill, beyond the big halls. Out of the stream valley. I pull my hair to cover my face. Skin will shine in moonbeams.

I stop when I hear people shouting. Drop to my haunches. Press my spine into the wickerwork fence nearby. Curl my arms tight about me.

But the shouts move away.

I crawl forward. I want to run home, hole up in the darkness and never come out. But my sister is there, in pain. Dying, maybe. I push myself to standing. Walk faster.

The hide-acre is full of shadow, bush and branch bent into beasts. The children who normally throw stones at the crows are gone.

I hurry. Keep my head down. Mouse-quick and unseen. The low fence is meant for keeping dogs out, not people, and I step over the wattle easily. I am tall now, taller than Haf. My heart is full and heavy. Is this the end of our last night together?

I notice, as I lift my skirt that I can see more brown than grey. The sky is no longer black. It's deep blue, softening to milky yellow through the trees. The sun will arc soon.

I have to be quicker. I run to the right furrow and the raspberry bushes growing there.

The fruits are hard, green lumps. But it's the leaves I want. I tug and rip at the shoots and stems too. I don't know how much Sara needs so I tear the row of thin plants, shredding them. I hope no other woman comes to birth for many days, I have taken all the medicine. I stuff it into the folds of my sleeves.

God is good and forever is long. I cross myself and leave the hide-acre as fast as I can.

I head back to give Sara what she needs.

7

LATE AUTUMN, AD454

WE ALL THREE curled up together in one of the stalls of the byre. The two chickens and the rooster were sleeping sound there too, knowing less of the danger than moles know of sunshine. But I kept my short knife in my hand, clutched tight, through the night. I fell into wary fox-sleep.

Sometime in the spine of the night, I heard Haf climb up to the rafters. The cross, her small treasures, she must be fetching them. I thought I heard her crying, but it might have been my dreams.

The cold woke me.

It was still dark, but I could feel the moon was low and the sun not too far below the tree-line.

Tad lay sleeping still. Haf stood at the open door staring out. She had let in the dawn air.

'Tad, Tad,' I whispered.

'Don't wake him, Mai,' Haf snapped. 'Not until we have to.'

But his eyes were already open. 'Are you girls already fighting teeth to teeth? It's too early to argue.'

'Tad, how do you feel?'

He tried to answer, but coughed instead, wincing at the pain.

'Let me check the wound,' I told him. 'Does it hurt?'

No answer.

The red gash was crusting to brown. The worst of the dirt had washed away with well water, but the skin looked tight and pink around the wound.

'Oh, Tad.'

Haf gripped my arm and part-lifted, part-dragged me out of the byre. Once we were away from Tad she leaned her face in close and said, 'Scavengers will come soon. They'll see the smoke once the sun's up. Ditch dunmen from the woods. We should leave.'

Haf pushed back her hair. I saw she was wearing bruise bracelets at her wrists.

'Where will we go?'

There weren't many choices. Saxons spread across the east. Algar – the thought of his name sent me half-sensed – had said the land was full of them. I thought of something else he had said. 'The Britons are in the hills. He –' I didn't want to say his name to Haf – 'he said so.'

'There's over the river too. If we can get across, the Britons of Gwent might take us in.'

'We can't cross,' I said. 'Tad says it's as wide as the sea.' He'd told me of mud banks that sucked men down to their deaths, water wider than any man could swim that ran cunning and slippery, changing its course with its mood. And pirates sailing up and down, stealing slaves away to Spain and further.

'He's just been herding stories for you. We can cross. Rivers aren't seas.'

'Sure certain?' I asked.

'I don't know, Mai! I don't know everything.'

'You act like you do.'

Haf hung her head. 'I know. But I don't, do I? We both know it. This is my fault. I gave them cider. I was foolish.' She reached for me, grabbed my shoulders too hard. 'But I won't be foolish again. Not ever. Do you hear? I promise you that.'

I was stunned to silence. Haf never took any blame if she could help it.

'We'll gather what we can and go,' she told me.

'Can I find Rat-cat?' I asked.

'No. She's run from the fire as sensible beasts should.'

'Are you sure we have to go?'

'Have you seen the wound Tad has? It needs medicine. Ours is burned; the leaves in the woods are dead. We need to find people who can help him, because we can't, Mai. We can't do it alone.'

I hung my head. She had the right of it, I knew.

I didn't want to leave Rat-cat, or the farm, or the spot where Mam was buried. But Algar had left us no choice.

*

We left with slow steps. The hall still smouldered and its stone footings looked like teeth thrust through the jaws of the earth. We gathered what we could in three small sacks, then followed the farm track to the road that had brought the trouble. It had once been wide and smooth, but was shattered now. The flagstones had been lifted by plants or people, leaving pockmarks. Its stones had gone to be hearths or thresholds in the mud huts of peasants, or had tumbled into the ditch. Thick layers of leaf fall hid the surface. Twigs and branches rolled and cracked underfoot.

'Which way?' I asked Haf.

'Not along the road. We'll cross into the woods and follow the stream. It will lead to the river then the harbour, or we'll see the fires of the Britons on the hills. We'll find people if we follow the stream.'

It seemed to me that she was promising me the sea and scree, with no way to give me either. I decided not to argue.

Tad didn't want to go. It was written on every inch of him, his slow steps, his eyes cast back to the byre and burned hall. I understood. This land had belonged to his father, and his before that. He knew the soil, ploughed with his own arm and shoulder. He knew the hedges, the earthworms and beetles, the blackbirds and bluebirds on the walls. The earth had got so deep into the folds and creases of his hands that no amount of fat and lavender could lift it. He wanted to stay.

45

'Scavengers will come, Tad,' Haf said.

'I know.'

'There's no choice.'

He dropped his head. 'I know.'

We crossed the road from one gutter to the other and then into the trees beyond. The woods were where goblins and wild men lived, where giant boar and wolves snuffled and sniffed for food, and herds of winter pigs got fat on autumn acorns. Tad was on his own feet, but it was clear how much it cost him. His breathing was the loudest sound in the wood, and despite the cold his skin was slick with sweat. He struggled to put one foot in front of the other.

'It will be well,' I whispered to him.

He managed to smile in reply.

We heard the stream before we reached it, its song was calm as it ran over the rocks. The trees beside it were thin-pin bristles, cut to grow that way for fences and posts.

Bone-straight white birch streaked skywards

Oak leaves lay coke-black and red

Mouldering in mole-hill mounds.

Tad kept his eyes cast down to avoid the sticks and rocks that littered our way. 'I've tried to keep you safe. Hidden away from the world. But looking for safety is like looking for melted snow. Now our luck's run out.'

'We'll find new luck,' I told him.

'I should have fought those men. I should have died before letting them hurt you.'

Tad sounded beaten. I felt the heat of my blood race, the *bwr-lwm, bwr-lwm* of it drowning out the sounds of the cold wood. I was all pulse. Tad had always held that, whatever the troubles of the day, it would all end well. He was smiles and stories in the face of misery, songs to stop tears. But not now. I stumbled over unseen roots. My arm flew out to stop my fall. But I landed hard, the air knocked from my lungs. My face scraped something cold and I felt stinging pain.

'Mai?' Haf asked from the back.

'I'm all right,' I said. My face was wet. My hand came away red.

'You're bleeding,' Tad said.

'It's nothing.'

I stood quickly and marched ahead, wide strides taking me away from them. I could feel my face swelling already. My cheekbone throbbed. I dashed at the cut with the neck of my sack, smearing the brown to red.

'Wait!' Haf called.

They were nearly out of sight behind me. One or two more twists of the stream and I would be gone. I wanted to run, to outpace Tad and his soft tales that had wrapped us up for so long.

I moved faster, beating back branches.

And stepped into weak sunlight. The trees thinned to open space, grey limbs around the mossy circle.

Space with people in it.

Two people, one man, one woman, sat beside their small fire. They must have been burning year-old windfall, as the sticks gave off little smoke. At the sound of my footsteps, they looked up. They had dark hair and eyes, made darker by dirt. I saw fear, creased lines and tight mouths. The woman reached for bundled swaddling beside her. I understood then what she was fearful of. I must be streaked with soot and there was blood on my cheek. I spread my hands, dropping my sack. I wouldn't hurt their baby.

Tad, then Haf, stepped from the trees. We stood like ancient stones, wary and suspicious. My want to be away from Tad was gone like dew rising. I needed him. I ran back to his side and took his hand.

His free hand went to his stomach, pressed tight against it. Out from tree-shadow, the sweat on his cheeks was clear to see.

The woman noticed. She looked at Haf. 'What's wrong with him? Is he sick? Stay back,' she snapped.

'He's hurt,' Haf said. 'Burned.'

'I'm right,' Tad said. 'Tired, that's all.' He stepped further into the clearing. There were jumbled rocks, set back from the stream, turning to green and yellow with moss and lichen. He lowered himself onto one slowly. He couldn't stop the sigh that came with the effort.

The woman spoke. 'How was he burned?' She had her swaddling cradled in her arms and came warily closer.

As she got close, I smelled her, sour and sweet, with rot laced through it.

'Our home burned,' Haf said.

The woman nodded slowly.

'Where are you headed?' the man asked. He wanted us gone, that was clear.

'To the hills to find the Britons,' I said. 'Or the river.'

'*Isht*,' Haf hissed at me.

The man scratched his neck where dirt lay in tidelines. 'Is it Gwrtheyrn you want?'

I hadn't heard the name before. It sounded growling fierce, defiant. I liked it.

'Maybe,' Haf replied.

'He leads what's left of the Britons around here. Is that you?' the man asked.

'Briton? Yes. And Roman too,' Tad said almost to himself.

The man inclined his head. 'We were Britons. Now we're dogs and weasels. Running on rabbit trails. We have our own ways in the woods.'

I didn't know what he meant. 'Is it far to reach Gwrtheyrn?' I asked. Tad had walked not even one morning and he looked tired as death.

The man shrugged. 'Two days. West. Into the setting sun. You want to join his warband, do you? You want to fight the Saxons, little girl?'

The beat of my heart quickened. I thought of Algar.

I did. I did want to join Gwrtheyrn and fight Saxons. I would stand beside men, tall and strong as oak, with shields and real swords and bring terror to the men who had hurt us. I could have stories told about me one day.

'Do you have any food you might share?' the woman asked. 'For the sake of my baby?'

There was little in the sacks: apples and roots. I pressed my lips closed.

'We left at speed,' Haf replied. 'We have nothing.'

The man stepped towards us.

Haf moved in front of Tad.

The woods were silent. Even the clacking of the branches in the wind seemed to hush. The air felt tight as loom strings. Haf stared at the man. There was power in her glare, as though she had taken all the anger she felt, all the sadness and guilt and was aiming it square at him.

The woman turned away and sat heavy on the cold ground. The baby in her arms stayed quiet despite the jolt.

And I felt my heart ache again. It wasn't true we had nothing. There had been some small scraps in the barn, and we were headed towards the hills to join people who would look after us. 'We can give them one of the apples,' I said to Haf.

'Mai!'

But I didn't care. I opened my sack and took one out. They could mash it for the baby.

I carried it to the woman. She raised both hands above her head to take it, leaving the baby lying in her lap. And that's when I saw the child properly.

The smell of rot wasn't from their unwashed clothes, their matted hair. It came from the little corpse they were carrying about with them. It couldn't have been dead that long, and was better preserved in the cold air, but dead it was. Its eyes were sunken and grey as the leaden sky. Its skin tight and swollen yellow.

The woman took the apple and bit, letting the juice drip down her chin. She rocked the swaddling gently as she chewed.

I stepped back, stumbling on rocks, stumbling over my own feet, clawing to get back to Haf and Tad. 'Let's go,' I whispered. 'Now. Now.'

My need killed Haf's anger. She helped Tad to his feet. 'We wish you well,' she said. We hurried back into the trees, as fast as Tad could walk. I kept looking back and back and back, over my shoulder, until the clearing was far gone from view.

8

THE CLEARING WAS far behind us by the time my heart slowed its beating, but the horror stayed – flashes of swollen yellow skin every time I blinked. The ground beneath my feet was cold and wet, splashing black up my legs and tunic hem. Coarse reeds rattled stems in the cold. Bog-rosemary scented the air with its heavy spice as the stream grew wider and the ground wetter.

'We should stop for the night,' Haf said much later. The sky was turning purple blue with fast-coming dusk.

I shivered as I realised we would have to sleep outdoors.

I hadn't slept outdoors in the cold before. We did in summer sometimes. When the heat of the day throbbed back from the earth and the sun barely dipped beyond the hills before rising again. When the world was like that, Haf and I would often work all day, then swim in the stream and eat fresh-caught dove or rabbit over burning wood while Tad sang or told tales. We'd all sleep with the stars in the Heaven above us.

Tonight would not be like that. I had to work fast to

build some shelter. Haf and I leaned thick sticks against the trunk of the nearest wind-felled tree. The space it made was small, and full of holes, but there was enough room for the three of us to puppy-huddle close, with the trunk at our backs.

Haf handed out apples, cutting the pieces for Tad with her knife. Tad ate slowly, chewing and swallowing with care.

Despite the pain in his side Tad pulled Haf into the crook of his arm. I rested my head on her lap. We sat together for many moments.

'I think the sun will rise in the morning and it will all seem better,' Tad said, his voice weak. 'I've kept you both well and safe for all these years. I can't believe that the Lord Iesu would stop watching out for us.'

I sent up one quick prayer, to help Iesu find us.

'Tell one of your tales.' Haf sounded younger than she had in many moons.

'Which one? Buddug defending her people? Constantine taking up the cross?'

They were some of my favourites. I liked to imagine the roar of battle and swords held high in victory. I especially liked Buddug because she was queen of her people, not the king, and still she had led her army against the Romans.

But they weren't the ones Haf liked. She preferred Moses and the plagues of Egypt, God striking fear into the heart of the king. I didn't want to hear about plagues, not today.

'I'll tell you about Adam and Eve leaving the garden,' Tad said.

I lay back to listen. Tad told his tales like witches cast spells; the words almost sung. The sounds shifting and fitting together to make magic. I wished I could tell those stories so well. Tonight, he began,

> *'In Eden, long ago, God*
> *Formed, from good clay, Adam.*
> *From Adam, God took one rib*
> *Bade it wrapped with flesh and skin*
> *To make his kin, his wife, Eve.'*

As I pressed into the warmth made by Tad and Haf all huddled close, I saw that first family in my mind.

'Go on,' I said, 'get to the snake.'

'*Isht*,' Haf said.

Tad rested his hand on the top of my head. It was big enough to hold all my worries, in that moment.

> *'God told Adam the garden*
> *Was his home, to tend, to treat*
> *With care: stock, stalk, seed and bean.*
> *With but one fruit forbidden.'*

I felt my eyes droop, lids heavy with the weight of the walk and the warmth. I forced them wide. I wanted to hear the best bit – the hiss of the treacherous snake.

Tad coughed, hard. Covered his mouth and pulled in air. More coughs.

'Tad?' Haf asked.

His coughs calmed. 'I'm well,' he said. 'I'm well. Don't worry.' He breathed as though his throat was too small. The sound wheezed.

'I'll do it,' Haf said. 'I know it.'

'No!' I was wide awake now. If I couldn't have Buddug, then I at least wanted Tad to keep going. 'I don't want Haf to tell it.'

Tad stroked my hair, soothing me. 'Your sister tells it as well,' he said. His voice wheezed again. 'Let her. For me?'

I nodded, my head still resting on Haf.

She picked up the tale. Slowly, carefully, trying to weave the sounds as Tad did. But her voice was too soft, too high. I stopped listening. Instead, I let my eyes close, my heart found its regular beat – *sib-rood, sib-rood* – and I drifted into sleep.

After that first night, we walked. Following the stream until the ground began to rise. We stopped to gather food where we saw it – watercress near the bank, and wild garlic bulbs dug up where the earth was soft enough. We saw no more people, and I was glad.

I walked further from home than I'd ever been before. It made me feel brave. I'd only played at being brave before. When Haf was young, before we gave any thought to the threats beyond the road, she had thrown her bed blanket over the trunk of the biggest tree and ridden her brave charger as Buddug leading the Britons. I remember Haf, stick-sword in hand, yelling, 'Mai, you're the invading Romans!'

'What, all of them?'

'Yes, all of them. Prepare for the underworld!'

She kicked the tree in its haunches and galloped into battle among the barley.

She was fearless for her fabled people.

And I was the brave leader of the Romans, ready to face her charge.

This was not play any more.

On the fifth day of slow, slow walking, as evening fell again and the forest thinned to fields, high on one of the distant hills we saw the light of fires burning.

9

SUMMER SOLSTICE, AD455,
BEFORE DAWN.

I CLUTCH THE raspberry leaves tight in my sleeve.
The sweet fruit smell is better than the smoke that
taints all the air around me. The hide-acre will smell of
it for weeks to come.

I have to stay mouse-quiet to get back to my sister
without being seen. Brown cloth, brown hair, brown
skin blend with the brown of the huts and the earth.

Then I realise that I can see the colours now. The
first light of the midsummer sun is close. I don't want
my body to betray me, to give me away to the hunters
in the hills and woods all about. I keep to the shadows.
But is that enough to stay safe?

I've learned that there are traitors everywhere.
Everyone can betray. Even me. I've seen my own sister
look at me in pain, pain from thorns that I sowed. I saw
it tonight.

My eyes are pulled back to the white path that leads
out of the village. I can't look away, even though I know
there's nothing for me that way.

I force my feet to take me back to the barn.

10

THE FIRES OF the fort glowed like the red star on the edge of night. I stopped walking and stared. The Britons didn't mind who saw their fires in the evening dark. They weren't hiding. They were right there for the world to see. I felt my back straighten, the weight of the world seemed less.

Haf, ahead of me on the path, stopped and looked back. 'Afraid?' she asked.

'No! Why would I be?'

Haf walked back to where I waited for Tad. He had had to stop for breath every few steps this last day.

'Mai,' Haf said, 'these people are our kin, but we don't know them. We've never shared bread, or slept beneath the same beams. We have to watch and listen more than we speak.'

Tad reached us. 'She'll learn,' he said. 'Mai's quick, aren't you?'

I slipped my hand through his arm. 'I'll learn to ride horses and chariots and fight with sword and spear. I'll have my own sword, you know. Forged in fire to fight Saxons.'

'Will you?' Tad leaned on my arm. His smile was weak, but it was there.

'Come down from the clouds,' Haf snapped.

I was ready to snap back that I hadn't been daydreaming, but then, I realised she was right, so I shut the door on my teeth.

Soon enough, the forest was behind us and ahead lay the open field that skirted the hill, mud-churned and slippery. I couldn't see cattle, nor sheep in the darkness, but it was hooves that had cut up the ground like that. At the bottom of the slab-dark way up the hill I caught sight of their graveyard. Man-sized mounds of earth still fresh, wooden crosses and cairned crags aligned with the setting sun. I crossed myself.

'Slow down,' Tad said, though I hadn't been walking fast.

As we followed the mud path, ditches and fences funnelled all-comers into the tiny square in front of the gatehouse. I searched the slope for the movement of people, or animals. Nothing shifted.

'Where are the people?' I whispered.

'They can't be far,' Haf replied, 'not with so many fires lit.'

It was strange. There were enough fires here to keep dozens of people warm, and yet there was no one with their nose to the heat.

'Let me go first,' Haf said.

'Not alone,' I replied. 'I'm coming too.'

'We'll all go,' Tad said.

'No.' Haf shook her head. 'I should go. Tad, they might think you're sick, like that woman in the woods. They might not let us in.'

I bit my lip, unhappy. I hadn't thought of it, but Haf was right.

Tad shook his head. 'I don't want to leave this to you. You're so young.'

'No. I'm fifteen. Almost grown. Please, Tad, let me do this.'

He frowned, but saw the sense in what she said. He moved to where thick stakes of wood lay in piles nearby, ready to form extra fences. Tad dropped down heavily onto one. We could be seen from the gate, I was sure certain, but we weren't spies, or thieves, we were no threat.

'Stay together,' he said. 'Say as little as you can.'

I wasn't sure what he was warning me of, but I knew his caution was no wasted step. I nodded.

Haf took my hand as we walked. Her palm felt warm and clammy, despite the fallen night. She was nervous. We followed the turning path of the fence and ditch. The people who lived here were warriors now, whatever they had been in the past. The farmers, farriers and fieldworkers were gone and only fighters remained. I hoped they would let me stand beside them.

The crackling of the fires was the only sound we heard. That and our own steps, wetly pulling feet through mud.

'Haf, where are the people in the camp?' As we walked, I remembered other stories Tad had told us, of wraiths and fair folk walking from their barrows and stealing sleepers to the lands beneath the earth. Had the fair folk been here and whisked everyone away?

'*Isht*. Be brave. The bravest you've ever been. But cautious too. We can't make any more mistakes.'

I tried to be like Buddug, but in the emptiness I was frightened clean.

We followed the twists and turns of the trail until we came to the great gate. It stood higher even than our hall. Roman nails held the two thick horizontal planks in place. Two stone pillars flanked the gate, then the banks of earthworks stretched in either direction into the darkness. I smelled the strong stench of the ditches now we were so close. There *must* be people within – the midden-stink was fresh.

Then, I sensed movement above us. Life. People. I breathed freely again. We heard footsteps, quick and light. Platforms or walkways must run along the inside of the defences.

'Hold still,' Haf said. 'Wait.'

I had no other choice. Though I wanted, with every hair on my head, to call out to our kin, to shout for them to let us in, I knew that was foolish. They didn't know us. Any true ties we had were far in the past, no more real than stories. They might not even believe in Iesu Grist! The thought sent my heart pounding.

'Who are you?' the hidden watcher shouted, harsh and deep-voiced.

'Haf, and Mai, *ap* Ioan,' Haf called. I was impressed by the steadiness of her voice. 'Our tad awaits too. Our farm was destroyed, burned by Saxon men.'

'What business is that of ours?'

'We are Britons, if that still holds meaning. We're your kin.'

Their pause was long. Then we heard the rasp of wood on wood as the great bar of the gate lifted. Slowly, the gate swung open.

'Fetch your tad,' the voice said.

The three of us stepped through as one, arms tight around each other, holding and leaning at the same time. We waited in the muddy yard. Hundreds of feet had churned and ploughed at the black earth. Water puddled in the pockmarked ground. Fires burned on either side and we could see huddled shapes against the light of the flames. People. Finally. Perhaps one dozen bodies spread in the dark.

Footsteps dropped from the walkway. The man who appeared before us was thin, scrawny, with his skin loose and wrinkled on his face. But still he looked fierce. His hair was black, pulled back; the sword at his side worn on show, to frighten, I guessed.

'You carry weapons?' he asked.

We shook our heads. Though we all had knives at our belts, they were no more weapons than the hairpins I'd seen at the market. The only skin they'd pierce was that on hot milk.

'Diseases?' The man looked watchful at Tad.

'He's injured, not sick. He was burned. The wound needs to be treated,' Haf replied.

'We have the priest,' the man said. 'He can see to it.'

We waited. Had I understood his meaning?

The man raised his eyebrows. 'You can stay. We'll talk more in the morning.'

We had leave to stay.

I'd not realised how much worry I held until he said those words. They were true balm. We could stay.

My hope-fuelled heart free-floated.

Behind earthworks and gates and men with swords, we were welcome. No one could come to our home and make us feel fear again. And they had their own religious man. We could pray to the baby and the Father and the Ghost for Tad.

'I'm Rhodri,' the man said sourly. 'My boy, Bryn, can show you to the priest. Bryn!' he called into the darkness.

We were blessed to have come.

In my mind, I saw the coming days. I'd join the silent watchers guarding the wall. I'd have my own sword. I'd be one of the Britons who raided and tormented the Saxons.

'Bryn!' he called again, impatient.

The boy who stepped away from his fire, Bryn, was young. Thin, like his tad, and wiry, like the runt running with the hunting pack.

'Take them to the chapel and get them soup,' Rhodri said.

Proper dark had fallen as we moved away from the gate. Stars and moon swept along the sky, offering pale light to see. Bryn strode ahead. Away from his tad, he seemed to feel bolder, ducking back now and again to stare at us.

'What age are you?' he asked me. 'What are you called? Where are you from?'

'He's restless as goats in thunder,' Haf muttered, annoyed by him.

I didn't mind. 'I'm Mai. I'm thirteen.'

'Older than me by one year,' he said sadly. 'But you're little enough.'

'For what?'

We passed low buildings, roundhouses thrown up against the wind and rain, but not doing the best job of it. They had no foundations and the roofs were pitched askew. I hoped they were for animals, not people. The buildings hugged the path on either side.

'I'm little enough for what?' I asked when Bryn didn't reply.

'For scavenging. They send the little ones into the narrow spaces, to see what we can find.'

'Narrow spaces?'

'There's all sorts of places we go. Empty villas for miles about. People rushing for safety hid all kinds of treasures. You can find them if you look. Not just houses, either, there are Roman tombs we go in sometimes.'

I wondered if our own hall had been picked clean by now. My nails cut into my fists.

'Pecking over corpses like carrion birds,' Haf said. 'Heathen.'

I hadn't thought she was listening. She had Tad leaning on her shoulder, arm around his waist. He looked too tired for talking.

'I'm no oak-grove heathen,' Bryn said, smiling lopsided. 'I cross myself at least three times every day. Ask Father Ambrose.'

'Is that the priest here?' I asked.

Bryn nodded.

The bank and ditch ran the whole way around the hill, as though it wore bands of torcs. The earthworks protected the huge flat space at the top, too huge for me to see the other end in the darkness. Cattle moaned out in the black. The roundhouses of the Britons were clustered at the near end like unploughed anthills. I couldn't count the number of homes: twenty, fifty?

I felt frightened all over again. I had rarely seen people all together like this. But Tad had told me stories of cities like Rome and Antioch and Alexandria. I tried to be excited. I tried to feel safe.

'What's that?' I asked Bryn, who had scampered closer. I pointed to one building larger than the others. It was square, in the Roman style, with two smaller roundhouses beside it like villa wings.

'Gwrtheyrn holds his court there,' Bryn said. 'He's the bravest man in the camp. In the whole land, maybe. I'm training with him.'

I tried to glimpse the great warrior, but Bryn pulled us past the hall too swiftly. Past the silent homes, and shuttered workshops. Out into the darkness on the other side.

'This way,' he said. We crossed another ditch and bank. Rough-cut planks formed the bridge. 'That's our chapel.'

The roundhouse he pointed to was set apart from the village. It had no fire burning, so was hard to make out. Somehow the edges of the roundhouse seemed to shimmer and move. Snakes, it seemed, adders, slowworms, shoals of silver fish, maybe, writhed about.

Its walls were moving. There was no two times about it. I stopped and stared.

'Streamers,' Bryn said.

Streamers? The word, said in that whispering night, meant nothing. I had no notion what he was trying to say.

'Streamers,' Bryn said again, 'leather strips cut to look like streams. It's to ward off the fair folk. They won't cross water.'

Now, I understood. The wall moved because it was covered with thin strips that flapped in the breeze, made to look like waves. I wasn't sure that they weren't heathens, after all.

This strange, writhing place was like no chapel I had ever heard of.

This place was like nothing I had known before.

11

'YOU WANT US to go in there?' Haf asked Bryn. She didn't like the chapel any more than I did.

'It's where Father Ambrose is. You scared?'

'No.'

'Come on then.'

We followed him under the leather streamers that licked and slapped above. 'Stupid lollin boy,' Haf muttered.

The only light in the darkness came from three burning wicks floating in bowls of tallow, like the wooden boats Tad made for me when I was small. I could sense, rather than see the space. Big blocks of wood, some pillars, some carvings, glowered in the dark. Then, one of the pillars moved. My heart leaped, but I saw wood become flesh as the man walked closer. He wore dark robes and his skin was dark too, like old beams. He held his palms open in greeting, the skin pink and clean.

'Father Ambrose,' Bryn said, 'new arrivals. This one is sick. My tad said you could help him.'

Father Ambrose took Tad by the hand. '*Wél cwm, mae son.*' His accent was thick as autumn mud and just as hard to wade through. It wasn't British, nor Saxon. I wondered if he was from over the southern sea.

'Thank you,' Tad said. 'My girls and I thank you.'

'*Syt. Syt.*' Father Ambrose waved to the narrow settle, one of the few pieces of furniture in the chapel. He was telling us to sit.

'Bryn, they nud ffwd,' Father Ambrose said. I concentrated hard on his mouth as he spoke, watching his lips, willing myself to follow. 'Ffwd, Ffood, food, quickly now. Ddaear should be hot cawl bubbling somewhere.'

He wanted to feed us. My stomach growled like wolves in winter and Father Ambrose smiled. He helped Tad to sit on the bench. Haf dropped beside him, her head drooping against his shoulder.

'You lwc as though you need to shed tears, not words,' the priest said. I was getting used to his accent.

'We've been walking for days,' Tad replied.

'Our hall was attacked,' Haf added. 'My tad is hurt.'

'I'm sore for you. The world goes from low to lower, I know. And ffowc give no mor thought for the holy altar than if it were dirty stones heaped high. But, Gwrtheyrn is set-tyn things right. Once you haf eaten, you must rest. You wyl sleep in the capel tonight.'

I wasn't sure I wanted to sleep in this strange place, but I definitely didn't want another night outdoors.

'Let me si your wound.'

Tad pulled aside his torn tunic. The priest peered closer.

'Hmm. I've something that wyl help.' He fumbled in the pouch at his waist. 'It ys from Rome. It's the very arrowhead that pierced Saint Sebastien through the heart and yet did not kill him – laudator Iesu Grist.'

'Amen,' Tad replied, taking the small bundle from Father Ambrose.

'Have you any willow bark?' Haf asked.

'Patience is the mother of wisdom,' Father Ambrose answered, his words clearer and clearer. 'With the brow of day, I wyl take you to Gwrtheyrn. He wyl find you your new home and put you to work, no doubt. He is the lord here, and the lands about. After the One Lord, of course.' Father Ambrose chuckled at his mild joke. 'Gwrtheyrn wyl take good care of you, as wyl Saint Sebastien.' Ambrose patted Haf indulgently. She shrank from his touch.

Bryn returned, balancing two bowls of steaming cawl, the tang of vegetables sweet in the air. He handed me the first bowl, the second he gave to Haf. We shared between the three of us. There were tiny pieces of meat in the broth and my whole body shivered with the warmth of it.

'Privy pits are dug near the wall,' Father Ambrose said. 'Settle down to sleep hir for the night and I wyl see you when comes the day. Come, Bryn, let them rest.'

Father Ambrose smiled as he lifted the bowls from us.

I closed my eyes not moments later, and we curled up like curs on the straw-strewn floor. Sleep came slowly. What help were old trinkets, even if they were from Rome? Tad needed rest and medicine and time to heal. I had to hope we would find that here.

12

THE MORNING BROUGHT new sounds to wake me: women shouting, children yelping, the hoof-haw of animals being pushed and ushered into pens. Inside the chapel, the tallow lights were out and sunshine poured through the window holes. Tiny gaps in the thatch let in pinpricks of light, daytime stars.

I rolled on my side. Tad lay close by, his eyes closed in sleep.

So I lay back too and listened. Such sang-de-fang sounds! More people than I had ever seen before living elbow to elbow. I swivelled to see if Haf and Tad still slept.

Tad had his eyes closed, and looked pale. Haf lay still. I kicked her with my bare foot.

'Hey,' she moaned. 'Leave me quiet.'

'Are you awake?'

'Are you the devil himself?'

'No.' I sat up. Tad slept still.

I pushed back the blanket and stood. My bladder was full. I wanted to see the people in the camp, the life that was here. But some small part of me needed my sister to come too.

'We should look about the village,' I told her. Her eyes were closed, but I knew she could hear me.

'We should find Gwrtheyrn,' I suggested. *Or Bryn, or any of the men who might give me my Saxon-slaying sword*, I wanted to add.

Haf threw back her blanket in anger. 'Mai, we are not going to do any such thing. Sit down. Don't be foolish.' She kept her voice low, so as not to wake Tad. I felt bad for my noise and sat as she said.

She put her hand on my face, moth light. Then it was gone again. 'Mai, we have to be careful here too.'

'Why? What do you mean?' What made her wary? Did she think the sun was coming back to our hill, or not?

'We just need to watch, that's all,' Haf said. 'Men can't always be trusted. And we aren't always as wise as we think we are.'

Before she could say more, Tad stirred with the sounds of the day. His eyes fluttered open. He smiled. 'Are you two bickering before breakfast?' he asked. He tried to sit up, but his breathing laboured with the effort. Saint Sebastien hadn't helped.

'Tad?' Haf put her hand to his brow and frowned. 'He's fevered, his skin is hot,' she said anxiously. 'We need the priest back. We need medicine. They must have some.'

'We can ask Bryn, when he comes.' He hadn't said he'd

return, but I felt sure certain that he would. He'd seemed like someone who enjoyed the new, and had his ear to the earth. We were new enough to catch his interest.

I left to visit the foul-smelling privy pit by myself. Its wattle and daub fencing was private, and sturdily built. But the air around it made me gag. Back home, Tad always kept our outhouse fresh with layers of dirt and ash. Here, my eyes watered with the stink.

I glanced at the people I passed. I saw old men, boys not much older than me, dark-haired like bulls; women whose clothes hung longer than mine, cut differently; children whose stick-thin arms looked like birch switches. Now I was out with them, they didn't feel like my people any more. They felt odd; strangers. I hurried back to the chapel.

In the daylight its leather strips fluttering about looked more like fishscales than snakes. Shades of grey, tan and brown moved together. I saw other decoration too, that I'd missed in the darkness – three head-stones, set in carved wooden alcoves above the door. Their eye-holes were cattle-belly dark and their teeth were clamped shut together, keeping the secrets of the dead.

Inside, Bryn was back. I felt pleased to have judged him right. He'd brought more cawl and hard bread.

'I'm to take you to Gwrtheyrn as soon as you've eaten,' Bryn said. 'Father Ambrose will be here shortly.'

'Is he bringing your healer?'

'He is our healer. Don't worry, he's good.'

'What's he like? Gwrtheyrn?' I asked. 'Does he train his warriors himself?'

Bryn pulled his short knife from his belt and cut the air right through. 'He trains me with his own sword. Ha!' He lunged towards me.

'Don't do that in chapel,' Haf said.

Bryn reddened.

She helped Tad sit upright and lean against the settle. 'You have to eat, Tad,' she said. She held the bowl of cawl up to his lips again and again, willing him to drink, but he took too few mouthfuls.

Bryn settled beside me on the sleeping rug, sitting cross-legged and eager. If people had tails, his would be wagging.

'Can you leave us for one moment, please?' Haf said. 'I need to change my clothes.' I knew for sure that Haf had not one single stitch with her that she wasn't already wearing, but I held my tongue.

Bryn got up and left in silence.

'Haf!' I said as soon as he was gone. 'That was rude.'

'*Isht*. I need to talk to you without the Britons hearing.'

'Why?'

She pulled me up and dragged me to the altar, as far from Tad as we could go. Her blue eyes seemed grey with storms. 'We should go and see Gwrtheyrn together. Just me and you. If he sees how sick Tad is, he might think us fresh burdens. He might make us leave. There's no need to raise the subject of Tad to the air.'

'Would Gwrtheyrn send us away? Don't we belong?'

'Sometime, somehow, we were kin once. Back before the Romans left and all ties were cut right through. But do you know how you're related to Bryn, or Rhodri, or anyone else here? No, you don't. We can't rely on ties of family. Gwrtheyrn has to want to keep us here.'

'Why would he want us though? Me and you?' Maybe Rhodri had seen what kind of soldier I could be when he looked me up and down the night before.

She didn't answer. She just let go of my arm. Then she pinched both of my cheeks, hard.

'Ow!'

'You need more colour. You need to look healthy. Our future here might depend on it.'

I hadn't been scared before – Ambrose had welcomed us, Bryn had fed us. Even Rhodri had let us in without much pausing. But now I was afraid.

The leather at the doorway flapped. Father Ambrose appeared.

'Good morning,' he said. 'I've brought herbs from the fforest for your pater. They're from last summer but it should keep need at bai. How ys he? Bryn says he ys weak.'

'That boy,' Haf said under her teeth, before saying, louder, 'Tad's doing much better, I think. Though he feels warm, maybe.'

I gawped at her lie, but she ignored me.

'We're to go to Gwrtheyrn, Mai and me,' Haf said, standing awkwardly before the priest.

He nodded, already untying the mouth of the cloth sack he was carrying. 'Impress him. Now the name Rome is empty of meaning, he is the hope of all Britons.'

I swallowed down my rising fear.

Bryn waited outside. 'Come on then,' he said, mouth churlish – sulking perhaps. He looked at the clothes Haf wore. 'Those tunics are as torn as your other ones. I can't see any difference.' Sulking, sure certain.

We crossed back over the boundary ditch. People walked everywhere; grey-haired men carrying tools and urgency, women with tightly held bundles that might have been food or clothes or children. They all had tasks, so much was clear. This was no clasped-handed amble, but the hard march of men with masters. I looked carefully to see if I could see the likeness of Haf in the face of any of the women, or Tad in the bodies of the men. Most people were tanned brown with dark eyes, as I was. But they didn't feel like family. Not the smallest bit.

I ran to keep up with Bryn.

I held my breath in my fists as we approached the hall. In daylight, it looked both grand and poor. It had four square corners set with thick, dressed stone. But the mortar to hold the foundations together was simple mud. It would wash away before spring was through. One wall was stone entirely, but I could see carved symbols of Latin letters – slabs stolen from elsewhere. The three others were freshly hewn planks, still pale and unweathered. Above, the roof was part thatch, part stone tile. Traveller-tales came to mind, of beasts with fur and scales both. The building was confused.

Would the man who'd built it be so too?

Bryn walked straight in without pause.

Haf took my hand, hers felt icy cold. 'Be brave,' she said.

'Yes.'

'But be watchful too.'

'I'll try.'

We went inside.

Three men stood around the fire that burned in the centre of the hall. I looked for the warriors, but it was just these three. Tall men, with their dark beards trimmed and hair to their shoulders. None looked like the hero of any story. I recognised Rhodri; now I knew Bryn better, the resemblance between him and his father was clear as sunlight on stumps. The second man wore the same brown wool as Rhodri, the shades woven in repeating patterns across their chest and arms, like fish bones. The work was well-done, but simple. The third wore brighter clothes, the wools richly dyed with rose madder – the red set him apart from the hedgerow colours of the rest of the camp. He was the speaker in the chair, sure certain.

Haf curtsied low to him. Gwrtheyrn. The man who

had brought the people to the hill as flowers turn to the sun. I joined her with bent knees and kept my eyes to the rushes on the ground.

'The new family,' he said, with warmth in his voice. 'Or two of them at least. Where is your father?'

'At chapel,' Haf said, her voice stronger than mine would have been.

'He likes to keep the company of that Lord, does he?'

Rhodri laughed as though it were the best joke. I wasn't sure why it was funny.

'He would have come if he could,' Haf replied. 'He was injured. He's getting stronger every hour, but Father Ambrose is tending him.'

'So,' Gwrtheyrn said, 'you have but one man, and he is injured. What else have you brought with you?'

'Little,' Haf was forced to admit. 'We left at pace. But we can work hard, we have skills.'

I thought of the sacks we had left at the chapel. They were mostly empty now, save for the little silver cross Haf had saved, all that was left of Mam. It wasn't true that we had nothing. We just had nothing we were willing to share.

Gwrtheyrn was silent for many moments. I felt the heat of his look on every inch of my skin.

'What skills do you have?' he asked finally.

I wanted to say I could train and fight Saxons, but I could say neither boo nor be, now it came to it.

'Tad can tell stories,' Haf said. 'As good as any bard.'

'Stories?' Gwrtheyrn laughed. 'I need soldiers, not storytellers.'

Haf curtsied low again, keen not to give offence. 'You're right, my Lord, but once the battles are won, they will become legends that need telling.'

Gwrtheyrn laughed, surprising us all, I think. 'It seems you can turn pretty tales too.' He clapped his hands. 'You will stay in the house near the bank, the one left by Eleri. It still stands empty?'

The man to his left nodded.

'Good. Bryn, show them where it is. Girl, you've bought yourself three days of grace. After that I want to see your tad standing in front of me with either weapon or shovel in hand. I don't care if he sings while he does it. Is that clear?'

I didn't ask what would happen if Tad could not stand, and neither did Haf.

'Until then, you both make yourself useful. There are more jobs than hands. Go wherever your skills lie. You'll not be unwelcome.'

We backed away with another curtsy. I reached for Haf, took her hand in mine. She gripped me back, tight. Our hands stayed fixed-firm together as we left the hall, clinging to each other, urging the other on. We had to get Tad fit enough to stand, or this would be no refuge at all.

13

WE STOPPED OUTSIDE the hall. Would we have to stand by our word? We'd sworn to have Tad standing fit and hale before Gwrtheyrn within three days. He could barely sit upright.

'What will we do?' I asked Haf.

'*Isht*, I need to think,' she said.

'We can farm and weave and cook. That will be of use. Even if Tad isn't well.'

Haf didn't reply pin-quick. I could feel her mind working. 'We could buy our place here. We have silver too,' she said, soft as snow feathers.

She was thinking of the silver cross.

'No, we don't,' I said.

'We do.'

'It's not for trading.'

'It might have to be.'

'That cross is all we have left of Mam,' I said.

'We have memories.'

She had memories, I didn't. Not really. But, I didn't

argue any more. There was nothing to argue over. I was right.

From the top of the hill I could see the dark green stretch of woodland to the north and east – the trees we'd trekked through like lost sheep. To the west was the slightest sliver of silver – the broad river flowing into the sea. Above us the sky arched blue and bright. I could see promise here, with hard work.

Bryn was on his way to us. But he paused to talk to one of the greybeards headed inside. It struck me that Bryn was the robin in this tangle of trees, his beak in every business, his eyes open and watchful.

'Mai! Haf!' Bryn said when he had finished pecking over seed with the man. 'This way.'

'Where are we going?' I trotted close to him.

'Your new home.'

He led us to the edge of the camp, where the smell of the midden ditches was strong. The homes on this side were not so well kept. The few people we passed looked weary. One woman, huddled on her own threshold was so thin she was no more than eyes and clogs. Dogs ran, ribs visible, between walls and willow-weave fences searching for dropped scraps, relentless. Bryn stopped beside one of the most heart-lost houses we had passed. Its round, dung wall was low and wretched, holes and loose mudwork patterned around the posts. Above, the thin thatch was wind-blown; it had shifted like mud flats at the river-mouth.

There were no window holes and the door was narrow. It had been built with hurry at its heels and had been cared for by no one.

'Whose is this?' Haf asked, her voice thick with contempt.

'It belonged to Eleri. She had no family,' Bryn replied, 'no one to take her in. Some of the others helped her with this, but you're right, it was done on wild hooves.'

'Where's Eleri now?' I said.

Bryn didn't answer. We understood. Eleri had stretched out her feet one last time and been carried out of here, no doubt.

We went inside reluctantly. I felt no difference in warmth – it was the same cold inside as out. But it was darker; no spring sun had ever reached in here. The air smelled of the damp breath of coming winter.

There was nothing inside to speak of. Whatever Eleri may have once owned was long gone. Even the hearthstones in the middle of the house had been taken.

'It needs some work,' Bryn said.

'Is it to test us?' Haf wondered. 'Does Gwrtheyrn want to see what we can make from nothing?'

'It isn't nothing,' Bryn replied keenly. He peered out through one of the bigger holes in the wall at the camp beyond. 'People gave their time to help Eleri build this. If you don't want it, the road is just there.'

'We want it,' I said.

'We do,' Haf agreed. 'I meant no offence.'

'None taken.' Bryn sniffed. 'There's dung and clay for repairs in the cattle field.'

'Where are the cattle?' Haf asked.

Bryn stepped out. We followed, blinking in the cold light. He pointed. 'Go past the chapel, to the far ditch. The cattle are kept just beyond. I've got to train now.'

He stalked away and didn't glance back; Haf had annoyed him.

Haf sighed. She hadn't wanted to make enemies, not even of small boys, I realised.

'I'll check on Tad,' Haf said. 'You go to the cattle field. I'll meet you back here. We'll need stones too, big ones, for the hearth. And something to burn. It's freezing. I'll see what I can find.'

I reached the cattle field following the path that weaved igam-ogam between huts. Another wattle fence and ditch marked the boundary. Few cattle were grazing, perhaps fifteen or twenty. More than we'd ever owned, of course, but not enough to give milk and butter and cheese for the whole camp. It was obvious why there were so few; the field was safe, but the grass was worn bare, nibbled to moth-eaten patches. Was it really too dangerous to let them creep and drop into the valley to graze?

I knew the answer myself in the moment. Of course it was too dangerous. The cattle and their keepers wouldn't be seen again if they went too near the wood. Saxons, like

Algar, would have them in heartbeats. So the poor beasts were stuck cropping chaff.

'Hey. What do you want?' The cattle were watched by two small boys, dwarfed by the black flanks of the beasts. The bigger one called again. 'What's your business?'

I walked closer, my feet sucked into fist-sized pockets of mud where the cows had trodden.

'I want to take some mud and dung for building. Are there buckets?'

'What will you give me for the loan?' the boy asked, sullen as floodwater.

I had nothing. Putting the truth first, we were beggared.

The boy must have seen something of that in my face. He shook his head. 'Well. I'll bring you buckets. But you'll owe me. Next time you have bread, I want some. So does my brother.'

There was nothing I could do but agree.

I stood in the field while the boy went to fetch his bucket. The cows ambled over, dark eyed and hopeful for some extra food. I patted the sides of one or two who came close. Their hides were dull, their bones like rocks under suede.

'Here.' The boy was back. He carried two buckets, both made from old leather, not coopered wood. It seemed we were all beggared on this hill. I thanked him.

For the next few hours, I carried mud and dung back and forth to the house. Haf joined me. Together we pushed chewed grass and clay-mud into all the holes we could see. The house soon smelled of drying earth and the sweetness of cattle. The tips of my fingers shrivelled with the wetness of the job, and my stomach rumbled with hunger. Sweat dried to salt on my skin. But within the half-day, the house was sealed again.

Bryn had been right. The gift from Gwrtheyrn was not nothing. I wondered if we owed him too. It was unpleasant to think we were in his debt already.

Haf came back from one trip with three hearthstones and some kindling.

'Who gave you those?' I asked.

'One of the families near the hall. They do better there.'

'You went back there without me?'

She shrugged. 'We'll need friends. You'll thank me once night falls.'

When the house was wind-tight and the fire crackled, we fetched Tad. It was the work of the devil to get him there, though the walk wasn't long. He couldn't stand unaided and Haf and me took his weight between us. He was getting worse. Father Ambrose took back the arrowhead that had pierced saint-flesh before we left.

We settled Tad around the meagre hearth, tucking the sacks tight around him.

'They'll help you?' Tad asked. I didn't understand what he meant, but Haf seemed to.

'All's well,' she said. 'Mai and me are to make ourselves

useful while you get better.' Her eyes warned me to say nothing more.

'Good,' he said. The effort of speaking seemed too much. His eyes closed mid-thought, it seemed.

Just as the sun dropped from the sky, Bryn pulled aside the sack we'd hung over the doorway. 'Am I welcome?' he asked.

Were all boys like this? Puppy-playful one moment, sulking the next, then playing at being manly? I couldn't make rope nor wreaths of it. Until I saw his cheeks redden when Haf smiled, and then I understood. He liked her. He was lollin daft.

'Come in,' she said. 'The welcome's warm, not blue.'

'I brought you food, from the hall.' He carried one big wooden bowl. I took it gratefully. Then I noticed how thin it was, with more water than broth and no meat at all.

Bryn caught my look. 'I feel bad over this.' His eyes watched Tad to make sure he was asleep before he added, 'Gwrtheyrn says no meat for your house until it's been earned. He wants to know your tad will live first.'

I looked at Haf, wild-minded.

Tad needed good food if he was to get better.

She didn't look surprised. I realised she had been expecting this. She was quicker at knowing what was in the minds of others than me, the few times we'd been to market together, I'd seen that: she easily bartered down where I would have taken the trade. I took the cawl with my thanks kept tight behind my teeth.

Gwrtheyrn was serious about seeing Tad stand before him. Our time here was marked.

With morning came work. Tad needed food better than the puddle water Bryn had brought, and to get it, we had to earn it. Haf was full of gorse-fire quickness.

'Trade your time and skills,' she said to me. 'There will be people here about who need help with their crops, or animals, or babies. Find out how it works.'

'What will you do?' I asked.

'Tad won't be well enough to stand in the hall when Gwrtheyrn asks for him.'

'You don't think so?' Tad had shivered through the night. I hoped that meant his fever was gone.

'I don't think so. No,' Haf said, as though it was nothing. 'We'll need to trade too for herbs to help him get better. Work, Mai, harder than you ever have before.'

Me! She was the one who hid from the wife-work! 'What will you do?' I asked again.

She pulled her fingers through her hair then braided it neatly. My hair felt like tangled bushes beside hers. 'I'll try to persuade Gwrtheyrn to give us more time.'

'How?' I asked.

'I don't know yet. You see about work.'

I had wanted to talk to Bryn about his training.

Perhaps I could watch the warriors? But Haf was right. Better food was what Tad needed. So that's what I would get.

The roundhouse beside ours was home to the woman I'd noticed yesterday, all eyes and clogs.

'I'm looking for work in exchange for food,' I told her.

She laughed, hollow-cheeked.

'I work hard,' I said. 'I'd never lift any lazy loads.'

'There's nothing here for you.' The woman turned to go back inside.

'Wait! I need to find food. Could you see to help me?'

'Try nearer the big hall. This end of the camp, it's thorns and thickets. But Gwrtheyrn and the men around him don't starve.'

I didn't want Gwrtheyrn to see me. I wanted my whole family gone from his mind like morning mist in sunshine. But I had to go where there was hope of work. So, I stepped cautiously through the camp. The woman was right. As the houses neared the hall, the walls were straighter, the thatch thicker and the cheeks of the people were rounder.

The first family I asked gave me winter wood in exchange for chopping kindling. Another gave me flour once I'd sat at their grinding stone long enough to blister my hands. I had no excuse not to give bread to the cattle boys now. I would pay my debt.

By the time the sun had arced the sky, I could return to

the house with food to share. The people felt less like strangers and more like neighbours.

I found Tad fevered again.

'Does it hurt?' I asked as I peeled back the edge of his tunic and lifted the binding. The burn below was pink as dawn with yellow and black flecks seeping at its edges.

'It's not so bad,' he said. His teeth chattered despite the heat that burned within him.

'Have you eaten? Drunk?'

'I've no hunger.'

'You have to drink. Come.' I helped him with the water, but much of it ran down his chin. I wetted the torn sack and held it to his face and neck to cool him, but his skin was aflame.

Haf came back before dark. She looked at Tad without speaking, then opened the pouch at her waist and took out something leaf-wrapped. 'Willow bark,' she said. 'Mix it with hot water.'

The small fire was little more than embers, but there was enough heat to prepare the mixture.

I was helping Tad to sip it down when the sack-cloth door opened. Bryn stood awkwardly, feet shifting beneath him. 'Gwrtheyrn says your tad is to come,' he said.

Tad looked up, but there was tiredness scored in every line of his face.

'Why?' Haf snapped. 'Our time isn't up yet.'

Bryn shrugged. 'He wants to hear new tales around his fire. You said your tad was as good as any bard.'

He was. But not now, not tonight.

Tad tried to move, to stand.

'No!' Haf pressed him back down.

'I have to,' Tad said. 'We can't make him angry.'

They looked at each other deeply, right in the life of their eyes, fighting silently. I felt useless beside them, looking to them both to lead.

'I'll do it,' Haf said. 'I'll go.'

'It's not what Gwrtheyrn asked for,' Bryn warned from the doorway.

'Well, it's what he's getting,' Haf said, as if that decided the business. She pulled her fingers through her hair, fluffing out the dark curls. 'Is my face clean?' she asked me.

I nodded.

Could she do this? Would Gwrtheyrn let her?

My skin prickled with worry.

But Haf had decided. She was up and at the door. 'Watch Tad.' She threw the words over her shoulder like salt, and was gone.

It was dawn before I saw her again. Tad and I slept badly. I could feel him in the dark, trying not to worry.

But Haf crept in with the blue of day. She settled on to the ground beside me and sighed.

'What happened?' I asked, on thorns with worry.

She reached out her hand for mine and held it. 'I told the tale of Caesar defeating the Gauls – and the Caesar of my story was bearded, with dark hair and he wore red wool tunics.'

I could see her eyes glitter with mischief.

'Gwrtheyrn!' I laughed.

'We're safe for today,' she said, and fell asleep.

Mid-morning, Haf found me at the winter woodpile, chipping kindling.

'Mai, Rhodri has work for you,' she said.

'I have work.' I pointed to the thin splints of wood at my feet with the tip of my short knife.

'What did you agree for it?'

I looked at the tall, war-scarred man who managed the woodpile like hawks watch their chicks. 'Three old carrots for every knee-high pile. His knee, not mine,' I told her.

'This work is better. Rhodri says to meet him in the hall.'

'What's the task that Rhodri wants?'

Haf glanced skyward before saying, 'I don't know. But Rhodri is important here. Second only to Gwrtheyrn. If he wants us to do something, we do it. Understood?'

'But I gave my word to cut these logs.'

'Perhaps, if you leave it, then one of the fair folk from

the tales will take pity on you and cut them while you're gone.'

I put my hand on my hip. 'Even if they did help me, you know they always want something awful in return, like my first-born child.'

Haf grinned, despite herself. 'Who'd want your child? It's bound to be ugly as chopped liver.'

'I'll give them your first born, then,' I grinned.

'These logs will still be here when you get back, I'm sure. Tad needs more medicine as well as carrots. Rhodri can give it to us.'

She was right. 'Has Rhodri promised it?'

'He has.'

So, I slid my knife back into my belt and abandoned my post and my carrots.

I headed towards the clobyn hall – I couldn't help seeing it as monstrous, like the half-formed beasts of stories. People were at work in every open space between homes. Young men placed hand-coiled pots in ovens, or twined ropes. Women tended to bundled babies, or picked over wool in baskets. There were no soldiers that I could see. No arms training or ranks of men marching in time. Was Gwrtheyrn really battling the Saxons? I had seen no sign, but then, it had only been two days.

I smelled the cook-house before I saw it. Smoke and meat and stock made my belly groan. I moved faster. It was another roundhouse, more solid than ours, with stone foundations. The store beside it was the same design, though with no windows and the door heavy, barred shut and guarded. I plunged inside into smoky darkness. My eyes stung. Three hearths burned at once with hot, low embers. Metal hooks hung from the roof and cauldrons, rolling boiling, were suspended from them. Four women hurried between the fires.

Rhodri guarded them all, chest puffed and crowing like the master of middens. Like his son, he seemed to be everywhere, though the haste of the women made me think he was more feared than Bryn would have been.

He saw me and spread his arms wide. 'The new girl,' he said. 'The small one. Good.'

'You sent for me?' I managed to curtsy.

'I did.' Rhodri strolled to the nearest fire. The woman who minded the hanging cauldron stepped aside for him. He took hold of the heavy wooden spoon and stirred the stew inside. I saw chunks of onion and swede pushing through thick gravy, strands of tender meat floating up to the surface. The smell made my mouth wet with want. 'I need someone small,' he said. 'Someone with sense, who knows their cawl from their oats. Is that you?'

I wanted to nod and say of course it was me, that I was bright and brave as heroes should be. There was something about the glint in his eye that held me back.

But Haf had sent me. And the stew smelled so good. So I nodded.

'It seemed to me you might join me and Bryn and one or two others on our task for the day. It will be enough to earn your bread. Meat to go in your cawl.'

'What are we doing?' I asked.

'Supply run. We need stone and goods for trading.'

We were leaving the camp? My heart fluttered in my chest like nestling birds. Leaving Haf and Tad, even for one day, would feel like terror. What if something happened while I was gone?

'Go find Bryn. Ask for clothes for scavenging.'

Scavenging?

I stayed planted-still. My legs couldn't decide which way to walk.

'Were you raised under buckets?' Rhodri snapped. 'When your elders and betters tell you what to do, you do it. Especially if you need favours from them. Is your tad standing yet?'

I kept my eyes down and shook my head.

'Then go and find Bryn. Tell him we're going to the Roman burial ground. We'll see what we can find in the unopened tombs.'

His words stank in my nostrils, but I did as he said.

14

SUMMER SOLSTICE, AD455,
BEFORE DAWN.

ALL THE WAY back to the barn, I duck between dogs and ditch, staying unseen. The new baby might be there when I get back. My heart fills with respectful fear at the idea. But I am same-filled with the thought that the barn will be silent, that Sara will be in there alone. The raspberry leaves crushed in my hands seem so weak against the size of the struggle.

I kick the leather aside and enter.

Sara bustles over and rips the leaves clean from my hands. Checks that I have brought the right thing.

'How is she?' I ask.

'Still here.'

'The baby?'

'Not here yet.'

I hear low moans, like unmilked cattle, heavy with pain. She sounds exhausted.

'How much longer?' I ask.

Sara shrugs. 'There's no way to know.' She hands back the leaves. 'Brew these.'

The fire is low, but still warm enough to heat water.

I drop one of the hot hearthstones into the full crock pot and it steams and hisses. I add the shredded leaves that smell melting sweet and bright. The water grows pale green. I wonder if Mam had had anyone to help when Haf and I came. I don't know. I'd never thought to ask Tad. Had she been frightened?

I pick up the pot carefully. The leaves should steep for as long as can be before the water goes cold. But I don't want to wait. I want her to drink it all down and be strong enough to finish this. I fish the cooled stone from the brew.

Deep breath.

Sack curtain pushed aside.

I see her. Lying pale as fish bones and slick with the sweat of hard, hard work.

I fill with hot loathing for the man who did this to her. Algar. I wish worms in his eyes and his dead skin soiled and gnawed by foxes.

'Mai!' Sara sees the anger on my face. There's no place for it here. She takes the cup and my poor *cariad*-love sips, her arms too weak to hold the brew herself. Her honey hair is dark with sweat. Her belly bulges gross under her loosest tunic.

'Drink this,' Sara says. 'Drink it, please.'

Dry, cracked lips gulp the fast-cooling liquid. Her head falls back on the stuffed sacking bed. She is silent, too dragged-tired to shout. Please live, please, please.

I beg Iesu the baby, the Father and the Ghost and all the saints and bishops of Rome.

Sara takes my arm and leads me back into the body of the barn. I see her eyes sparkle and realise, with shock, that she is crying.

Of course she is.

This night is full of sadness. The baby unlooked for, unwanted. Coming into the world after so many have left it.

Sara knows there is no life waiting for this mite. Nor for its mam.

'Who did you see out there?' she asks, nods at the doorway. 'Rowan? Horse? Oak?'

I shake my head. 'No one. I saw no one. I hid.'

'Good. It was good to do that. But . . .' she trails off. She wants to know what's happening. By reason, I want to know too. Who lived? Who died? Who was hurt when our neighbours turned enemies?

'Well news will be put out wide, soon enough,' she sighs. 'We've bigger things to worry our thoughts.'

My mind flicks back to the path. I will stay here. I must. I've promised. But the path, the way out, while the village is empty, calls to me.

'Sara!' the cry is sharp, slicing air. 'Mam!'

It comes from behind the curtain. She's calling for her mam. I think of the mam I barely remember. Dark hair, like Haf, spinning in sunlight, dancing with the air. She's long done.

'Mam!'

Sara stumbles through to hush her.

I've chosen to stay. I've chosen this. It wasn't forced upon me. The thought feels, for one moment, like freedom.

Sara lifts the curtain, gestures to me, without taking her eyes off my sister. 'Fetch water,' she says. 'And something to bite down on. She has to stay as quiet as she can. But it's crowning. The baby's nearly here.'

15

CURSE RHODRI TO the skies. I had folded to his orders like wet straw in the wind. I should have argued, begged, persuaded. Instead I'd been maid-meek and weak. And now I was ordered to do the dirtiest of work, scavenging in burial grounds. The thought made me sick.

'It isn't as bad as you think,' Bryn said, when I found him. 'There's nothing to be afraid of.'

'I'm not afraid! I'm ashamed.'

'Who are you ashamed for?'

I trotted to keep up. We wound through the camp to one of the bigger roundhouses near the hall.

'The dead Romans, what about them?' I asked.

'They've gone to meet their answer. They're mouldering old bones now.'

'You don't think the dead are still watching us?'

He didn't answer me. Instead he ducked inside, and I followed.

The house was warm and cosy, despite the cold outside. His mother, I supposed, stood threading her loom, with small children playing at her feet. She smiled at Bryn, but didn't stop her work. His home was round and mud-walled like mine, but richer. There were furs hanging on the walls, airing or drying. He had his own box-bed and cist for his things. His parents had their own bed screened away with woven willow. The air smelled of woodsmoke and ewe-skins and drying herbs. If only I could choose to stay here. To stand with his mother at her loom and keep the weights straight, or mind the little ones who gurgled and lolled with rag dolls.

'Here,' Bryn threw clothes at me. Trousers and stouter shoes with hard soles. 'Get changed behind the screen.'

Even as I pulled on clothes borrowed from Bryn, I wanted to run to Tad and bury my face in his shoulder and beg him go hinder me. But I was doing this for Tad, so he could have medicine and get better. My hands shook as I tied the laces on my borrowed shoes. The legs of the trousers flapped like raven wings. It was unnatural. The task. The tools. The terror. All wrong. The dead trusted us to let them rest. Bargains were struck when their tombs were sealed – stay away from us and we'll stay away from you. Now I was going to break that trust.

For Tad. I was doing it for Tad.

'Ready?' Bryn asked.

I followed him awkwardly, my legs felt freer and more stiff both at once.

'You're walking like ducks on ice,' he laughed.

'Well, you walk like chickens on hot coals.'

We bickered, spitting pebbles and pips at each other, all the way to the gatehouse. It reminded me of talking to Haf. Rhodri and another man I didn't know waited there for us. The man was so like Rhodri, dark and squarely built, that they must be brothers, or cousins. Family, anyway.

'March, this is Mai,' Rhodri said. I was surprised he had remembered my name, surely he had more important things to worry his head. March stayed silent. We headed out of the gate.

The low sun shone bright on my skin. It didn't know what I was doing, otherwise it would have hidden its face in shame and made us walk in darkness.

'Keep up!' Rhodri called.

We followed the red path, the grass worn to clay by many feet. The tree trunks and bare branches were dappled in light. We walked towards the half day. Old oaks and ash guarded the clearing beyond, the ground beneath my feet hissed and crunched with their dry leaves. Then I saw the first tomb. I had seen things similar before, of course, on the road into Cwmnant. But I'd never gone near one thinking to open it. My hands shook. I stuffed them under my armpits so Bryn and the men wouldn't see.

The tombs were grown over with winter green. Bramble wrapped the brick around with its thorny arms. Ivy clambered up, trying to snatch some sun. I shivered.

'This one's empty,' Rhodri said, as though talking about flour bins or water troughs – not the homes of the dead. People who had lived and breathed as we did.

'Try over there,' March replied. He was talking to me. His thick, hairy finger pointed to another tomb, almost sunk under briar. It looked like the burial mounds on the plains hereabouts that Tad said were the homes of sprites and wights.

March reached for his short knife. I cowered back, but the small blade was for the climbing, sucking plants. He slashed their stalks. The green rustled and fell, the blade singing as he nicked stone.

He'd found the entrance. It was small and narrow, the wood rotten and black. I could see why they wanted thin creatures like me for the job.

March aimed two or three solid kicks at the wood. It crumpled with little fight left. I felt my eyes well with tears at the smell. It wasn't of rot, as I feared, it was sadder than that. It was the smell of dark, and silence, and forgetting. It was the smell of promises broken.

'Go,' March said.

'With no light?' I asked.

'Go on.' He ignored my question. 'There's no choice here. Go in, girl.'

I bit back the panic that threatened to send me wasp-wild. I had to do it. For Tad. For food. For the taste of stewed meat. But the moment I stepped inside I wouldn't be the girl Tad was proud of any more. The girl who worked hard, and treasured what little had been handed down to her – tales of Iesu in far-off lands, or fair folk closer to home. I'd be someone else. Someone who stole from the dead, who had no respect. I would be someone Tad wouldn't like.

'There's nothing that can hurt you,' Bryn whispered.

I forced myself to step into the tumbling ash-darkness.

My toes gripped the insides of my shoes as I dropped my head and squeezed inside. I stayed still, waiting for my eyes to get used to the gloom. Something scurried across my cheek. I bit back my screech and tasted blood.

The black became grave grey, slowly. I saw years of dirt, churned up by woodlice and worms, dropped down through the roof tiles. I saw something solid in the centre of the tight space. My mind leaped from it, but my frozen body stood still. Stone. Cragged sides, cragged lid. Stone that should have held its contents, untouched, for ever.

My breath came fast and fierce.

I wanted to run. Plunge out into the clean air.

But the way out was blocked by Bryn. My toe-tips touched the edge of the stone cist and every hair on my head wanted to scream.

'Did you find anything?' Bryn tried to peer around me. The flesh of his shape pressed against me. Pushing me against the stone. 'It's still closed tight. That's good.'

The meat of him muttering. 'Mai?' he asked. 'We have to open it. Help me.'

I had to do this. I had come this far. I had to reach into the coffin and find something that would make Rhodri pleased. I had to get herbs that would build Tad up and make him strong again.

My shaking hands wouldn't do what I asked.

In the pressing dark I heard bones clatter. The dead waking. Sitting up. Their empty eyes turned on me in rage. Bone-needle fingers stretched out to touch me. I couldn't see them, but I could feel them close, in the stone black. Rage, rage, rage that they were being robbed. I felt their cold scratch my cheek.

The light shrank until I was looking at stars through pinholes. I felt blood rush as I fell.

'Mai!' I heard Bryn shout, then, nothing.

16

LEAF MOULD. THE dank smell of it against my skin.
Cold. Biting nips at my ears and fingertips. Tingling pain.
Then, head-slamming bursts of it. Boulders of pain.

'Mai? Are you dead?'

I tried to open my eyes, but they were blind-shut.

'Stay still,' I heard Bryn say.

Then, I felt cold water on my face, my eyes stung
and soothed. The world was tinged pink until I blinked
it away.

'You're bleeding. Your forehead.' Bryn leaned over me,
his eyes washed with worry. 'Can you sit up?'

He hooked his hand under my shoulder and lifted me
upright. The bare trees and flat earth staggered sideways.
I thought I was going to be sick, though there was nothing
in my stomach to come back up. I folded forward.

'You hit your head.'

I could feel that clear as corner-posts. 'What happened?'

'The tomb . . . You fainted.'

That was the right of it. I had been busy robbing the
dead when the dead reached out and robbed me right

back. I looped my arms around my knees, the dampness of the earth seeped through the wool I wore.

The world steadied enough for me to be able to lift my head. We were still in the woods, just steps away from the open tomb. Only Bryn was beside me. There was no sign of Rhodri or March. Bryn noticed my watchfulness.

'They left me here to bring you back. They said if you didn't wake by nightfall I was to leave you. But it hasn't been long. I waited.'

The men had left us here.

'They were angry?'

'Not angry,' Bryn looked up at the trees with their bony branches. It was clear he didn't want to speak, to say what he thought.

'They just don't see what use I am,' I finished his thought for him.

He shrugged. I had it at all points.

I tried to stand. I was wet-calf wayward on my feet. He shouldered my weight for more heartbeats than I wanted.

I was useless. I had been given one task and I had melted like ice in spring. Perhaps it was good that I'd failed, the task was rotten-rancid. But then I remembered Tad. I'd been doing it for him.

Bryn moved to help me walk, but I pushed him back. 'I can do it,' I said.

He let go. The trees stayed upright and me alongside them. Each step I took, each movement, pulsed in my head, but we had to get back. I had to save their opinion of me, before word reached Gwrtheyrn.

We walked in silence. I was too sore to speak. I don't know what kept Bryn quiet. We made it home as the sun slid towards the distant shore.

Bryn left me inside the gate. 'I don't think you should come and collect your clothes with me. I'll bring them to you when I'm able,' he said.

He didn't want me near his home, or his father. He didn't want to be tainted by my failure.

'What will you say?' I asked. 'We came back with nothing.'

He reached into the pouch at his belt. 'No, I found something.' The brooch he held was beast-shaped, snouted, with round eyes either side of the pin. 'It was by her shoulders,' he said.

Her?

The Roman.

He had searched her bones. As I lay, with blood on my face and my head cracked on stone, he had stopped to hunt for trinkets.

I felt sick again.

'I have to tell my tad that it was me that found it,' Bryn said, uncomfortable, head down. 'I can't say it was you. He'll be pink-fit furious if I come back with nothing.'

'I don't want to share it,' I snapped. 'It's all yours.'

I made my way back to the house that Gwrtheyrn had given us over-while, until he knew if we were worth keeping. Haf had sent me to help Tad by helping Rhodri. I'd done neither.

There was smoke rising through the thatch of our hut. I stumbled inside.

Haf sat with her head low, gazing at thin flames. Tad slept, though his skin looked less waxy.

She didn't turn to me, and I knew then that she had had the bones of the tale already. Rhodri must have sent the story wide, keen to tell the world how useless I was. I cursed him to the skies. How could Bryn be his son, they were nothing alike?

'I didn't mean to do so badly,' I said.

She looked at me, her eyes blazing like the fire. 'So, it's true? Oh, Mai. Why do you have to breed beatings? Aren't we in enough trouble?'

'It wasn't done deliberate,' I said, elbows in palms.

'It doesn't matter if it was or wasn't. The end is the same. I spent the whole night building up his opinion of us with songs and smiles, and you knock it all down the next day.'

She had the right, I knew that. But that didn't make her words burn any less. It wasn't her place to serve tongues at me. I'd had no choice to go into the tomb, and I'd not chosen to faint inside. None of it was my own doing. I looked to Tad to defend me, but he lay still as if he'd already been laid in the long home.

I stumbled to the fire. The flames were as thin as

the logs that fed them, they gave off little heat. I still wore the clothes I'd taken from Bryn. I felt as though everything had shifted leftwards. It wasn't just the walls we'd lost in the fire. Each of us was less somehow, than we had been.

'Tad is meant to stand before Gwrtheyrn with weapon in hand come dawn,' Haf said. 'I had hoped to get him more time.'

'It's my fault Rhodri's angry,' I said. 'I should have said no when I heard what he wanted.'

'Said no?' Haf snapped. 'Are you half-sensed?' She turned away from the weak fire and pinched my shoulder tight between her fingers. There was anger in her face, anger and fear snake-coiled together. 'You shouldn't have said no, you should have said yes, and gladly, and then gone and done the thing, all smiles and honey.'

The tips of her fingers dug deep into muscle, grinding me. I gripped her wrist with my free hand and squeezed as hard as I could. I felt her bones shift and creak. She gasped and let go.

But that wasn't her last word. 'You're no child any more,' Haf said. 'You need to be more careful.'

I was web-caught and wriggling, even though I had loosened her grip. She wished I'd gone through with it: rifled through the dead as though they were nothing but wind-blown twigs piled for kindling. My mouth opened but no words came out.

'You have to plead mercy from Rhodri and Gwrtheyrn as soon as the sun rises,' Haf said. 'And even that might not be enough.'

'What do you mean?' I asked.

'We have something else we can trade for more time. We can offer Gwrtheyrn the silver cross.'

'You can't,' I said pin-straight. 'It belonged to Mam.'

'What choice is there?'

'We don't have to stay. We can go somewhere else. We can cross the river-mouth, to Gwent.'

'And step from the smoke into the flames? How can we leave here with Tad still ill? We're as stuck here as if we'd walked through tar and been glued to this hill.'

I pulled my knees up under my chin and wrapped my arms tight about myself. The heat from the fire reached my shins, but no further. My back felt damp with the chill. The coming night would be cold as the feet of the dead.

I pushed myself to standing and went over to Tad. He slept, as though Haf and I had been whispering lullabies, not snapping at each other like whips.

I'd made things worse for him today.

'We'll take the cross to Gwrtheyrn in the morning,' Haf said, firm-final. 'It's us who have to save Tad.'

I slept badly. It was cold and the ground was hard. But it wasn't just that. The ghosts of the disturbed dead were walking. The woman whose brooch Bryn had taken led their march. I felt them at the edges of our camp. To leave now would be to walk among them. We wouldn't reach Gwent. The dead and the living would stop us. From the smoke into the fire was right. I'd hoped we'd find welcome here, but we'd only found more trouble and I could see no way to fix it.

I woke with pale light creeping in through the gaps to hear shallow gasps from Tad. I was awake on the instant. His lungs sounded mud-filled. I shook Haf.

'Wake up, you have to help me lift him,' I said.

Together we pulled and pushed him into sitting. Something shifted in his chest and he breathed easier.

'Tad? Can you hear me? Tad?' I said in his ear.

His eyes opened. 'Mai?' he said faintly. 'My chest feels heavy.'

'We must fetch Father Ambrose,' I said. 'He can give us more herbs. We can ask for the holy arrowhead again.'

Haf let Tad lie back and pulled the sacks close about him. 'Rest, Tad. We can see Ambrose on the way to see Gwrtheyrn,' she said to me.

'One of us should stay with Tad, while the other fetches the priest.' As far as I cared the day could age as long as it wanted before I went to look for Gwrtheyrn.

She looked at me, her blue eyes stern. 'We both have to go. It will be worse for Tad if Gwrtheyrn has to come looking for us. We aren't guests here. His respect will parch if we ignore his order. Three days to get Tad standing, remember?'

My eyes turned to Tad, slipping back into sleep, getting frailer as I watched, it seemed.

'I don't want to leave him alone either, but we've no choice,' Haf said. 'We're between the devil and his sty.' She didn't need to say that it was me who'd put us there. Me. I'd undone her good work.

Her words were slaps on my cheek.

I held myself still and level like dished water, but I was afraid my fear and anger were ready to spill. She was right. It was my fault.

That decided me. 'Let's go together,' I said. 'Bring the silver cross.'

I hadn't eaten since the morning before and my stomach cramped with want as we walked to the great hall. My head ached too. The air held the taste of first frost.

Mud dragged at my feet, but we reached the hall together.

It was fuller than I'd seen it, with those seeking favour, maybe, and servants, certainly. And one or two men who might have been fighters. So Bryn hadn't been lying, there were some warriors here. Those two, who might once have been farriers or farmers like Tad, now stood in the shadows, watching it all with their fingers never far from their swords. They were big and bearded. It was foolish dreaming to think I could ever join them. I was scared to even look at them. Mouse-meek. The air was sweat-filled from the heat of the bodies.

Gwrtheyrn sat in his high carved chair, barely watching the people in his hall, so sure of their loyalty that he paid them no mind. He threw knucklebones with Rhodri at his side, betting on the outcome.

Haf walked with sure-certain steps to stand before him. How could she not be afraid of him? But it seemed she wasn't. The bones rattling in his palm sounded like distant laughter. He tossed them up, the white shapes glinted before he caught them neatly on the back of his hand. He clapped Rhodri on his shoulder. 'That's another slice of silver you owe me!'

'You make it seem as simple as drawing your hand across your face,' Haf said. Then she dipped to curtsy and added, 'my lord.'

At the interruption, he clatter-dropped the knucklebones onto the calfskin stool beside him. His eyes were rimmed red and his mouth was stained the same. 'Ah!' he said, looking at Haf from feet to top, 'it's the nightingale returned. Here to tell us another of your tales?'

'That's the one I told you about,' Rhodri said, pointing to me. 'She makes pets of her cattle that one.'

'That useless?' Gwrtheyrn asked.

I felt myself shake under their stare.

'Worse,' Rhodri said.

'No, with my respect, lords, no, she isn't,' Haf said. She kept her eyes down on the bones. Her dark hair clouded around soft features. 'Although she holds high thoughts of you and your men, the task you gave was hard for her.'

Hard? It wasn't hard, it was wrong. Just wrong.

But I found I couldn't bring myself to say so. Not in front of these men and the warriors of the hall. I felt tears prick my eyes. I was weak and stupid. Algar had made me angry, but these men made me foolish.

'She has no hold in her,' Rhodri said with scorn. 'She gives at the slightest weight.'

Haf lifted her head and smiled at him. 'She's young,' Haf said. 'She'll learn.'

Gwrtheyrn stood and edged forward, leaning towards her, sapling-supple. 'And your tad? Where is he? I expected to see him here in good health.'

Haf curtsied again. 'He gets stronger by the hour and hopes to stand before you soon.'

'I'm to wait, is that it?' Gwrtheyrn growled. He planted his hands on his hips, taking up more of the space. 'I'm to feed and clothe you all, while your sister grows some sense and your tad grows well. Are your tidy tales worth that?'

Haf reached to her belt. She pulled out the cross that rested in her pouch there. Its simple silver arms shone in the light from the hearth. Silver looked golden under flame-light.

At the sight of the cross, Gwrtheyrn folded. His full lips softened. He reached out to touch the metal, knuckles dark with hair. Lifted it from her fingers. He smiled at us both. Then he pressed his thumbnail against the silver, searching for the give.

His nail made no mark on it.

His grin broadened, showing tongue and teeth. 'Are you buying my protection?'

'We hoped you would accept the gift in exchange for our stay?' Haf asked.

Gwrtheyrn tossed the cross that Mam had guarded so fondly to Rhodri. 'It's worth weeks, not months,' he warned. 'Food and shelter for your family from now until the shortest day. That's all. Then either your tad stands in my hall or you all stand outside the gate.'

We were at the end of autumn, the last month of the year was here or hereabouts, and the days were racing towards darkness. The shortest day was some four weeks away, I wasn't sure certain when exactly.

'We'll make ourselves useful,' Haf said. 'I swear.'

17

SUMMER SOLSTICE, AD455,
BEFORE DAWN.

I PRESS HER hand between mine. She squeezes hard. Knuckles white. Skin pulled tight. The first rays of morning shine through mouseholes in the shingle. I pray fast, hard, as the pinpricks of light touch us, stars on skin.

Iesu, in your name, help her.

Iesu, in your name, help her.

My sister screams, the stick she was biting tumbles to the floor.

18

EARLY WINTER, AD454

GWRTHEYRN HAD GIVEN us some four weeks of his protection. That was all. We had thrown the cross Mam loved across the table for almost nothing. He could go and hang. I kicked hard at the frozen clumps of grass outside his hall.

'Stop that. We have to prove that we're worth keeping,' Haf said as we walked back to our hut. 'From today out, we are all smiles and honey at everyone. You understand? We make ourselves valuable here.'

So, I did.

I worked, and I fed Tad, and washed him, and tried to pull him back to the world. I chopped kindling and boiled the carrots I earned, feeding them mashed to Tad. In time, he held the spoon himself, and sat up to eat; he took steps without my help. I hoped soon he would be able to walk to the hall and astonish Gwrtheyrn with his tales and stories. He would be the best storyteller the camp had ever seen. As soon as he was well.

Haf would wake with the settling dew and be out before

it dried. One day she brought back wooden spoons, the next, two bowls. I tried to ask her where she got them from, but she just smiled and told me not to worry. Another time she brought my tunic back from Bryn. Someone was giving her extra food too, it seemed. Her face had filled out, her cheeks rosy with health, not cold. She was using her wits and wiles.

I was just using the strength of my arm and elbow. I hunted chores, not Saxons.

There were men training. I saw Bryn with them one afternoon. They fought on open ground behind the hall and cook-house which was grazed by one or two bad-tempered goats and picked over by toddlers gathering goat dung for meagre fuel.

Not quite one dozen men struck swords and sticks together in clattering glee. Gwrtheyrn wasn't there. But I recognised Rhodri and March. The others were of the same sort, roosters strutting on their own farmyards, crowing atop their middens. One man would dart, the other block the blow with stout oak and roar as though he had crossed the Hafren in one bound.

'Is this the army?' I asked Bryn. It was more brawl than battle.

'Some of them! Most are out raiding.'

Bryn leaped away from me to grab for one of the smaller sticks. He threw himself into the fight with whoops and laughter. Men clapped him on the back in welcome.

There was no place for me there. Not while there was work to do. Babies needed minding, grain needed grinding, all manner of things needed to be fetched. There was bartering over the job and its payment – flour, store-apples, wind-fallen nuts were all traded for my time.

And I went to the chapel. Not to ask Father Ambrose for more herbs, but to pray for Tad, to ask the child Iesu to make him strong again.

Some days there would be women there, praying for their men who were out in the world. Praying for their safe return. Everyone wanted something, it seemed.

Nearly ten days had passed in this way, when I went to chapel and stepped under the hissing streamers and the empty eye-sockets of the head stones. Inside, the smell of damp and cold was untouched by the small tallow flames. I looked about. No Father Ambrose. No worshippers, and no hide nor hair of anyone. I crossed myself, then kneeled on the cold ground near the altar. The frost of the morning was clinging to the earthen floor. Could I pray for thick socks to warm me this winter? I squished the thought like bedbugs. I was here for Tad.

I whispered the prayer over and over into the dark. *Help him get better.*

I didn't hear Father Ambrose until he spoke: 'Suffer the little children.'

It made me jump. I turned quickly and saw his face wrinkle as he smiled.

'How goes it wyth our waif from the woods?' he asked.

Did he mean me? 'I'm not from the woods. I'm from our farm.' It felt strange to talk to him from the ground, twisting around to look up. So, I crossed myself and stood. Iesu wouldn't mind that I'd stopped in the middle of my prayer.

Father Ambrose smiled again. He took the short knife from his belt and cut the small hunk of dried meat he held, he handed half to me.

'Thank you,' I said. 'I'll keep it for my tad.'

Father Ambrose nodded. He moved towards one of the benches near the curved wall and sat heavily. He pushed off his shoes and wiggled his toes. 'The ground ys damp,' he said. 'My feet swell.'

I didn't think that could be true, but I smiled anyway, and slid the dried meat into my pouch.

'Are you settling into your new home?' Father Ambrose asked.

I thought about Gwrtheyrn and his threat to cast us out – I wasn't sure certain that this was my home. Or even if I wanted it to be.

Father Ambrose must have seen the doubt written on my face. 'It takes time,' he said. 'I felt the saim, when I arrived. And I knew no British. I had Latin and Greek and some smattering of Saxon.'

'You speak Saxon?' I asked.

'I've travelled from Carthage, to Rome, to Constantinople

and more. The roads are safer when you understand what ys being said.'

I thought of the road and the danger it had brought us. Would Tad have been safe if he'd spoken Saxon? I wasn't sure it was true. But Father Ambrose knew more of the world than I did.

'Tad's getting better,' I said.

'Praise be.'

'But the nights are getting colder. There might be snow soon. And he has only sacking to sleep under.'

The priest laughed. 'Are you asking me for blankets?'

I shrugged. I was.

He pointed to the wall beyond the altar. 'There are sheepskins in there. They belonged to one of the families I ministered to. You can take one.'

'Don't the family need them?'

'Not any môr. Sickness took the last of them this summer.'

Iesu had answered my prayers! I went to the cist and lifted out one of the skins; it smelled sheep-sour and there were stains on it.

I was pleased with myself as I tucked Tad in warm that night.

Five more days passed and the sun waned earlier and earlier.

I saw Haf in the mornings, but she was gone by noon

and came home after I slept. I wondered where she went, but there was never time to talk. It was work and more work. Grinding flour was the hardest job. It was work to shorten bones, pushing and pulling the heavy top stone back and forth. As the two stones rubbed, I dropped the round grains in handfuls between them. Slowly, flour formed. My arms ached. My fingers were nipped and cut where I was careless with the stones, but the job was done, in the end. The woman whose flour it was inspected the work.

'It's coarse,' she complained.

'I could put it through the stones again.'

'What? And get more of your blood mixed in with it?' she said. 'No thank you. But you'll understand if I pay you one loaf not two.'

'We agreed two!'

'We agreed you would grind it, not stroke it.'

I felt my cheeks redden with anger. 'It's to feed three of us and my tad is ill.'

Her mouth puckered, hard as winter. 'Your sister is filling her own belly well enough.'

'What does that mean?' I asked.

'She's made herself at home in the great hall, that's all. Though I'm not one to herd tales.' She puckered her mouth again, the old witch, and only gave me one loaf for my troubles.

But what she'd said grew like mould on cheese. Where

was Haf? Was she working at the hall, or was she just playing the lady at the sleeves of the big men?

I had to know.

I went to the hall to look for Haf. The space outside looked different, more cheerful somehow. Men, women and children scurried, busy as lamb-tails about the place. The doorway had been entwined with waxy green holly boughs, the tiles dripped with ivy plaited with faded red ribbons. There were sounds coming from the cook-house too: the clamouring of knives on wood, women talking or arguing, firewood crackling and belching.

I found Haf napping on black bearskins, close to the empty seat of the lord.

I dropped down beside her and lay near the warmth of her body. Then I reached out and shook her gently. 'Haf, Haf, wake up.'

Her eyes fluttered open. 'Mai?' She smiled at me. Her hair had come loose from its tie and she pushed it clear of her cheeks. 'What is it?'

'What are you doing here?' I asked, keeping my voice low, for the hall had many ears.

'I was resting, but I suppose now I'm not.'

'Why didn't you come home to rest?'

She looked at me full serious and pushed herself to sit. 'There's no rest there, and I feel so tired. They said I could close my eyes here, so I did.'

'Why are you tired? Have you been working?'

She drew her hands through her hair, teasing it flat. 'What's this about?'

'I don't like the hall, or Rhodri and Gwrtheyrn.'

Her eyes darted, worried over who was listening. 'Don't say things like that. That's why I can't bring you. You can't control your tongue.'

'Why are you being so cruel?' I felt the bear fur beneath my palms and dug my fingers into fists. Haf noticed. She reached out and pulled my hands free. '*Isht.* I'm not being cruel. I'm watching out for you.'

It didn't feel like it.

'How's Tad?'

She was changing the topic. My lungs felt too small, so I let her. 'He isn't eating as much as he should.'

Haf stood and stretched her arms above her head. Amid the clamour in the hall she was pool-calm. She bent to lift her shawl. Under the dun-coloured wool was something wrapped in dirty cloth. She handed the parcel to me. 'Ground meadowsweet,' she said. 'Boil water and make Tad drink it. It will help.'

'Where did you get it from?' I asked. It was valuable – any herb was during the sleep of winter.

'Honey words and tall tales,' she said. She rubbed her face, casting sleep from her eyes. 'I need to wash and eat.'

'Tall tales?'

She nodded.

'The ones Tad tells?'

'Some of them.'

So that was it. I looked around. The fire in the pit was low now, but I could imagine it at night, flames leaping while Haf kept the crowd laughing or gasping or crying as she weaved fine words.

'That was what Tad was going to do,' I said flatly.

She smiled and cuffed my arm gently. 'I know. As soon as he's well again, I'll stop. He can do it.'

My sister was stone stupid.

'And will Gwrtheyrn want Tad to sing or to fight, do you think? When he has you being his nightingale?'

'He'll want Tad. Of course he will. When he hears how good he is.'

She sounded certain, but I could see doubt in her eyes.

I took the meadowsweet and didn't look back.

19

THE SHORTENING OF the days made everyone rush to get their tasks done. There was no time for idling, and the wind blew too cold for standing still. So, I was surprised when Bryn came to find me. I was laying winter fodder out for the cattle when he called me to the ditch. I walked to him, dragging my feet.

'You're still here, then,' Bryn said.

'That's as clear as mud on sheep,' I said.

'You still have my spare clothes,' he said. 'From that day at the . . .'

It was true. I had forgotten. I'd had my mind on my own pots.

'I'll come with you now,' Bryn said. 'I'll get them back.'

'I'm not done here,' I said.

'Owain will do it. Owain!' he yelled and one of the many small boys who seemed to run like dogs around the camp scurried to us. 'Feed the cattle,' Bryn told him. 'Don't eat the grass, it will make you sick.'

We walked in silence. I heard woodcocks call to each other beyond the hill. Somewhere, men laughed loudly.

'Your head. It healed?' he asked, eventually.

I bit my tongue. I was standing there, wasn't I? I wasn't dead. I pushed down my irritation. Maybe all boys were like this. I hadn't met enough of them to know. 'It did.'

We'd talked easily before, but the memory of his hand in the coffin of the dead woman set me on edge. We moved in silence through the daytime gloom of nearly-midwinter.

'Gwrtheyrn wants my tad to be well by mid-winter,' I blurted.

'I know,' Bryn said.

'Haf told you?'

He nodded. 'She's worried.'

'She should be.'

'Is he no better?'

I didn't answer. I kept my eyes straight ahead and pretended I hadn't heard.

'I wanted to say sorry,' he said.

'Why?' I was nothing to him.

'You didn't want to scavenge in the tombs. They made you. I told my tad afterwards that it was wrong to make you. He . . . he didn't agree with me.'

Had Bryn been beaten for disobedience? I stole looks at him. He seemed lost-hearted.

'I wanted to tell you that you shouldn't have been made to do it,' he said.

'It isn't your fault. You had no choice either,' I said.

128

He stopped walking. I stopped too. There were feelings on his face I couldn't read. Feelings I'd not seen in my family, or heard about in the tales Tad told. It seemed like misery, and bravery, mixed together.

'Your tad needs food and herbs. To help him get better,' Bryn said.

I nodded, wary.

'There's something I want to show you.'

'What?'

'Come with me.'

Bryn turned off the mud-churned path that led to my hut. He took us instead towards the great hall. He took long strides and I had to rush to keep up.

'Where are we going?'

I had no want to see Gwrtheyrn or Rhodri today. Nor even Haf. The great hall was full of noise and people and creeping fears.

But we didn't go into the hall. Instead we turned left and walked around the roundhouse that held the cookhouse stores. It had stone walls and thatch that reached almost to the ground. There were no windows, and only one door which was shut tighter than our barn at home, with heavy wooden bars. One of the fighters from the hall stood beside it, watchful.

Bryn slowed down, strolling as though we were searching for daisies. The guard said nothing and let us walk on.

Four or five scraggly trees grew not far from the hut. Bryn headed there. I followed. Bryn grabbed one of the thin branches. It bent, but held his weight. He leaped and hooked his knees over the thicker branch above. He dangled, upside down, with his hair falling towards the earth. His mouth was where his forehead should be.

'What are you doing?' I snapped. 'I haven't got time to play.'

'I'm not playing. I'm pretending to play, in case anyone looks our way,' Bryn said, gasping uncomfortably.

'Why?'

'I want you to look at the hut. See where the wall is dark? By the bigger stone?'

I did. It was as though the wall was stained.

'It's wettest there because the foundation is weak. I explored one night, when the men were drinking and I wouldn't be missed. The wall has dropped, broken. The hole isn't big, but enough for someone small to crawl inside. I covered the hole with reeds and dirt, so no one would notice.'

'Why are you telling me this?' I asked. I could feel the blood in my body, hot and quick. If I could sneak into the store while no one was watching, I could feed Tad something worth eating.

Could I trust him?

'I'm just telling you,' Bryn said.

'Why?'

He shrugged. 'Your tad's ill. And they made you do something you didn't want to. Family shouldn't do that.'

'Family?'

'Well, we are, aren't we? Britons against the Saxons?'

I thought of Algar. He was worse than Gwrtheyrn, it was true.

I let silence fall. Bryn wasn't telling me what to do. He was just telling me what might be done, if I chose to. I could creep, mouse-quiet into the store and take just enough to help Tad get better. No more.

If I was caught, they would kill me. I was sure. We might all be Britons, but my time here had showed me that that would mean little if I broke their rules. Thieves would be punished harshly, I was sure certain.

Bryn dropped down from the tree and strolled back towards the camp, as though nothing had happened. I chased to catch him.

'Mind, it's nearly empty just now,' Bryn said.

I kicked at the nearest stone. What was the use of knowing the way in if there was nothing inside?

'But there will be more food soon,' he said. 'Raiders are on their way home. They've been in Caerfaddon, hunting whatever they could find.'

Caerfaddon was the biggest city for miles about. Though I'd never been there, I knew of it. It had been mighty once, Tad said. He'd gone there in his youth, and he'd told me of temples and baths, markets and grand houses. It would be rotting to stumps now. 'What were they looking for? The raiders?' I asked.

He shrugged. 'Slaves, I think. To sell for salted pork and wine at the west harbour. Traders from beyond the sea are buying there.'

Slaves? Like the Israelites in Egypt? I felt cold despite the fire. Gwrtheyrn had had his men rip people from their homes and families in exchange for wine? So he could revel in his cups? Perhaps he was as bad as Algar, after all.

'They'll be back in time for the shortest day. We'll celebrate the sun coming back with wrestling matches and food!' Bryn spoke with eagerness. 'We'll eat roast pork. Have you had that? Can you remember the taste of it?'

I could. Tad had caught wild boar in the forest three summers ago, when he was strong and healthy and could lift the whole beast above his head with one hand. We'd roasted it and ate it for many days. The thought made my mouth water – warm fat and crispy skin and juicy strands of meat that slid off the bone.

But in exchange for what? The lives of the people the warriors had taken? Sold as slaves?

'Now,' Bryn said, 'where are my clothes? I've been wearing these drewy rags for too long.'

Haf didn't care.

I waited that night, stayed awake until she came to the hut. It wasn't hard. Tad was fevered again. It had flared up that morning and his skin felt like embers. I spent the evening wetting his brow and waiting for Haf.

'Did you know?' I asked her as soon as she stepped inside. 'Did you know about the raiders?'

'What about them?' She sounded tired.

'Gwrtheyrn's sent his men out to raid farms, empty stores, steal slaves for all we know.'

Haf narrowed her eyes. 'Do you see fields here? Furrows ready for spring seed?'

I shook my head. There were grazing cattle and smaller stock, but no ploughed earth.

'Where did you think the bread came from?' Haf tutted at me. *Soup-stupid, Mai,* the sound said.

I hadn't thought. I hadn't even wondered. But she had. And had made peace with it.

'You can't think it's right?' I whispered.

'I don't think it's right. Of course not. But what else is there? How else will we – you, me, Tad – get through to summer? Our farm is gone, Mai.'

'We could leave.'

'The snow will be here soon, and then what? Where will we go where strong men don't prey on the weak? Where is that, Mai, do you know?'

'It's no world for children,' Tad said.

We had almost forgotten he was there. He lay shivering under the sheepskin I'd begged from Father Ambrose, his eyes open and shining.

'Tad?' I dropped to his side. He didn't look at me.

'Carys,' he said. 'Carys.'

Mam. He was talking to Mam.

'Carys, I can't do this without you. Don't go. Don't go!'

I looked to Haf. She looked as wild with worry as I felt.

Then, late though it was, Bryn moved aside the sackcloth and stepped in. Had he known Tad was worse? What was he doing here?

He looked to Haf, not me, before he spoke. 'Saxons have ambushed the returning raiders,' he said, his voice as flat as river stones. 'Gwrtheyrn is sending out men to help them. He's called for every man in the camp to rally. Your tad has to come.'

20

'TAD CAN'T COME,' Haf said. 'He can't.'

Bryn nodded. 'I know. But he has to.'

There was no way on the good green earth that Tad could stand and fight. No way at all. But if he didn't go with Bryn then Gwrtheyrn would throw us out of the camp – me and Tad, at least.

Haf twined her fingers, pressed her palms together. Praying, or thinking? She paced the width of the hut.

'I hate him,' I snapped. 'I hate him and the way he thinks he can strike the fear of God into everyone here. He thinks he's Moses leading his people, but he's no better than the dunmen in the woods.'

She stood stock-still.

Looked at me in wonder. 'That's it!' she said.

'What's it?'

'Mai. Stay here. Look after Tad. I need to speak to Gwrtheyrn.'

'I'm coming with you.' If there was pleading to be done, I would do it on both knees and willing.

We rushed like wind howling through the camp. Bryn,

Haf and me, weaving through the paths between huts, into the gloaming. I could see bursts of white breath from us as we ran. At the hall we pushed into the throng of people. The news came in ragged pieces: raiders on the road . . . Saxons lying in wait . . . circling wolves . . . battle brewing . . . scouts sent to bring reinforcements before the two sides clashed like rutting stags.

Gwrtheyrn was in the centre. He puffed up his chest, rooster-ready to strut into battle. Men circled before him – Rhodri, March, the half dozen others I'd seen. The meagre might he had here on the hill.

The men spoke earnestly together. But Haf walked through their ranks as though they weren't there. She curtsied deep and long before Gwrtheyrn.

'My Lord,' she said.

I wanted to run up and stand by her side, but I in no way wanted the notice of these men on me. So, I hopped from foot to foot at the back, praying to Iesu that she knew what she was doing. Bryn had no such worries – this was his world. He moved to stand beside his father.

'Ah,' Gwrtheyrn said, seeing Haf, 'my storyteller is here, with her shrewd words.'

Shrewd? Haf?

'With your leave, my Lord, I have something I'd like to say.'

He gestured for her to get up, as she was still in the

curtsy. When she stood, she still held her body meek, arms at her side, head bowed, as though she was awestruck by these men. How did she know to do that? Perhaps she was more shrewd than I knew.

'My Lord, your fighters are strong and skilled, but they are few. If you send them all out, there will be no one to defend the camp.'

Gwrtheyrn was not smiling now. 'You tell me nothing I don't already know,' he said. The men around humphed and muttered, pawing like dogs at the ground.

Haf brushed her hair back, flattening the curls. 'There is another way.'

'Go on.'

'When Moses commanded the King of Egypt to release his people, it wasn't soldiers he used.' Haf was excited now, slipping under the spell of the story. It was one we all knew – the Israelites and the plagues. 'Moses didn't need soldiers because he had God on his side.'

Gwrtheyrn was interested, but his eyes narrowed. 'You suggest I send locusts to attack the Saxons?'

'No, my Lord,' Haf said. 'But let them know you have God on your side by filling their hearts with fear. The Saxons are in the forest, in the dark, with enemies close by. They will already be fearful. Add to their fear. Send out trumpets and bellows and make the sounds of monsters in the woods; take leather streamers from the chapel and fill the trees with the sound of hissing snakes; take drums and make them think that the very earth is cracking open beneath their feet.

'Frighten them witless, my Lord. For that, you don't need soldiers, you need small boys.'

Gwrtheyrn laughed, quietly at first, then louder until the roar of it reached the rafters.

21

IT WAS DONE. It was done just as Haf suggested. And it had gone just as she said it would. The Saxons fled as if the jaws of Hell had opened behind them, with boys like Bryn laughing in the trees. I'd wanted to go too, to frighten the Saxons like the weasels they were. But there was no question of it. When I'd asked Rhodri if I could go with Bryn my voice had quivered with fear – of the man, not the task! I'd tried again, my voice more bold, but he had pushed me aside, growling at me to stay out of the way, not even listening to me.

Haf had led me out the hall. Full of glee that her plan had worked, not noticing for one heartbeat how Rhodri had treated me. She told me to wait with Tad.

I tried to remember that Tad was the important thing. He hadn't had to fight for Gwrtheyrn. It didn't matter what Rhodri did or said to me, it was Tad that mattered. But it was hard to remember that with Haf at the hall.

The raiding party came back on the shortest day, sacks full of whatever they had stolen and mouths full of wild tales that Haf had helped put there.

Gwrtheyrn praised her. The whole camp did. Her and the men who returned laden with food and stolen treasures. Tonight the camp would celebrate. Already, I could hear legends forming. The kind of tale that would be told at feasts and festivals for generations. Each listener knowing the names of the heroes: Hywel Brynglas, Morgan Dda, Gwynfor Gwawrddyn . . .

Even at noon, the sun reached no more than thumb-height above the horizon. Gwrtheyrn was all honeyed smiles at Haf and her wisdom, as he called it. She stayed close to the hall.

I stayed with Tad. As evening fell his breathing sounded wet and mud-rattling in his chest.

'Tad,' I shook him. Harder.

His body burned hot as fire,

His skin contained his own pyre.

The fever burned from the inside. There was no rousing him. I doused him with water, but the drops rolled off in vain.

'Tad! Wake up.'

Nothing. He was breathing, but he wouldn't wake.

I needed Haf. I needed to find her and bring her here and make her help him. I needed my sister.

'I'll be back, Tad, I'll be back soon,' I promised.

As the sun settled into its cradle in the west, the camp began to move. It was as though they could sense the coming violence of the revels and were drawn towards it. Bodies strayed from huts, wandering igam-ogam towards the cattle field. For tonight, the cattle had been corralled between the bank and ditch, leaving their grazing free. Small boys had cleared the ground of dung and had done their best to flatten the field where they could.

I knew where to go to find Haf. I dropped myself into the stream of people. There were so many. More men had returned. Many and more. Haf would be with them at the heart of the feasting.

I let the crowd guide my feet, I bent to them like wheat in the wind. The smell of skin and old clothes was strong, sour in my nostrils. The sounds too were louder than anything I had heard in many months – sounds and songs rising to the starry black. Deep voices shook the air, while higher voices struck harmonies. The song spread through the crowd.

'Sea-hey-loo, lee-babby,

His ship is on the waves.'

I recognised the words. Mam had sung it to Haf when she was back in the arms of childhood. Haf had sung it to me. It had been our song to sleep by. I wondered where Mam had learned it. I had no one to ask. But if these people knew it too, then we shared something important, didn't we?

I whispered the chorus as I walked.

'Loolee, loolee, the men have set sail,
Loolee loolee, the captain won't fail.
Loolee loolee, on seas without end,
Loolee loolee, they'll turn homewards again.'

I fell into step with the people beside me. One woman caught my eye and smiled with warmth in our shared song. It went to my heart, then I felt as though it would break my heart.

These people, broken and hungry and frightened as they were, they were my people. We shared the same song.

I slowed as I carried the weight of the thought. This crowd could be my family. My future. I might grow up here, marry, raise children of my own, one day.

But tonight, now, Tad lay wakeless in the hut. I quickened my pace. Where was Haf?

The crowd parted as we reached the cattle field, it spread like open arms about the edges of the space. Four fires burned pyre-high in the centre. Yellow light spilled over us all. I wiped my face and found there were tears there.

'Friends!' the shout came from the centre of the circle. Someone was serving as herald, like John the Baptist announcing the coming of Iesu. He was young, but tall and held his hands wide, welcoming us all. 'Friends!' he cried again, 'Welcome! You are all welcome! Tonight we will see such celebration so as to make the halls of Heaven shake. Raise your voice to greet our leader and the man who has given us the gifts we enjoy so handsomely – Lord Gwrtheyrn!'

The cheer went up, loud and strong. Not one voice held back, despite the empty bellies and sunken-eyed babies that the crowd carried.

Gwrtheyrn entered the field, dressed like Caesar from the stories. Gold chains hung over his red-wool cloak. His hand, raised and waving, had rings on every finger.

I wondered which graves those rings had come from.

Then his companions followed him, Rhodri two steps behind, Bryn behind him, and, following right at the back, was Haf.

22

GWRTHEYRN WALKED WITH power and pride. Haf held her head too as though she had left our troubled times behind.

'Gwrtheyrn! Gwrtheyrn!' the crowd roared as though their bellies were full and their cattle fat.

Haf smiled, perhaps thinking the shouts were for her and her stories.

My head felt wasp-wild, buzzing louder than the people around me.

I needed Haf to come with me, to help me bring Tad back. Her real family needed her. I called her name, but the sound was drowned.

I couldn't get close. The crowd around me pressed too tight. 'Let me past,' I hissed at the wall of backs and elbows that penned me in. But all eyes were on the lords – and lady.

Gwrtheyrn led his group across the open ground in the centre to the platform and chairs that had been raised for them above the crowd. Gwrtheyrn stepped up onto it to sit and the rest sat in order of rank, Rhodri closest, Bryn furthest away. On the last chair, right at the edge of the platform, Haf took her place.

More men marched into the centre, ten or twelve. The crowd pitched and shifted, filling the edges of the circle. 'Hywel,' some voices called. 'Morgan, Gwynfor.' More voices took up the calls. I ducked and twisted, trying to push my way through to reach Haf. What did I care for these brawls? The people around me shouted for their favourites. I caught glimpses of fire-light on oiled skin. Warriors. Bare-chested, bare-footed, ready to grip the earth with their toes. Ready to maul men who had been their friend that morning.

'Haf!' I called to her. But my voice was weak as wren-piss in the sea compared to the swell of the crowd.

The men reached the centre of the ring. With his horn to his lips, the herald blew for silence. The crowd around me stilled into eager quiet, their whispers were like waves on the shore. I heard night-birds shriek somewhere to the west.

'Our champions!' the herald called. 'Returned to us with wealth and goods to share. But one will end the night as our Champion among Champions. The first pairs have been drawn. Roar now for the battle!'

The crowd gave the call – loud, angry yells to frighten the dark. My skin prickled.

Six pairs of fighters took their stance, face to face, spread out across the field so all could see. Then, the horn blew again and the fights began.

The crowd surged and tightened around me. They weren't the same people who had sung lullabies on their way here. They were bull-bent on blood. I could see the field through crooked elbows and over shoulders. Two men fighting closest to us had grabbed each other at the waist and were heaving to pull the other down. Within moments sweat sheened in firelight, spittle sprayed. The thump of flesh on flesh could be heard between the screams of the crowd.

I tried to push back, to free myself from the press of bodies, but it was like pushing tides. I was swept in and forward. The heat was solid, the air tasted of other mouths. I was surrounded by people who were as strangers to me.

Tad was alone, slipping from the world while we watched this sport.

'Let me through, let me through! My tad is sick!' I yelled in the face of the woman behind me. But she didn't hear. Her eyes were fixed on the blooded lip, the swollen jaw of one of the fighters. Beside her, men crowded in, their teeth bared, mud-mean.

'Grasp the game, girl,' one of the men said to me. His hand fell heavy on my shoulder and he tried to turn me back to face the fight.

'No! Let me be.' I dropped my shoulder away from his touch and pushed into the pack. I slithered through narrow gaps in the scrum, into the cold air beyond.

I had to get to Haf. She had to come now. She was on

the other side of the arena, up on the platform. I ran, following the edge of the field. My feet stumbled. I fell twice, sliding to the wet grass.

Then I reached the platform where she sat. Gwrtheyrn and the others had their backs to me.

Haf too, sat watching, leaning forward slightly. Her hair was loose, the dark curls veiled her shoulders. They had been washed and combed, somehow. I didn't recognise the tunic she wore, or the draped fabric and pin that held it in place.

I wondered who had owned those clothes yesterday.

'Haf!' I whispered. The sound died in the vibrating air. 'Haf!' I said, louder.

She turned. As she saw me, she smiled. Then her eyes darted to the men on her left. She was deciding what to do. Me or them. She rose from her stool and stepped off the platform, joining me on the grass.

'You came!' she said. 'I wasn't sure you would.'

'I didn't come for the brawling. I came to find you. You have to come with me.'

'Now?' her head was bowed towards me. I could smell spiced oil and something like flowers.

'Yes, now. Tad needs you. He won't wake up.'

She paused. Her hands reached for my wrists and she held them as if cradling something small and weak. 'If I leave now, it will be noticed.'

'So what? What do you care?'

'Don't be childish. I can't insult him.' Her eyes flashed over her shoulder to where the men sat. They roared at the bouts before them.

'He won't notice. You have to come.'

'He notices everything. I'll come as soon as I can.'

'There isn't any time.' I hated myself for even thinking it. But it was true. Tad was standing at the edge of the deep pool and might plunge at any moment. My stomach shifted, I felt sick. 'He needs more willow bark. The fever is back. It's worse, please, Haf. You have to ask them for more. You have to.'

'And I will. But look about you. No one will leave the arena, not until the fighting's done.'

'You have to come now.' I was begging now. Begging my own sister.

She lifted up my hands and held them too tight. 'I can't leave my place empty for more than this moment. We can't embarrass Gwrtheyrn. It would be dangerous. Why can't you understand that?'

She let go of my hands, dropping them as though they were burning.

'So, you won't come?' I said.

'Not now. Not until this is all done. I can't risk his anger. Not if we want any kind of future here.'

She turned away from me and stepped back to her stool on the boards.

23

SUMMER SOLSTICE, AD455,
DAWN.

WITH ONE LAST struggle, the baby is here. It slithers out, head first, and lies on the soaked straw for too many moments, silent, unmoving. Sara rushes to catch it.

My breath catches.

Will the baby stay with us or not? And what of its mother?

Is there one more death to add to the deaths beyond number? Time stands still, as though we had walked through cracked rock and found ourselves bewitched.

And then, the baby twitches, stutters itself into life. And it cries out, lamb-weak and needy.

It's alive. Despite everything.

My sister laughs. Despite everything.

24

THE CAMP WAS empty as I made my way back from the arena to Tad. They were all there, watching the fighting, waiting for spilled blood and spit-roast pig. I hurried from them under cold starlight, with my head down. Haf was too frightened to leave the side of the men. Too frightened of what they would say or do. This was no home. No one was free to choose for themselves.

Our old life, that Tad had given us, was nothing like this. He always had soft smiles and stories ready to lessen hurts or heal sadness. He would let us do as we pleased on the farm, as long as the chores were finished.

But it was different here. It was no wonder that Tad had always kept us from straying too far into the wood. He had been keeping us safe.

Thoughts of him quickened my steps. Was he still sleeping? Would he wake with the dawn?

The hut was dark. The fire had dwindled and nearly gone out. But there was nothing left to feed to the embers. The air tasted stale and drewy.

'Tad?' I spoke into the gloom.

Nothing stirred. I rushed in. I felt worry to the tips of my hair. I dropped down beside the bundle of furs that seemed so small compared to the giant he had once been to me. I drew back the cover.

'Tad? Are you sleeping?'

His skin was pale in the dark. I touched him.

There was still heat in his cheeks. Not much, but enough for my cold fingers to sense. He hadn't gone. Relief poured through me.

'They sang the lullaby Mam loved tonight,' I told him. 'The one Haf sings sometimes.' He didn't move, but I felt maybe his breathing was stronger as he listened.

'When you're well,' I told him, 'you can sing them your songs. You can stand in the hall and make everyone laugh with the story of Owain the Giant. You can tell them about Buddug, and all the stories you know of Iesu. Do you remember last spring when you told the story of Owain so well that Haf was nearly sick with laughing? You'll be well enough to do that again, you'll see.'

I settled down to sleep beside him.

In the narrow hours of the dark, someone shook my shoulder. 'What?' I swam up to waking.

'Mai, wake up.' It was Haf. 'I brought something.'

'What?'

'Dried poppy seeds.'

I couldn't see her hand, it was too dark, but I felt her

reach for mine. She put something small and round into my palm, some kind of box.

'Poppy seeds,' she said again. 'It will take his pain away.'

I struggled to sit. My back ached from the hard ground. I patted the place beside me, feeling for Tad. My fingers curled on his woollen tunic. 'Tad, can you hear me?' I whispered.

He didn't move. There was no sound, no sign he had heard.

'Tad.' I shook him gently. Nothing. 'Haf, fetch light.'

I heard her stand and the cloth moved aside, letting in the grey light of stars. Her shape filled the gap, then was gone. I could see Tad, lump-black as rocks dropped on the earth. I rolled him onto his back. 'Tad? Wake up.'

Haf was back on the instant with light, one wick burning in tallow. I had no idea where she had taken it from. I was angry at myself for even wondering. Now was not the time for worrying over such small things.

Haf brought the tallow lamp closer to Tad so that its pale amber light shone across his face.

His eyes were open, but there was no life in them. His mouth had fallen open too and the pink tip of his tongue looked dry. There was no breath, his black pupils stayed wide, even as the light reflected in them.

He was gone. Tad was dead. And he had left this earth

all alone, without either of his daughters to hold his hand as he went.

The thought kicked at my chest, blackness burst from my heart.

He had died alone.

25

'TAD? TAD?' HAF leaned in closer with her lamp. His eyes were too dry to reflect the light back. They drank it in and turned it to black nothing.

'He's gone,' I said from the hole I had crept into.

'He hasn't. I've got poppy seeds. They'll help.' She put down the lamp and pawed the ground for the box I'd dropped.

'Leave him!' The anger flared in me, torch-hot. 'Leave him be. You weren't even here. You didn't come. Leave him be.'

She staggered back from the fire of my words.

I scrabbled across Tad, my arms over his chest, my hair falling on his face. I pressed myself into his hard body as though I could give him some of the life I had in me.

Haf pulled at me. Her nails sharp.

But I didn't let go.

He had died alone.

'Get away from me!' I hurled the words at her. 'Get away from Tad. Where were you, Haf? Where were you?' I buried my face in the smell of his neck. Sick and sweet and laced with something dark, but still Tad at the end of the song.

I ignored her sob. I heard her leave.

I don't know where she went. My head felt that it weighed more than I could ever hold. The wool Tad wore soaked up my tears.

We stayed like that until the sun rose. My legs were pins and thorns, and cold as earth. It felt wrong to notice such ordinary pain.

The sack moved in the doorway. I looked for Haf, but it was Father Ambrose who stepped in. 'Our brother has left us?' he said. 'The groans of the Britons are unending. All is loss. All is loss.'

I heard him mutter the prayers for the dead. Then his hand was on my shoulder. 'There's work to be done. You will prepare his body. I will have someone open the earth for the burial. *Mori vita.* To live is to die.'

He left. Where was Haf? My fury burned when I thought of her. I hated her, I hated her, I hated her. But I still wanted her here. Where was she?

I couldn't move, but I had to. It was impossible, but I had no choice. Tad had to be washed, ready for the long home.

'Tad,' I whispered. 'Tad, please come back.'

He lay like wood, like wax.

I couldn't do what needed to be done. I couldn't. Not without Haf to do it with me.

I sat, watching Tad, watching his chest in case it rose again. Watching the colour of his cheeks in case they should rose again. Waiting for Haf to come and help me.

But she didn't come. No one did. It was just me now.

There was no wood left to heat water. Cold would have to do. That and wool gathered from brambles. It was enough to get the task done. I began. First, his hands. I cradled his rough, work-worn palms as I wiped water between and around his solid knuckles. I pulled the worn leather shoes from his feet and washed his soles. His face would be the last thing. I couldn't bear to do it. I poured the used water away and fetched fresh. The wool too, I plucked new from the basket.

I sat beside him for what felt like eons, as though whole cycles of the moon came and went. Could I bear to say goodbye? He was not always strong, or clued, or right, but he was Tad. He had been Tad and he had kept me safe for thirteen long years.

I dipped the wool and began to wash the planes of his cheeks, the sweep of his forehead. My tears dripped onto his skin.

'Let me help,' Haf said, standing in the doorway.

'It's done,' I said, cold as Tad himself. I dashed my sleeve against my face.

'You should have waited for me.'

'You weren't here.'

Damp curls clung to his cheeks. I smoothed them back with the tips of my fingernails.

Haf walked in. The light dimmed as she dropped the sack behind her. 'Everyone knows,' she said. 'Our news has spread on horns and pipes. I don't know how. It seems the wind speaks here.'

I shrugged. I didn't care who knew or who didn't.

'Gwrtheyrn will hear before the first grave cut is made,' she said. She reached out and smoothed his hair too. Her hand sent the stray curl bobbing loose again.

'So? What if he hears?' I snapped. Having her here made the pain worse, not better.

'We've done one good thing in his eyes. Our stories saved the raiders.'

'Your stories,' I said.

She inclined her head. 'He might come to see our value, given time. But it's men he respects, not girls. And now we're just two girls with no family and no name to speak of.'

I rocked back on my heels. The bowl jolted and water splashed the floor. 'Is that what you're worried about? What people will think of us?'

Her eyes flashed angry. 'No, of course not. I'm worried about what people will *do* to us. We are still proving ourselves. They haven't forgotten about your nonsense at the tomb, you know. If Tad had got better he could have fought for Gwrtheyrn, or farmed for him, or built for him. Gwrtheyrn might look at us now and just see two mouths he has to feed. It would have been better to draw no attention to Tad in any way at all.'

She wanted to hide Tad in the ditches or middens hereabouts, instead of letting him have the final blessing. She wanted to pretend our world hadn't collapsed. I couldn't look at her.

'You're angry,' she said simply.

'You're one of the horrors of the world,' I whispered.

'I'm all you have left in it.' She straightened and stood. 'I'm going to go to the hall now. And while I'm there I'll be singing and smiling, though my heart is just as broken as yours. Just as broken, you hear? I'll be doing it so that Gwrtheyrn doubts the news he'll hear of my father being buried today. I'll be doing it to keep both of us safe.'

In the dim light she looked tall and hard as the dolmen stones of the ancients.

'You can paint your grave white as much as you like,' I threw the accusation at her, 'but I see what you're really doing.'

'And what's that?'

'You're finding riches for yourself. I saw the new tunic you wore.'

She quivered with anger, I could feel the air around her beat with it. 'You fool,' was all she said. The door flapped behind her.

I turned back to Tad. His hair needed combing, but we had no bone comb. I pulled my fingers through his greying hair for the last time. Loose strands came free. They felt oddly alive, tickling my palm. Tad had no respectable clothes to wear. We two had only what we stood up in. So, once he was clean, there was nothing else to do but wait.

The shadows were shorter when Father Ambrose returned with Bryn. 'Are you ready?' he asked. 'We will carry him to the base of the hill.'

Carry Tad? I felt panicked then at the thought of lifting him myself. Or even with Bryn. I couldn't do it. Tad was too big. And I couldn't bear to drag him, his body ploughing the mud with his heels.

Bryn reached for my arm and held it. 'I feel bad over your tad,' he muttered. 'There are boys outside who'll help. We can carry him.'

Somehow I walked outside. There, three young men waited, sapling-bent in discomfort at my grief. They scuttled into the hut and I heard Bryn issue orders.

We began our slow walk through the camp. I glanced back once or twice. Tad was carried between them lightly. They kept his arms folded across his chest, which I was glad of. I wanted none of him to trail in dirt, though we were about to wrap him in it until kingdom come. The boys moved forward with such solemn grace. How did they know how to carry him like that? Was it something they were practised at? People stood in doorways or bowed their heads as we passed. If Haf had had her way, this would have been done in secret, in darkness. But there was no way to hide it, what was done at night would be spoken of in day eventually.

We were allowed through the gate without question. The sky was bright blue but the sun felt weak on my skin. The air smelled of snow. Winter whiteness would settle soon.

And Tad wouldn't see it.

I saw the mound of earth then. It was more red than I expected. When it touched his skin, Tad would be bathed in ochre. Like some ancient warrior of old, taking his place in their stories. I stood oak-straight as we walked closer to the hole.

The grave-digger had worked hard to move the hard ground. He stood, some way off, his wooden shovel in hand. I would have to find some way to pay him later. Or ask Haf to do it. She sat beside wealth these days. She was already planning her days to come, while I could hardly get through these moments.

Father Ambrose was ready. He had added adornments to his usual brown tunic. He wore skeins of shells around his shoulders. Perhaps for the one who walked on water, perhaps just to mark the day. 'Lay him down,' Father Ambrose told the saplings.

The young men moved as one, lowering Tad into the newly cut grave. As he disappeared below the edge, I felt my chest yawn open wet and dark. Anyone could have reached in and touched my heart in that moment. I wanted to throw myself in beside him and let the dirt cover us both.

But I stood straight and still.

Father Ambrose began. He spoke Latin and British. I was too tired to follow it all, but his words were solemn-serious and full of the blessing of our Lord.

'*Pulvis et umbrus* we are,' he said. 'Dust and shadow *sumus*. And to dust we will go, until the light of the Lord will raise us to stand by his side under the surer domes of Heaven.'

I looked up. The clouds looked too flimsy to hold the domes of Heaven. The treetops looked stronger. That would be where I would go, if I had that choice. Into the branches of the tallest tree, looking down at the blanket of the earth.

Above the brown mud, boughs bent,

Wrought about with new green buds.

Life brought back to the dead wood.

It was time to throw the first sod of earth. Father Ambrose looked to me to do it. So, I did. But I looked away as I let go my handful. I couldn't watch it fall onto his body. Instead, I watched the waiting, whispering trees.

It was done quickly, the earth shovelled back in. The idea of it settling in the creases of his skin, dusting into his hair, pressing down on his mouth, made me want to scream.

But not in pain, in anger.

At the person who had done this. At the men who had allowed him to slip away unaided. Algar, Gwrtheyrn, Rhodri. They had black hearts, each one.

Even Haf, who hadn't come when she was needed.

I swept from the grave like storm clouds on the heath, alone. I felt so tired, as though the bones of me were worn through. Back in the hut, I dropped beside the cold hearth, though the day was not yet done, and I slept and wept and slept.

Haf was there when I opened my eyes. She said nothing, but offered warm bread. I took it, suddenly hungry as carrion crows. She waited until I'd finished, then she said, 'I have news. There's work, if you want it. I heard just now.'

'What work?'

'The raiding party is going out again. They think to find the Saxons near Cair Pensa. They want to trade, not fight. There's to be negotiations. They want someone to go with them, to peel and chop and run errands for their cook. You'd eat well.'

'You want me to leave?'

'No. I want you to eat well.'

'You think you'll be better off without me. You want

me away from here.' How could she ask me to go? How could she want to stay? How could she have made her home here so easily? My head ached with the whirl of thoughts that rushed in. I wasn't ready to think about tomorrow. The troubles of today were enough.

Her lips pressed tight together, white worms. Then she sighed. 'I want you to eat, Mai. I want us both to eat. And I want you to keep out of trouble, out of the mind of Gwrtheyrn. If you're not here, he won't think of you. He sees some value in me. I've been useful and he thinks me wise. He's less sure of you. Rhodri spoke ill of you. I want to keep you safe. What's so wrong with that?'

It felt as though there were floodwaters rising between us. She was on one side of the river and I was on the other and rapids were forming as we spoke. I wanted to reach out and take her hand, but she kept them folded tight in her lap.

'The raiders take slaves and sell them. They burn homes.'

'How do you know?' she asked.

'I can guess.'

She rocked back away from me in anger. 'Well I can guess too. I can guess what Gwrtheyrn will do if he decides you're no use. He'll give you to one of his captains for one or two nights and then throw you out of the camp. He has no use for idle hands.'

I sat up, angry too. My palms still had blisters from

grinding quern-stones. My muscles ached from carrying water. 'I'm not idle.'

'I know, I know. But he isn't building one farmstead here, he's building his kingdom. He doesn't need peasants, he needs his nation.'

'You've been listening to him talk,' I said.

'*You* should listen to *me*.' She stood suddenly, and dusted down the back of her skirt. I noticed it was new, the fabric brighter than her old tunic, tighter on her hips. 'You need to get up, get presentable and be strong, Mai. You have to. Even if you are just pretending. Even if it's just lies to fit in. If you don't, you'll be alone in that forest out there. I'm going back to the hall. You should meet me there when you're ready.'

I wanted to walk, run, tear at the sky, cry at the earth. I wanted to fall down and sleep deep as hawthorn roots. And she was asking me to pretend my pain away. To be meek and quiet and not disturb still water.

'I won't be coming,' I said. 'Never. I'm not going near that hall. I'm not staying in this hut either.' My words surprised us both.

Her face was clouded, confused. She spread her arms, clutching the doorframe as though she wanted to keep me inside. 'Where will you go? What choice do you have?'

I had no idea. There was nowhere but the woods. I thought of the man and woman we'd met, and their dead baby. 'I'll find somewhere,' I said.

'I don't want you to leave. Not like that.'

'You could come with me.'

'You could stay.'

The gulf between us opened as wide as the banks of the Hafren river. She huffed as though I was six years old again and had taken the rag doll Tad had made for her.

Maybe it was childish. But I did know that if I stayed on this floor, seeping back into the earth, I'd be just like Eleri. Dead before the season changed. On the cold floor of the hut, I knew, I couldn't leave with the raiders, and I couldn't stay where I was.

The earth pressed into my back. The sheepskin Tad had slept on was close, but my hand wouldn't reach for it. It smelled of him and his sickness. I preferred the cold. I sat up.

'Where will you go? Who will be your people?' Haf was still speaking.

I covered my eyes with my palms and tried not to think of the cold earth at the bottom of the hill where Tad slept. He should have been with Mam, in the top field of the farm between the hill and the sky.

'You need friends,' Haf said, 'you need family. Your elbow is closer than your wrist.'

'And what use have relatives been to me?' I spat, without looking at her. 'I'm surrounded by people on all sides, but I've never been more alone.'

'You've got me.'

I lurched to standing. 'I barely know who you are here. You shift like smoke, meek lamb one moment, wolf the next. Where were you when I needed you? When Tad needed you? You were playing the lady beside Gwrtheyrn!'

Her palm struck my cheek. Teeth rattling, ear singing, skin on skin.

I was shocked silent. My hands flew up to where my cheek burned.

'I am helping you,' Haf snarled. 'And you are too stupid to see it. Well, one of these days one of the people here will properly clout some sense into you and I for one will be pleased to see it.'

She strode, swift as blows, from the hut.

I sat down hard. My body ached as though I had run for hours. My cheek stung. Swirling thoughts spun too quick. Tad. Haf. Gwrtheyrn and his raiders. I couldn't stay. I couldn't. But leaving was just as frightening.

26

THE HUT GREW dark. Outside, I heard the camp settle from day into evening. There were still some who were drunk from the night before, and others nursing sore heads.

Haf didn't come back.

And Tad was never coming back. Nor the Romans he so believed in. Nor Mam. Nor the farm. The world belonged to people like Algar and Gwrtheyrn now. And Haf wanted to be just like them, she was halfway there already.

As I sat, I felt my anger harden. Like ice sheets forming over river torrents, my anger turned cold. Determined.

I was leaving.

I didn't know where to, maybe to the people of Gwent, or Cernyw, maybe I would cross the sea and find the place where they spoke like Father Ambrose. I didn't care where it was, as long as it wasn't here.

I had few supplies. The poppy seeds Haf had left would be worth something on the road. I could trade them. There were roots I had worked hard for and not yet turned into soup. I heard the sound of beer-filled singing from outside. The stores were full thanks to the raiders. I paused.

I couldn't steal from the dead, but I could steal from Gwrtheyrn and Rhodri. Bryn had told me how.

It had to be done quickly, while anger gave me strength. The sack I'd carried from the farm was near the hut wall. The harsh weave scratched my palms, but I squeezed it tight until it bit into my skin. It helped me feel real, not all mist and fog and pretence as Haf was.

Then I headed to the great hall and the stores beside it.

With my eyes cast down, anyone I passed paid no more notice than if I were one of the worms.

As I got nearer the hall, I saw bones gnawed clean on the ground. Vomit and splashed beer stank the air. The revels had continued here with battle songs spilling from within. The hall itself looked tired. The green boughs had wilted in the smoke and heat. Men lolled outside. The damage from the night before was carved on their faces – bloodshot eyes were set in bruised sockets. I turned my own face away.

'Mai!'

I stopped at the sound of my name.

'Mai, how is it with you?' It was Bryn. He stepped half-smiling from the cook-house. He carried bread, one small, pale disk in the dark.

I clutched my empty sack to my stomach. 'I'm well,'

I said. My sister wanted me to become adder-low, raiding on the road. But I said nothing of that.

'You should come into the hall,' he said. 'It might cheer you. There will be dancing soon. You could sit with the other girls until then.'

'I don't want to dance,' I said. 'I have to go.'

'Do you?'

'I have chores to do. Flour to grind.'

'In the dark?' Bryn didn't believe me.

'Yes.'

I stepped away from Bryn without farewell. Over my shoulder, I stole glances of him stepping into the hall to join the rest of the men singing. There was no place for me here.

In the purple light of the evening, I circled the back of the storage hut, keeping clear of the guard who looked half-drunk himself. The hole Bryn had pointed out was barely visible, even though I knew where to look. Grass grew in thick ribbons over it. I eased the grass aside. Planks of wood that should have sunk into the earth were rotted away. All that was left was dank sadness. I put my hand into the hole. No adult could squeeze through. It would be tight for me, more suited to mice and rats. But I had to try. I dropped onto my belly. The grass seeped wet and cold through my woollen tunic, my short knife dug into my hip. I plunged, swimming into the soil, belly-wriggling with the jaws of wood scraping along my back. Then, I was through.

The smell of the hut stopped me still. Food. More food than I had ever seen in one place. My nose could tell better than my eyes in the darkness. I smelled dried fruit, grain — sacks of it, smelling of full stomachs. Meat and mead. Something sour as pondweed beneath the good smells, moonshine from the dunmen in the woods.

Food that had been stolen. Food that might have cost the farmer his life. Food that Gwrtheyrn would kill to protect. I was snake-slithering into his store.

My hands slicked wet with sweat. It was hard to breathe.

I had to work fast.

The sack shook as I dropped things into it. Roots, carrots, turnips. They were fine raw. Hard cheeses smelled strong and sour from their wrappings on the dirt floor. I took my short knife and cut one in half, then quarters, slicing through the meat of it.

When I had enough for six or seven lean meals, I crept back the way I came. Shaking like new leaves.

Night had fallen, cow-belly black. I teased the stalks of grass upright with my fingers. Dew and night winds would hide my tracks. But I would be long gone by morning. I headed to the gate. The sack was heavy, but it gave me strength to know what was inside. I had my way out prepared. I could escape and make my own home somewhere I chose. Maybe even go back to the farm and rebuild?

All the huts on the path down were shut up, just as they had been on the night we arrived. But so much had changed since then. The gate was in sight. Fires burned beside the path, so I went wide, heading into the shadows. I wanted to see how the gate was guarded before they noticed me there.

I crept closer.

The gate was maybe twenty steps away, and I could see no guards, no watchmen. Maybe I could unbar the gate and slip out unnoticed? I felt my heart lift – one piece of good luck!

Then, I felt hands grab me from behind, someone stepping silently from the shadows.

I struggled. The sack fell from my grip.

But the hands were strong. I could smell meat grease and dirt and week-old beer as one hand covered my face, the other wrapped tight around my waist and lifted me from the ground.

I screamed. But the grip tightened, smothering the sound.

'Stay still.' The voice came from the darkness of the shadows, not from the man holding me. There were two men here. My eyes stared wildly, trying to hunt out their faces. The arms about me squeezed.

I was carried, still struggling, into the light of one of the fires. I could see the man before me – March. I twisted my head to see who carried me – Rhodri.

Rhodri held me tight while March leaned over the open sack.

'Thieving,' March said softly. 'Taking from the people who helped her and gave her somewhere to call home.'

'Ungrateful,' Rhodri said. His arms gripped so hard that it seemed I could only breathe with his say-so.

'You know what we do to thieves?' March asked, picking up the hunk of cheese and biting into it.

'We punish them,' Rhodri replied.

27

SUMMER SOLSTICE, AD455,
DAWN.

THERE IS NO other sound in my ears but the wails of the baby. The crackle of the fire becomes leaves rustling in distant forests. The wind becomes soft sighs. Everything but its joyous cries retreats.

And I feel love in my heart, carve-cutting itself there. With the fierceness of wolves. With the permanence of the earth. The baby is pink and red and covered in what looks like pond water, dark hair clings in wisps to its thin skull. It is small and shrivelled and the cord at its middle throbs blue and purple.

And yet, it is faultless.

Every inch of it, pinch-perfect, from toes to nose, newborn. Its shape tips into me and fills me. In love, living again.

I don't feel scared.

I should be scared. More scared than I have ever been.

But I'm not.

28

RHODRI CARRIED ME trussed on his shoulder like slaughtered deer. March tipped up the sack and everything in it. He pushed it roughly over my head.

'Let me go! Get off me!' I wrenched my arms free and slammed my fists into his back. I wanted him torn in wracks. I smashed at him, for Tad, for Mam, even for Haf, for all the pain that welled up and spilled out of me.

But it was like hitting oak. He could barely feel it.

'Shut her up,' Rhodri growled.

March hit me. One hard clout across my head.

I saw stars. The pain shocked through me and I tasted blood. My head lolled sideways and I lost sense of where was up or down.

I had no notion of how long we walked. It seemed unending. Blood pooled in my head, my eyes throbbed. The weight of us both crushed dry leaves and snapped twigs as Rhodri walked. I heard March behind us. Night-birds called and small creatures rattled branches. We were in the woods. I wished that the wolves who lived

174

here would pounce. But there was no rescue coming. And I was too small and weak to protect myself.

I hoped whatever they were going to do, it would be done quickly.

'Here,' March said. 'Stop here. This is what we do to whelps who can't keep their hands clean. Who have no loyalty.'

'Wait! Wait,' I begged. 'I was doing no harm.'

Rhodri laughed and the smell of beer was strong. 'You were caught with your hand in the spices. Your sister said you needed watching and so you did.'

Haf had said that?

Haf had told them to watch me?

Haf had sent them?

She had threatened it. Threatened to get one of the men to teach me sense. But I hadn't thought she meant it.

All the fight dropped from me.

Nearby, I heard the grating sound of wood dragged against stone. Rhodri dumped me down onto the mouldy leaf-litter. I moved at once. I crawled and crabbed away from his feet, ignoring torn knees and elbows. But he grabbed my ankle and pulled me back towards him. My face ploughed the ground.

'There's no wriggling away from us,' Rhodri said.

He lifted me again, around my waist. I was whirled around, then slung into blacker dark. I was inside somewhere. It smelled of caves: mushrooms and mould.

The space felt narrow with stone close on both sides. The square of dark grey, the entrance I'd been thrown through, vanished.

I heard wood splintering. The sound of hull-planks hitting rocks. Not far away.

Then hammering. Iron on wood.

They were shutting me in. I was being nailed inside this cave.

I pulled at the sack over my face, breathing free once it was gone.

But the darkness didn't lift.

I knew where I was.

This was their idea of justice.

One of the men slammed his hand on the wood of the door. From the other side, I heard him say, 'This is what happens to ungrateful little girls who steal from their own people. They get forgotten like the long-dead.'

Laughter.

Getting fainter as they walked away.

I was in the Roman tomb.

Shut in.

Tight.

I staggered back. My calf scraped against rough-hewn stone. I knew what the stone sheltered. The Roman woman whose brooch Bryn had taken.

No. No. No.

I flew to the door. Thumping my fists on the wood.

Hammering. My heart was wild-boiling in my chest. There was no air.

'Let me out!' My voice was nothing, no power in my lungs. No air at all. The world swam,
shifted,
     slipped.
          I heard whimpering,
               starved dog whimpers,
   that came from my own throat.
   I curled up on the floor, beaten.

29

ONCE, I'D KILLED one of the wood pigeons Tad had caught. I held the bird still in my hand, rock in the other, and crushed its skull. But, despite the blow, which had sure certain killed it, its heart still beat against the palm of my hand, five or six heavy, pounding beats that I swear were strong enough to break its ribs. It was as though there was nothing but heart inside that bird. It didn't know it was already dead.

My heart pounded like that now, full-heavy enough to bruise me on the inside.

I was trapped in the dark with the Roman dead and no one but March and Rhodri knew where I was. I could feel dirt beneath me, rough and dry on my face. No rain had fallen on this ground for tens of years. I could smell decay too. Mouldering bones. My body was curled into the small space between the nailed wooden door and the stone coffin of the woman whose place this rightly was.

I lay still and small for hours of night where all I could do was tell myself to breathe. To find space enough for air around the full beats of my heart.

My ears were alert as fort dogs.

I wasn't listening for the men returning. They weren't coming back. No, I listened instead for the woman in here with me. I was sure certain that at any moment, I would hear the *clack-de-hap* sound of bones shifting and moving. Her skull snapping its jaws, rattling loose its own teeth.

'Leave me be,' I whispered. 'Leave me be.'

But it wouldn't stop.

Click-clack-click-clack.

'It's just the trees,' I said. My own voice sounded too loud. She'd know I was here. I clapped my hand over my mouth.

Click-clack.

It was her jaws. I was sure of it. Teeth on teeth. Bone on bone.

I covered my ears. Pressed my face to my knees.

Something ran over my ankle.

I screamed.

  Screamed.

       Screamed.

Throat-red, tongue-ripped, torn-right-out

Sounds

That heaved hot and heavy shouting

Into nothing.

Later the screams became sobs.

  Stilled to gasps.

And I was still trapped in the dark.

I kicked at the door. It shook loose dust and dirt on my face. I was on my back, thighs bent, sending my feet straight out. But the nails held. The planks were thick.

The late sun came up. Thin shafts of light came through pinprick holes and narrow gaps in the wood. I could see better.

I didn't want to see.

The stone coffin was behind me. I had had my back to it all night, not wanting to know what was inside. Not wanting to see it move.

But with the light, I looked.

The coffin had once been sand coloured stone, now it was green with moss and probing ivy. The lid had fallen – been pushed – to the ground.

I could see inside. I could see the dead woman.

She was all grey. Grey rags over grey bones. Long leg bones. Tangled ribs that fanned out through the torn shroud. The small bones of her fingers and toes had fallen into gullies in the carved stone. And the skull: strands of thin hair still holding to it in places. Its eyes empty, black. Its teeth too long for its face.

I moaned. The sound was animal.

My back slid down the door.

I would die in here. I would rot to rattling bones.

My mouth already felt so dry, my lips thick and cracked.

How long could someone live without water? Days? Weeks? I didn't know. But my head ached and the sounds of the dry leaves shifting beyond the door sounded too loud.

I wished I hadn't cried in the night. The water was wasted on tears.

The day passed with my headache growing worse. Throbs of pain where I'd been hit. My tongue too thick, even when I licked at the sweat and salt on my arms.

When I had the strength, I shouted. 'Let me out! Please. Mercy! Mercy for what I did. Is there anyone there?' I heard ravens call in alarm. But no people. They'd left me. They really had.

My stomach growled as the day wore on, but it was the thirst that was worst. Soon, I could think of nothing but water. Rain, falling in drips from the thatch, puddles in the yard, the swell and crash of the stream on rocks.

The light began to fade.

Another night coming. Another night with the dead.

I couldn't do it.

I couldn't.

I had to get out. No one was coming for me. Not Rhodri, not March. Would they tell Haf what they'd done? Would she come looking?

Not if, as they'd said, it was by her doing that they'd caught me.

I fought against the idea. I was her *sister*.

'Haf!' I called. 'Haf!'

But she'd hit me. And had left Tad to my care when it suited her.

My mind darted like fish in sunlight. Perhaps Rhodri was lying.

I covered my ears, as though I could shut out the voices that argued in my head.

But one voice was louder than the other: Haf had told the men to watch me. I believed it.

Her whispers had got me nailed up in darkness. Algar had started this horror, but Haf had added to it. She couldn't keep her words behind her teeth. She had betrayed me.

I looked at the coffin. It seemed to me, in that short moment, that it was as well to die here as anywhere.

I moved closer to it, gripped its stone walls with both hands.

And, inside, I saw the shroud shift.

The cloth near one shoulder fluttered, as though the body had shrugged.

My bowels turned to water.

I felt piss run warm down my leg.

The shroud twitched again. Then I heard squeaking and small claws scampering. From under the cloth, whiskers twitched and the mouse they belonged to ran along the bone that stuck out from the folds.

'Mouse!' I snapped at it. 'You frightened me, you little horror.' Really, God entertained Himself in odd ways.

It twitched its nose, scenting me in the air. It clenched tiny fists before leaping up the stone side of the coffin and disappearing under the broken lid.

'That's right, you run,' I added. I heard it scramble, then rustle, then it was gone.

How had it got out?

The question seemed to ask itself, the voice clear in my mind.

If the mouse had got out, could I?

I moved to where it had disappeared, squeezing between the coffin and tomb wall. I heaved at the lid. It was as big as I was, but cracked in at least two places that I could see. Still, it was heavy. I felt the solid weight of it graze against my palms. 'Move,' I insisted. Leaning away from it, knees bent as far as I could manage. I heard stone grind on stone. It was moving! I doubled my effort. I felt one fingernail bend and tear free. The sudden burst of pain didn't stop me.

I would go where the mouse had gone.

I couldn't be Buddug, I couldn't lead my people. But I could be like the mouse, small and swift and able to scuttle wherever I wanted.

'Argh!' With one last gasping effort, the stone toppled and thudded to the flat ground.

There was green light behind it.

The wall had partly collapsed and ivy had pushed through, slowly, slowly, slowly shifting stone blocks as it grew. I worked on the thick ivy stems with my short knife, gouging out chunks. I twisted the weakened sections, pulling wet wood and broken stones away in nail-tearing handfuls.

I was hot with sweat and effort by the time the hole was big enough to snake-wriggle through.

Before I left the horror of the tomb, I stood over the coffin, looking at the woman who lay there. I dipped my head to pray. 'I'm sorry if I disturbed you. Please don't follow me. I'm nothing, no one, I'm just like the mouse that was here. Please, stay away. Amen,' I whispered. Then, on my belly, I forced my way out into the wood.

I started running.

I hurled myself through low-hanging branches. The winter sun was low and weak, so it was hard to avoid their whips. The muscles in my thighs drove down and out, pushing me on. I had to be beyond their reach if they came hunting.

I was deeper and deeper into the cold wood in moments. I tasted blood on my lips. Had I bitten myself? Or struck through thorns? I sucked the worst of it away. I was limping too. I couldn't remember falling.

I had to slow. The forest forced me to. The wind was

tight in my chest and I was gosling-gasping. I listened to see if I was being followed. There was nothing.

I walked without knowing where I was going. The farm was gone. The woods were home to scare-bods and mud men. The towns and cities were targets for raiders. I didn't belong anywhere. I had exiled myself like Iesu walking in the desert.

Where was home now?

I had nothing that could be called that. I was like the woman we'd met in the woods, with her dead child, knowing no shelter, no hearth.

I walked. Moving until I was too tired and achy to think at all.

At each step, birds above me bent their heads together and cawed danger on all sides. Small things scuttled and scurried from my path. They did all they could to stay hidden in the shadows, to let the threat pass over.

I wished, I *wished* with arm-and-elbow strength, that I could hide too, like the beasts in their mouseholes or badger sets. I'd roll my fur around me and pull straw and hay close and sleep until the winter had passed.

But I kept moving.

When I found water, I sat beside the little stream and splashed my face and neck gratefully, then drank and drank and drank.

I was alone. For the first time in my life, I was truly alone. No one knew where I was, or cared to think, not unless Rhodri had sent men after me. I was as rootless as the birds that sang above me. More so even, they had their nests, after all.

Though I hadn't eaten for days now, I wasn't hungry. When night came, I lay down with my head on the soft mossy bank. Despite the chill, I slipped into dreamless sleep. But the cold bit me hard in the night. I woke with chattering teeth and goose-pimpled skin in the dark.

I stood and jumped to send my blood around faster.

In the starlit night something crashed to my right. Tearing at the trip-tangled brambles. I heard the arms of young trees snap. Whatever it was came towards me. Twigs showered down. Birds disturbed from dreams dashed upwards. What was it? I couldn't see. There were just shapes plunging through the shadows. Wolves? Scare-bod men of the dark?

I turned and ran.

Ran as though the Midnight Hunt was upon me. It was gaining on me. I saw curving tusks, bright in shafts of moonlight. Dark, grizzly fur. Tiny eyes that seemed to glow like coals. Boar! My legs pounded. My hair caught and ripped free. My head stung with pain, with beating blood, with fear.

Then, I was falling.

Down, crashing on rocky ledges. I clawed at roots that dust-crumbled free.

Over and over, I rolled.

Then fell through bitter-coiled ferns and black-tongued garlic until I landed, facedown on wet earth.

I heard the boar sniff the air above me, high on the gully edge. I couldn't move. Everything hurt. I heard it scrape the ground with its hoof. Then snort and turn back into the forest.

I closed my eyes and felt grit under my lashes. The smell of rotting leaves was strong. In the dark and cold it felt as though I had fallen into my own grave. And I felt ready for it. Let the earth take me as it had Tad. For the last few weeks I had done nothing but walk from the smoke into the flames. And I'd had enough. I didn't care any more.

I dreamed I was being rocked, infant-small, in the arms of someone who smiled to see me there. *Loolee-loolee*, the voice sang. Haf? Mam? In my sleep I joined in the singing.

I woke to find myself being carried. My legs swayed from side to side and ached with every inch of motion. My eyes were glued shut with dirt and sleep and mud. Light got through, but no images that made sense. I was slung on the back of some swaying beast. The warm smell of ox-hide was sweet, despite my aching bones. Had I broken limbs? I tried to flex my hands and fingers, to see how deep the pain ran. And I found my hands were bound.

Someone spoke, but their words were just noise, lurching clacks and caws. Had beasts of the forest found me?

What were they saying? I felt cold. I had heard these sounds before.

Saxon. The man I could hear was speaking Saxon.

30

SARA PUSHES ME out of the way as if I were lumpen flour sacks. 'Clean water,' she says.

She wants to wash and swaddle this mewling newness.

I rush to fetch water from the wooden bucket and another warm rock. It can't be left in the pot too long. The water mustn't be so hot as to hurt. I grab rags left warming by the fire for this purpose. I take those too to help Sara wash the baby and my sister both.

She's holding the child when I get back. I have never seen her face so beautiful-strange as now, holding her infant. Hazel eyes full of kindness. Any cross word, or harsh thought we've ever had ebbs like mist in sunshine. My heart is full for her too.

I can't find love for the man who is responsible for all this. I never could do that. But even he seems small now, silent as death itself, in the face of the love I feel. Bull-strong beats of blood fill my ears.

We are all alive. 'Thanks to Iesu the baby, the Father and Ghost,' I say.

'Amen,' Sara says and takes the rags.

She wraps the liver-red afterbirth for burning.

My sister tries to sit up, still weak.

'Boy or girl?' I ask.

'Boy,' Sara tells me.

I'm glad of it. So glad. He won't live to be used as we've been, as drudges or dolls to be played with.

He will be chattel though. Owned by Horse or Rowan. Raised to raid, or plough, or soldier in fields that aren't his own.

'He's so small,' I say.

'That's the way babies come, especially when they're early,' Sara laughs, relieved he lives.

'When will she be well enough to move?' I ask Sara.

She frowns, her cheeks hollow into shadow. 'Move? Where do you mean for them to go?' she asks.

I have no plan to speak of. But I feel braver now than I have for eons. I feel like myself again, with my own words in my head. I feel like the girl I was before Algar set the fire blazing and our old home went up in flames. For the first time since then I have something real and good to live for – the baby and the mother holding him.

'I don't know yet. But the village is damned. The bad man walks its paths sowing dragon-teeth. You know it.'

Sara pulls me aside roughly. All tenderness gone, hard as sheep-feet. 'What are you thinking? You aren't fool enough to mean it. You know what they do to slaves who flee. You *know*.'

If we're caught, we're killed.

And not killed quickly, either.

I know that.

But what sort of life will the boy have, if we stay? Chance-child born and unwanted as he is, with only two girls to defend him.

He mewls softly, kitten-sweet, and my heart swells again. I feel it can't grow any bigger, but every breath that baby takes inflates it that little bit more.

I won't let him grow to manhood here. I'll do it somehow.

I stare Sara in the life of her eyes. 'He won't . . .' I can't say the word I'm thinking: *He won't die?*

Sara shrugs, then shakes her head. 'He plans to stay with us, I think.'

'He should have better than this then,' I say.

I push all thoughts of the risk from my mind.

31

I KEPT MY eyes closed. The ox swayed, with me thrown on its back. My hands and ankles were tied and my heart kicked in my chest, beast-wild. But I didn't let the fear show outwardly. I stayed still. Played dead. Pretending.

Men talked.

Three of them, I thought. Two spoke such jumbled sounds that I couldn't follow it from hearth to heath. Their words were like water crashing on rocks. They were like the ogres and coblyns of stories who would grind bones to bread. My skin shivered just listening.

But the third man was different.

He spoke as though he had trouble with the harsh sounds that might cut his tongue. He handled them carefully, slowly.

I was sure he wasn't Saxon-born. Was he British? Or from across the sea like Father Ambrose? Would he take pity on me?

Treacherous hope sprang unwished for.

I crushed it. Even if he did help me escape, then what?

There was nowhere for me. I felt blackness drag at me, pulling me under like the tides of the Hafren.

'Water?' I heard the strange man say, near my ear. I understood! He'd spoken British. I was scared to move. But my swollen tongue and dry throat forced me to turn my head towards the voice.

Water splashed my face. Crisp, cold, beautiful.

'Open,' he said.

I moved my jaw and pain sang across my face and chest. My ribs felt crushed. I must be bruised blue. The cold water flowed into my mouth. Swallowing was sore, but I had to drink. I'd drink to drowning if he'd let me. But the water stopped moments later.

My eyes were washed clear enough now to be able to open them. The man walking beside me, holding the water pouch, was flint-faced. The planes of his cheeks and jaw were hard-set with grey-looking skin. His dark eyes were sunk in their sockets, his brown hair flecked with white. He saw me looking and shook his head. 'Say nothing. Fools grow wise in silence.'

He had the right of it. I'd have to be watchful if I was to stay alive.

We stopped near sundown. The Saxon men spoke in what sounded to me like animal clicks, growls and grunts. Together they seemed to be deciding on the best place to unroll their beds. I was lifted down by the bigger of the two Saxons. His thick, black hair stretched across his head, his chin, his arms and fingers like pelt.

He dropped me to the ground. My knees buckled. It jarred my bruised ribs, making me catch my breath. I was still bound, so I pulled my knees up to my chin, curled up as tight as I could, despite my injury. If I was meek, I might melt myself into the nooks of the ground like rainwater. They might forget all about me and ride away.

'*Essenmädchen*,' the pelt man said. '*Essen*.'

He spoke right above me. I had to look up. His face was thick with black hair, eyebrows, cheeks, chin. His brown eyes peered like wet rocks in seaweed. He held flatbread and waved it at me.

I didn't move.

He clicked impatiently at Flintface.

'He says you must eat,' Flintface said slowly, in British. '*Essen*, it means food.'

My throat felt reed-thin, but I took the bread and held it.

'*Essen*,' Peltman insisted. I took the smallest bite.

He lost interest in me then. He and the smaller man who made up the third in their party began fire setting. They gathered windblown twigs and stouter branches.

Essen, I thought, as I swallowed, snake-watchful. Why were they feeding me? Not from kindness, I was sure.

Flintface said nothing, but took my wrists and worked

194

at the knot that bound them. Blood rushed back into my hands and I whimpered with the pain of it.

'Press them,' he told me. He held his hands, palm-to-palm in front of my face, showing me. '*Drück auf*.'

He was trying to teach me their sounds, I realised. '*Drück auf*,' I repeated. I copied him and gritted my teeth against the pain as the blood rushed in.

He strode away and returned with his water pouch full. '*Wasser*,' he said. He held it back. 'Repeat.'

He was putting their words in my mouth. I had no strength to stop it. '*Wasser*,' I responded, taking the dewy pouch. I sipped. My tight throat allowed only the slimmest dribble to pass.

'What's your name?' he asked, switching back to words I could understand. His voice was not unkind.

I thought about lying, or keeping silent, but I was too tired and sore to remember lies later. 'Mai,' I said.

'They call me Welsh,' he said. 'They'll call you Welsh too.'

'It's not my name,' I said, confused.

'It doesn't matter. Welsh is Saxon. It means *foreigner* or *slave*. They call us all Welsh. They'll find somewhere for you.'

Slave?

Then I realised what else he had said. 'Somewhere for me?' I looked at the trees around us, feeling mud-thick thoughts sloshing in my head.

'You look healthy enough. They checked your teeth while you were out cold. You're bruised, perhaps one of your ribs is cracked. They won't try to sell you before you heal. Damaged Welsh look like troublesome Welsh.'

Sell me? I had trouble understanding what he meant. I felt slow and stupid and my head ached. Haf was right. I'd run from the smoke into the flames. I'd thought I could choose who to be. Now there was no choice at all. I was caught captive by cave trolls.

'Where will I go?' I asked. I didn't know whether I meant now, to escape, or when my bruises healed and I could be sold.

Welsh thought I meant when I was slave-sold. 'There are many rich villages to the north with the market near the Hafren harbour. You are gift-given to them, they weren't looking, they just found you. So I don't know if they will change their plans or not.'

'What are their plans?'

He pushed the water pouch towards me again. I drank, though I didn't want anything of theirs. 'The one with all the hair, he leads his own village. That's where we were going. His full name is tricky to say, call him Horse, its sounds are close enough. We're headed back to our home. Horse wants to get back swiftly.'

'So, I'm going to his village?'

Welsh shrugged. 'He has news to share with his people. He's been making alliances. I don't think he'll change course just to sell you. But I can't be sure. You're his for the time being. You must learn their words. It's the only way to stay unwhipped.'

I swished the water pouch. '*Wasser*,' I said. I had no want to learn Saxon but the smallest bit of me was pleased to have remembered the word. I had no want to be whipped either.

'You'll do,' Welsh said, '*gut gemacht.*' He patted the hard earth. '*Schlaf. Schlaf.*' He pressed his palms together and rested his head upon them. I understood what he meant and lay down to sleep.

Schlaf, essen, wasser. I tested the words on my tongue like new food. The taste was sharp and bitter, like fresh-cut roots.

The girl who had dreamed of fighting alongside the British warriors, like Buddug, was gone. It seemed so long since she'd arrived with her tad and her sister at the camp, hoping to hold aloft her sword. And now, all that was left was this Welsh mouse with Saxon words in her mouth.

32

I SLEPT BADLY. All night the tree branches overhead clattered like the bones of the long dead. My chest ached. When I shut my eyes, I was back in the black tomb, nailed in by men I'd hoped were kin. I opened my eyes to lift the horror, but saw the hulking shapes of Saxons snoring nearby. I'd got out of the rain but under the waterfall. Should I have listened to Haf? Gone with the British scavengers, despite the hate in my heart for the task? Was there any difference between being captive there, and captive here? I missed the farm. The warm hearth, the hewn walls, even the hard work. And the people in it. I turned on my side and winced at the pain in my ribs.

With the arc of the low sun came Welsh, shaking me upright. He carried *wasser*. And *essen*. And he made me say the words twice before he gave them to me. This time I cut into the dark bread and hard cheese hungrily. Welsh watched me slice with my short knife. I noticed he had one too, at his waist. Blades too small for the Saxons to fear.

'Are you well enough to walk?' he asked me.

'I hurt all over,' I said. 'From the fall and from the rope.' My bones felt fused.

'Walking will do you good.'

Horse ignored us both as Welsh freed the rope from my ankles. Soon enough, we were on our way. I dragged myself along the path. The morning had found me goat-sullen. Every step hurt.

'Keep up!' Welsh insisted.

I hurried three or four steps, but soon slowed again.

'Mai!' Welsh stopped until I caught up. He gripped my arm. 'Horse is happy as deep trout today, he's traded with the Saxon leaders around and goes home loaded with guest-gifts and good news. But he's easily angered. You don't want to see him in temper. Keep up.'

The warning picked up my heels. I marched to their faster pace. As my feet hit the earth, words beat through my mind. Tad. Haf. Home.

Tad. Haf. Home.

Tad.

Haf.

Home.

'What's the Saxon for home?' I asked Welsh.

He smiled at my interest. '*Heimat*,' he told me. After that, there was no folding his mouth shut. He told me the names of the things I was seeing, giving new sounds to the shapes of the world. 'You can learn as we walk,' Welsh told me. '*Auf dem weg.*'

It was strange to me, that these two sets of words sat side by side in his thoughts. His own tongue, the one I shared, was of this land. Its sounds were the rising and falling of the hills, the melody and rhythm of running streams. It flowed as morning mist flowed into valleys, it was soft with blurred edges. Had learning the hard sounds of Saxon made him harder too? He was stiff and sharp in his movements. Perhaps there was iron where his spine should be. Perhaps that's what I needed too, to become hard and fixed so that the losses of the world couldn't hurt me.

'*Baum*,' he said, pointing to the bare branches that cast their net above us.

'*Baum*,' I repeated, not caring.

'*Himmel*,' he pointed to the heavens.

Tad. Haf. Home.

What was Haf doing right at this moment? Not learning Saxon, I was sure. Nor wondering where I was. No. She would be at the camp, standing at the sleeves of the big men. I was one problem she didn't have to think about any more. She'd be happy to be free of me. She could build her nest now however she wanted.

I stumbled, my foot caught on rain-washed roots. I gasped and the pain cut knife-sharp through me.

Welsh caught me before I hit the floor. 'Watch your step,' he warned.

Morning became afternoon. We stopped to eat more

bread and dried fruit from the bags the ox carried. The fruit tasted of harvest and sunshine and better times that made my eyes sting with the memory of it. With food in his stomach, Welsh seemed more cheerful. He sang as he walked. The tune was for marching to, it seemed, the beat falling on every other step. The sounds were Saxon, but the accent was all British. I listened as the notes rose on the breeze, carried up and up like the red kite riding the air.

'*Hört, von ger-dänen vergangener tage,*' he sang.

'*Klingt uns der könige ruhm,*

wie edelste krieger sich ehre erwarben.'

He prodded me. The chorus was coming around again. I opened my mouth and the faintest song came out, I hummed the tune, not the words.

His sharp glance made me try to catch the tail of the phrases as I sang, with no idea what they meant. Welsh sang the verse and chorus, again and again, prodding when I fell silent.

We walked, two Britons, singing marching songs in Saxon, through the wild wood. I hung my head with the shame of it, but there was no fight left in me at all.

The first day was over. My words still flocked above me – Tad, Haf, Home. But the calmness of walking, of having to put one tired foot in front of the other, lulled me. I slept better.

On the second day, I woke shivering. White snow-feathers were falling. Settling on the ground, making the stark winter branches plump and rounding the edges of the world.

I heard Welsh curse the change in weather. 'We'll have to clear the way for the ox,' he told me. 'Pray this doesn't last.'

The snow slowed us down. I pushed it from the path, brooming it into drifts, though my cracked ribs ached with the effort. I saw that we walked slant at the sun. East. We were headed away from the Hafren and the ship that might sail me far from here. At night, I clung to the blankets Welsh threw at me, cold stealing the sleep I craved.

On the third day, Horse pulled up the ox and turned to roar at Welsh, too quick for me to understand. Welsh whispered his reply and Horse roared again. They both glanced at me before Horse raised his thick fist and shook it at the low, grey sky. His temper made me want to curl up ash-bug tight and crawl under the nearest rock.

Once the shouting was over, Welsh turned back to me. He spoke slowly, in Saxon. 'We're not to speak British any more. It makes Horse angry. Saxon only from today out. Understand?' He said more, but too fast and flurried for sense.

I had to master Saxon. I felt lost again. Plunged into unknowing. Drowning in sounds that had no meaning.

As the day wore on, I crept back into myself. I listened to the three men. I sought the gaps between the words, slight places where I might wriggle my way in. I listened to more than the sounds, I tried to read the men too, hearing anger or confusion in their words and guessing the source of the trouble. Had we taken the wrong path? Was the *wasser* brackish, or running low? I acted on my guesses. I tugged Welsh in the direction of stream-song and fresh water. I watched the sky and caught the track of the sun. Father Ambrose had said that it was safer to understand what your enemy was saying, so I soaked up the words as my hem soaked up the snowmelt.

Days and nights of digging and tramping followed each other while I learned more and more.

I learned that the men were heading back to their *dorf*, their village. It was deep in the *wald*, the woods, between *zwei bäche*, two streams. They had *familien* there, even Welsh had his family.

I didn't want to be part of it, but I had nowhere else to go. I decided, while they fed me, and while my ribs were still bruise-wrapped from the fall, I would see where this road led.

Snow fell again. Settled. Thawed. The path was more mud than stone and even the ox struggled. Through the pulling and pushing, digging and bruising, I set myself to learn, asking Welsh for more and more Saxon. I was wolf-eating the words and spitting them back out half-chewed. Welsh described the Saxon world and I repeated it back to him.

He noticed how fast I learned. 'You're quick,' he told me. 'Be careful. Don't let people see your quickness.'

'Why?'

He didn't answer me. Instead he pointed to clouds and the sky, the hills and trees, the moon and the sun and told me about the Saxon gods who lived there, Woden and Thunor and more.

I listened to his tales, before finally, with winter still holding the land tight in its fist, we arrived at their village.

33

I LOOK AT the baby in my arms. He's sleeping now. The trauma of his birth is already being forgotten. His hair is drying to honey. He clenches and unclenches his fists as though testing the thickness of the air. I pull his swaddling closer about him. My sister is pale and quiet as sleep pulls her under too. The pain is like the tide running out of the estuary leaving new land behind. I settle him beside her. They should both rest together.

'You too,' Sara says. She shuffles around the floor, clicking her teeth and gathering the bloody rags into her basket.

'Me too what?' I ask, not too loud.

'You need to rest. The sun is rising. The longest day.'

I hadn't noticed until that moment, but the birds in the woods beyond have been calling to welcome the day. It's soft and golden and for one moment; I think of the baby Iesu and his mother and my heart bursts again.

'Come. Rest,' Sara says.

She pushes me past the sack curtain and tugs it

205

back into place behind us both as though it were fine bower-linen.

We are no longer alone in the hut. Some of the Welsh have slipped back, unheard and unannounced. Like Sara they look tired as Job. Elin and Anwen, usually heads together, telling fat stories, are silent. They hold hands, both sorry things.

I don't speak to them. There's nothing to say. They won't care about the baby. He's nothing to them.

The weight of my tiredness hits me and I let myself drop sack-heavy onto one of the stump stools. The heat from the fire is very welcome. Sara sits too.

'You said,' she begins quietly, 'you said you want better for him.'

I nod.

'What did you mean?'

I hold my hands out, warming them on the low flames. 'I don't know, not for certain. But I know I want him to be free to choose. I had Saxon words forced on me, they still feel too sharp in my mouth.'

Sara nods, listening.

So, I carry on, 'I am the words I speak. Saxon Mai is mouse-meek and scurrying. British Mai dreamed of fighting for her people. It's the words that make us, the stories we tell ourselves.'

'You want him to choose what he will be? Does anyone get to do that?' Sara asks.

'Tonight, I chose to stay, to be here. I might have chosen otherwise.'

'I know. I'm grateful.' She rests her hand on my shoulder.

'I want that for him. For him to decide who he is. We don't get that, do we?' I nod towards Elin and Anwen. 'We came back here, even when we might have run.'

'The dreams of witches get you nowhere,' Sara says.

'Wanting better isn't dreaming,' I say too loudly. Elin lifts her head and stares, empty-eyed. Whatever horror she's seeing, it isn't me she's looking at.

We've all seen horror tonight. The woods are still full of it. Saxon men with iron in their hands. Men I can't trust. The smoke still rises in the village. And, even if we could get past the fighters, there are wolves and thieves and cutthroats. The world is full of terrors. It's no place to take my sister and her son.

'You should rest, I'm heart-serious,' Sara says.

'I can't. I'm too full up with feelings.'

'Steal fox-sleep, then, just rest your eyes. Food. Bed.' She strokes my cheek.

I feel my eyes prickle. She is so kind. She need not have cared for us tonight, but she did. Sara gets to her feet slowly, sighing. Then moves to her sleeping mat.

She is asleep before I think to thank her.

I drop my head in my hands. Thoughts race like hares before dogs. We need to leave. But there's as much

danger beyond the village as inside it. We can't stay. The baby can't be raised here. We should go now, while the world is at driffs and draffs. But we'll be caught and the traitor tree waits. The choices are impossible, like bagging smoke. I don't know what to do.

I can't sleep. The path is calling to me.

I stand. Leave the hut. The air is damp in the midsummer dawn. Dew turns much of the ground silver, and webs glisten like fallen stars. The furnace of Hell might have opened last night, but the morning is born fresh.

There are more dogs than people in the village. I see the animals slink black-furred into shadows. But there are some people too, now. Women and children, mostly, coming back from the woods.

They ignore me; too full of their own fears. I stand at the head of the path. I won't follow it. I won't. Not alone, anyway.

I just want to see it. The way out.

Before I know it, I'm walking.

Soon, I'm in the open ground at the entrance to the village. The place where I arrived moons ago now, when the days were still short. I stand stock-still. Staring at the dusty chalk path that would lead me out. Beside the path, just at the village edge, are the smouldering funeral pyres I've been able to smell all night. They are low now: the bodies in them burned to nothing more than grey sticks, black twigs, ashen skulls. I keep back. I can't walk past them.

I hear someone cough. Gentle, delicate, determined. I turn and see that Rowan has been watching me.

And I know I will drown within reach of the river-bank.

34

I SAW THE village first through gaps in the trees. The path ran downhill, with the village nestled in the land-dip below. Someone had dug trenches on either side of the path, to carry off rainwater. And it was well-walked, no sleet or snow was allowed to settle anywhere along it. The trees were coppiced, farmed to become fence posts and roof pillars and spears. I could see homes between the straight stems. Glimpses to begin with, then full walls and roofs. All wood, long and narrow with square corners. There was wood everywhere. No reused Roman bricks or tiles, no rocks pulled from the belly of the earth. These were the homes of sawyers and carpenters; people starting anew, not stealing from the Roman dead.

Horse was wild with glee at the sight. He called at full skull-strength, plumes of white mist rose from his mouth as he yelled. Names, I supposed. They were not words I recognised from all the learning I'd done on the road.

The village answered. I heard dogs bark the alarm at our approach. Children squealed. Hammer blows on metal stopped. They knew we were coming.

Horse quickened our pace.

I felt my arms tighten at my sides as we entered the village. I snatched in the sights, fox-wary.

The path ran lazily through the middle of the village. Not Roman straight, but twisting Saxon. There were many halls along it, and more in sidewynds behind them. I couldn't see the streams, but I could smell them – cold marsh-murk and reedbeds somewhere close.

Two small children rushed from one of the halls, squealing like piglets. They hurled themselves at Horse and he grabbed them both, tucking one under each arm. Their shrieks became giggles as he spun them around. 'You're heavy!' he said. They were, their cheeks rounder than the children I'd left behind at the camp. There was food.

The children squealed their replies, too quickly for me to catch every word, but their delight in seeing him was plain. Horse was their father, then. With his children in his arms he was so different to the angry, coarse man he'd been this past fortnight. He roared with laughter this time, as he dangled the smallest upside down.

I was forgotten about.

I was grateful for it. I wanted no one to notice me again.

I stayed stump-still. There was danger here, sure certain, but there was food and somewhere dry to sleep, maybe. I would sooner take my chance here than die of cold and hunger on the road. At least while I felt so weak.

By now, twenty or thirty people had come from the halls and paths to greet Horse. There were many with light hair and light eyes – greys and blues instead of the browns and hazels I was used to. Their clothes were odd too. Tunics clasped with thick brooches, beads in reds and yellows and amber.

Then, in the roil and roll of the crowd, I saw dark hair, flecked with white, broad shoulders. Tad? Was it Tad? It looked just like him.

My heart was in my throat as I pushed forward to see. Tad! I wanted to yell at him, for him to turn and laugh and say I'd been dreaming these last weeks.

But when the man turned I saw my mistake. He was British, no doubt, but he was not Tad. His face was too young, his features wet-dough soft. Welsh, not British. Slave, not free.

I felt hope slip from me and unfallen tears burned my eyes.

'Mai, stand straight.' Welsh was at my side. 'Head up.'

Why? I couldn't think, but I did as he said. I was doing everything he said, I realised. He had spent short days and long nights dripping Saxon words into my ear. He'd seemed to be my friend, but all the while he'd been ploughing furrows in my mind, dropping Saxon seeds there.

'Look meek, but useful,' Welsh whispered.

What? To be the best slave I could be?

'Girl!' Horse had remembered me. He yelled and waved his thick paw. '*Vorerst*, you'll join my household. My daughter, Rowan, will you *dienen*.' I couldn't understand every word, but there was enough sense there for me to follow. I was being given my place. I watched the crowd. Who was I being gifted to?

One hailed me.

Rowan.

She had the height of her father. But was pale, like morning before the sun has given colour to the day. Her hair was the weak Saxon colour of fieldmice, her eyes hedge-green. I followed when she beckoned.

Walking two steps behind her, my eyes darted like little fish from her spine to the halls and back again. The village was bigger than I'd imagined from the glances stolen between bare trees. There was room for thirty families, pups, dogs and sires. The halls hadn't all been built at the same time, I saw the wear of winters on some, while others were saw-fresh. Horse was doing well here, drawing people to him, providing for those who were whelped under his rafters. So different from the hollowed faces at the British camp. They were reshaping the forest to suit themselves. I saw carvings on lintels and roof beams, strange creatures, serpents and adders with wings devouring their own tails.

Gwrtheyrn should fear this. I saw no tumble-down huts like the one that had belonged to Eleri and then us. I shivered for Bryn and the small boys who guarded the camp cattle – one day they would clash with these people, I was sure.

We climbed one of the sidewynds uphill.

Rowan stopped outside one of the larger halls. Chickens bothered the ground and the housecat purred in pale yellow sunshine. 'This is my home,' Rowan said. Her accent was easier to understand than that of Horse, she spoke slower. 'You will work here. You will also join the other women to grind, *weben*, mind the children. There are crops to farm. You understand?'

I nodded. I'd not caught every word, but had caught the meaning. I was to work, wherever I was told. I could do that. I could lose myself in work.

Tad. Haf. Home.

'Good. What's your name?'

'Mai,' I whispered.

'Mai? Mai,' she tested the name on her tongue. 'Come with me to the *werkraum*. The women there will instruct you.'

We dropped back down into the shadows. Dogs snuffled the path and the sound of Horse celebrating his return drifted towards us. But we didn't turn right to find the entrance to the village. Instead we headed to where the shade became damp and frosty, and the smell of marsh was stronger. Rowan stepped into one of the plainest buildings I'd seen so far. No carvings or paintings at all. She pulled aside the leather door. Inside, it was not laid out for living. One whole wall was open to the woods, the long side entirely missing. Women sat circled on the floor, working at quern-stones to grind grain. The air tasted of flour. The women kept up low, rhythmic singing, their arms and backs moving in time to the melody. My heart leaped. Tad had sung the same song as he worked, at least, the same tune. The words the women sang were strange to me. Saxon.

Rowan told me, 'I will send for you, when I have tasks I want you to do.'

I nodded.

She left, headed back to her kith and kin, and the warm welcoming party. I looked around awkwardly. I had not taken in the women properly until now. There were five of them in the room at the grinding stones. Two had dark hair, swept under scarves. One was lighter, more honey-coloured. Two looked older, silver and grey strands fell about their cheeks. Their clothes were all similar shades of brown, the simplest of dyes, cut hoop-de-hap to their bodies. The honey-brown girl watched me, the stone in her hands still. 'You can take over,' she said cheerfully, over the sound of the song. 'I need to visit the drop.'

She spoke Saxon, but her accent was British, I was sure certain. 'Yes, I can . . .' I began, in British.

The girl recoiled as though I had slapped her. 'You speak Saxon,' she scolded, 'always. It worries them to

215

hear British.' Her frown vanished and her face brimmed with laughter. She said more, but I couldn't follow.

Saxon, always? The words in my mind were British. To turn them to Saxon would make me seem slow and stupid as winter dormice. I remembered Welsh gave me just that advice. Be slow, be stupid, keep your head down.

I could do that. 'My name is Mai,' I said in my new-learned Saxon.

'Viola,' the girl said. 'My tad thought we were Roman!' She laughed though I couldn't spot the joke.

'Slow,' I said, 'speak slow.'

Her head tilted with sympathy. Remembering, perhaps, how she felt when the Saxon words were new and uncomfortable. She nodded, then said, much more slowly, 'My tad was Roman, Viola was Roman. But I might change to Bertha or Frida or some good Saxon name.' Her lips were full, her cheeks dimpled. She seemed happy as the cuckoo on its branch. I couldn't see why she would be so.

I felt pleased, and ashamed, to have understood her so well.

I was Welsh now, not British, not Roman.

Viola stood and stretched her arms above her head. 'You take that,' she said, pointing to the quern-stone. She stepped past me and out of the door, winking as she went.

I sat down in her place and held the stone. It was warm from work. The woman beside me, who had grey hair and lines deep across her face, broke from her song. She clicked disapproval at the door Viola had left through. 'Keep away from that one. She'll be making small bones before spring is through.'

I wondered if I'd caught the Saxon words right. I had no idea what the woman meant, but I smiled to show I'd listened.

'I'm Sara,' she said. 'The one there who walks on worn soles, is Gwennan.' She nodded towards the other old, grey-haired woman. Gwennan greeted me. No one broke from working as they spoke.

'Those two are Elin and Anwen. They're nearly as bad as Viola. So you're to join us, are you?'

I muddled through her tangle of words. Then replied as best as I could: 'I for Rowan work. I here finish then Rowan find?' It was harder to speak than to understand. I had the dizzying feeling that I would never sound like myself again.

'Find Rowan?' Elin laughed, breaking through my fear. 'No. Don't look up when acorns fall. If she wants you, she'll find you. Stay out of their way.'

That same advice. Be small. Be stupid. I felt raw as leeks. I had no clue what I was about. I was grateful that the singing began again and I could hide in the work. That I could understand.

The shadows swung about the room as we toiled. The *huss-huss* of the grinding beat out time and the droning song helped me to ignore the growing blisters on my fingers, the ache in my still-shifting ribs. I'd worked before, of course, but not for so long without breaking to tumble in the yard, or run with fresh air on my face. The work was hot and swamp-sticky. I realised why there was no side wall – the cold air rolled the furnace heat of the work aside. There was no sign of Viola for the rest of the morning. When she did return, she held her skirt before her with something carried in the pouch it made. 'Food!' she said joyfully.

My stomach growled.

Everyone stopped work and began to chatter. Words I could only snatch by the tail. With so many voices speaking, I understood nothing. I felt myself shrink into my space. How could they follow the flow of talk and reply without missing their moment? I wanted to cover my ears, to run and hide.

'Fruit!' Viola said with delight. 'One for each of us.' There were loud coos from Elin and Anwen. In the short silence, I understood Gwennan ask, 'Where is it from?'

'Don't check the teeth of free sheep.' Viola rolled her eyes at the question. 'It's fruit. Do you want it?'

'Sorry,' Gwennan replied. 'I want it.'

Viola doled out her treasure, one honey-stewed berry for every mouth. She had flatbread too, fresh from the oven. She stopped in front of me last of all. Her look was part pity, part humour. 'Mai, was it? How are your hands?'

I held them out for her to see. The palms were red, the knuckles chafed. Four blisters had formed where the fingers met the palm.

'I've seen worse,' Viola said. 'You need saltwater. Soak them. They'll hurt tomorrow too. And the day after. But after that . . .'

She added something I couldn't understand, then handed me the last sticky berry from her bread parcel. It was small and the red was tinged black in places. I took it and cradled it carefully in my palm.

'It's for eating,' Viola laughed.

I looked at her for three heartbeats, then I bit it in two. The juice was more honey than fruit, it was so sweet, but it was so welcome, like ice stream-water in midsummer. I felt my eyes sting.

Viola laughed. 'Don't make calf eyes, I've got no more to give.'

I felt myself blush rose. I hadn't meant to ask for more. 'Sorry,' I whispered.

'Well, maybe I do.' She handed me bread, then strode back to the chattering women.

35

THE OPEN WALL of the workroom let in the pale light of the winter sun. Viola wiped the pink juice of the berry from her lips and sat with her legs dangling over the ledge. She wrapped her arms around herself against the chill.

Everyone else sat back at their quern-stones.

'You should get back to work too, Viola,' Sara said gruffly.

'Sweet fruit should be *gefeiert*!' Viola insisted.

The women laughed gently. I didn't understand the word she used.

Viola smiled at the room, eager to have the audience, I thought. 'There should be more celebrations always. New fruit, new loves, new leaves – everything should have its feast day.'

Gefeiert, celebrated. I swallowed the word down with all the others. My hoard of Saxon words was growing with every breath.

Sara grumbled something about idle shepherds losing their sheep.

'What would you call holidays for?' Viola asked her.

Sara slowed her grinding, but didn't stop. 'Births?'

Elin and Anwen giggled, although I didn't know why.

Viola huffed at the idea. 'What would be the point? Babies can't celebrate, and you're too tired if you're the mother. Only fathers get to celebrate births.'

Sara said nothing. She just pushed one of the empty stones towards Viola. That was answer enough. Viola grimaced, but took her place and poured the grain with good humour. 'Fine,' she said, 'you can be sour as five-day milk if you like, but I won't join you.'

'Nothing changes,' Sara said.

The afternoon passed in the same way, work, work and more work, with Viola making the circle laugh, or herding tales of people I hadn't met. The sacks of new flour grew full. By twilight the bones in my back felt hard and brittle as stacked slate and my ribs ached. There was no call or sign that I spotted that meant work was over, but they all seemed to feel it in the same instant. The work songs stopped and the women crouched, crunched, clicked their bones comfortable. I copied them. Until I was stronger and could decide what to do, I would copy.

The women filed out of the workroom in ones and twos. Sara took my arm before I could follow.

'Help me with the wall,' she said.

The open side wall needed to be lifted back into place for the night. It lay flat on the ground. The wicker was light, but awkward and it took lots of huffing and puffing from Sara before she agreed it was in the right place. She untied her scarf and wiped her face with it. Her forehead was marked like mud banks with deep furrows. She wore her silver hair tied back tightly into plaits and pinned to her head.

'Now, we clean.' She mimed holding the broom so that I would understand. Soon the only sound was the *shh-shh* of our sweeping.

'Work faster, Mai. If we don't get to the Welsh barn soon, there will be no food left for us.'

I'd worked hard enough to kill snakes that day, so my arms ached. But the work was simple enough. Husks and grains of loose barley-corn and flour-dust spread around the abandoned stones. They were pale in the evening light.

Sara said something. The words slipped together like swill.

'I don't understand,' I said.

She paused, her eyes flicked to the leather door, the closed wall. 'Clear every last grain,' she said in British. She had to search for the words she needed. It was heavy work for her to remember them. I wondered how long it had been since she'd spoken British words. 'Clean well. Or we'll see mice where there should be none.'

I kept my eyes to the ground for every last husk.

We worked with only the sound of the broom bristles on the hard dirt floor to disturb us. The village felt ten miles away, as though it had forgotten we two existed. Sara crabbed between the abandoned grindstones. She bent now and then to fish out stray grains.

'We had chickens, when I was young,' she said, almost to herself, her words mixed British and Saxon, tripping neither of us up. 'And here I am, pecking grains like my old hens. Mam kept them, really. Well, Mam had servants back then, to mind them for her. Ha! That's surprised you. We were Roman. I've seen too many summers to count and my first ones were Roman.' Her voice sank like mist in the valley. She reminded me of Tad. The way she paused on the word Roman, as if it meant more to her than I could ever understand. I felt my heart burst with ache for him and all he'd lost. All I'd lost, now.

'My tad remembered the Romans. Or his tad did,' I said. My chest hurt, even to say his name, but I wanted to talk about him too. To believe he was still real enough to be talked of. 'He told me he remembered the soldiers. Did you ever see soldiers?' I asked.

It was dark now and my pale pile of dust seemed to glow.

'I saw them when I was as young as you are now. They marched in *reihen. Reihen.* Do you know what that means?'

I didn't. It wasn't one of the Saxon words I'd heard.

'You wouldn't know the word in British either. It isn't something we have any use for now. You've seen starlings

223

in spring? The way they fly together as if they were one mind on one wing? Thousands of them? That's what the army was like. They'd follow their wide, flat roads like one thousand-legged beasts. But when you looked closer, they were all different shapes and sizes of men. Some had skin pale like ice on well water, others were dark like otters. It was just the marching that made them look the same. The differences were lost in the belonging.'

'When I was young, I thought to join the warriors,' I said, almost to the broom.

Sara laughed. 'Young! You're getting on in days, not years. Young, indeed.' She wandered to the door where there were wooden buckets, with lids, lined up. Grain for the morning. Sara dropped her loose hoard into the nearest one. 'Put the floor dust out.' She passed me the wooden shovel that partnered the broom. 'Ten steps away at least,' she warned. 'I'll have no rodents in my workroom.'

'Yours?' I asked in surprise. I'd seen her working her bones short with everyone else.

'I watch over it, for Rowan and her father.'

I felt fleet surprise. If she was so trusted, allowed so much freedom, why didn't she just walk into the woods and never come back? Why didn't she run to safety? Was it because there was nowhere on this island that was safe any more?

She interrupted my thoughts, 'Come now. Let's get

some of that flour in you. You're thin, girl. Thin as the foreheads of hens.'

She shut up the workroom, tying the leather door shut. Outside we were in sea-dark twilight. Slips of pink and cream faded to dark blue at the bowl-lip of the sky. Sara began her own slow march through the village, with me chickling behind her. The yellow glow of fires came from half-closed shutters in the halls we passed.

'You'll sleep in the barn of the Welsh, and eat there too. We work together to stay fed and warm. As long as you work, you'll be fine.'

Welsh.

Slave.

I'd been trying not to think the word. But it landed like cold stones in my belly. Slave. That was what I was now. Not here to earn my keep in the workroom, or earn my food by cleaning clothes too rich for me to wear. I earned nothing. I was to do what I was told, just the same as at the camp.

What if I was told to steal or raid too?

I pressed my palm to my ribs and gasped with the pain of it.

'Hurry!' Sara said from somewhere in the darkness.

We walked right to the edge of the village, dropping into dank shade as we went. The path narrowed, so Sara walked ahead. Branches loomed on either side. On them, I saw the earliest signs of change, dark bumps that would bud on the thin stems of trees. And, faint as the fading light, I caught the buried scent of little white lilies and saffrwm leaves, though the green was still trapped deep under the earth. Winter wouldn't last for ever.

I wanted sleep and food and to be left alone with my British words – Tad, Haf, home.

The Welsh barn was small, the shingle roof low. The boards which formed the walls were set edge-to-edge, not overlapping like closed teeth. It saved wood, but it would also be colder. Wool had been pressed into the gaps where the boards didn't quite meet. Sara pushed the leather door aside. I followed her in.

Inside were more people than there had been in the workroom. Men and women both, and children. They sat around the one fire that lit and heated the space. They were speaking in Saxon, but there were British words too, dropped in where the Saxon wouldn't fit or flex to form the right meaning, like wooden teeth dropped into red gaps in gums.

These were the Welsh.

The Britons who hadn't joined men like Gwrtheyrn. Had they been pushed out, as I'd been? Or had they been captured in raids? Or, maybe – I remembered the man and woman in the woods carrying their dead baby – maybe this life was better than being free, but starving.

My eyes got used to the gloom. There were few windows

to let in starlight. Those that they had were set high in the wooden walls to let smoke leave.

'This is where we sleep,' Sara told me. 'And eat. And everything else when the work of the day is done. Take your food and sit quietly,' she said.

Gwennan served stew into bowls from the blackest cauldron I'd seen. Its battered and bent shape told of the thousands of fires it had touched. The Welsh sipped from their bowls, or stabbed chunks of turnip with their knives. I took the stew with nervous thanks and went to sit in the farthest corner to watch.

Viola was in the middle of everything. Her hair glowed honey in the firelight. Her laugh rose light as the seeds of the flowering lion-tooth. She had somehow lost the dust of the day from her clothes and face. I sipped from the bowl and kept my head down.

I thought I wouldn't sleep. *Tad, Haf, home*, still bit at my heart. But, with the stew inside me, and the warmth from the bodies and the burning logs, my eyes slowly closed.

My dream-torn seams unravelled.

Dread led me into the dark.

In my dream I was back in the tomb. But the body in the coffin wasn't the dried and shrivelled Roman woman. It was tall, and dark, and newly dead. And if it opened its eyes, I knew my heart would stop cold.

Tad.

I wanted him to wake.

I feared his waking with every hair on my head.

The walls pressed in. I choked and gasped for air. I fell. Hard on the stone floor with the coffin-cliff looming above me.

'Mai!' My name was spoken softly. 'Mai, wake up.' I felt sick and sore, with my ribs feeling cracked again. My head was being cradled. I could smell sour cloth. Someone leaned in close. I tried to open my eyes, but my lids felt heavy and I clean failed to move them.

'Don't worry, you're in the square field, you were sleeping,' I recognised the voice. Viola. I was on the floor of the barn; my head was in her lap and it was her fingers I could feel, cool and light, against my cheek. She stroked me and, for wonderful, woozy moments, I thought of my sister. Haf had soothed me like this when we were children.

I forced my eyes open. Viola looked down at me, her eyes merry. 'You leaped in your dream and dropped like dung from cattle,' she laughed.

The Welsh in the room were not all asleep, though the fire was low. The brow of day was still far off.

'It will be the heat and the smoke,' Sara said nearby.

'Yes, and the work,' Viola added, laughing too. 'Poor creature. She needs to eat and fill out her skin. She won't last unless she's better rested.'

'You and your rests,' Sara tutted. 'Get her to bed.'

'I can't lift her, she's the same size as me.'

'You've at least two summers on her. Don't be idle, Viola.'

Viola slipped her arms under mine and hoisted me. She was my hands and feet. I climbed up off the floor. Bodies slept on full sacks of straw at one end of the room. She led me there and sat me down.

'You need to sleep,' Viola said softly.

She was right. I was too sick and sore to do anything but sleep. I rested in the dip dented by dozens of bodies before mine. The coarse sacking smelled of men and work and poor washing. I closed my eyes. From the fireside, I heard Saxon drift from so many mouths. I was carried on the waves of it to the sea of sleep. I floated there without dreaming.

It was Sara who woke me hours later. She carried more dried fruit and flatbread. I took them gratefully. My arms hurt from the grinding work. Viola was right, I needed to get stronger before I could think about leaving. And there seemed to be food here, plentiful.

'Eat,' Sara said. 'There's water runs just beyond the barn, between here and the woods if you want to wash. The cold will help your sore bones. Did you find the long-drop?'

I suddenly realised how swollen my navel felt – I was bursting to piss. It hurt to move, I needed it that bad.

'Some people drop just off the path,' Sara said. 'It saves time, but smells like dead goats. Or there's the drop near the stream.'

I shot out of the barn, past the other people who milled like sheep, pulling on clothes and combing their hair. The morning felt cold, the ground white with frost. I could see footprints, dark on the grass, that showed me where people had gone. I rushed to follow, away from the village, into thin trees, coppiced straight. The smell of the drop took the skin off my teeth, but I went with relief.

Sara was waiting when I got back. 'Come,' she said when she saw me. 'We've work to do.'

That day and the days that followed had the regular pattern of loom-woven fabric. Meals and work were the upright warp, they were constant and unchanging. But the weft of colour was made by the conversations of the women.

Sara was not much of one for herding tales. She lived with her eye on today and cared little for what happened beyond the sleeping hall and workroom.

But Viola chewed the air with her stories, ambushing anyone who would listen. She sniffed out the tales throughout the village. She had all the news: who was spreading at the apron strings – and who had put the baby there; who had stolen glances at who at the feast table; who was betrothed, and who was getting over their shyness together. All her tales were of love, somehow. She could see it where I could not. Her stories helped my Saxon take root and grow. I wanted to understand the tales she had to tell me, so I listened and listened and listened. And the words I couldn't understand grew fewer and fewer. Welsh had taught me the words for hundreds of things I could see and touch as we'd walked to the village. Viola taught me the words for things I couldn't see: love and hope and dreaming.

Most days, Viola would sail into the workroom with the fair wind at her back. She'd settle slowly to her grindstone, willing to sit, unwilling to work. So like Haf. Whenever there was pause in our songs, she would pipe up with her gossip. 'This morning, Linn has her hair differently *frisiert*. I saw her. She tries to look like Synne, the wife of Wilfred.'

'What's *frisiert*?' I asked.

'Styled,' Viola told me, in British.

'What of it?' Anwen asks. 'It's her hair.'

'What if it isn't just her hair that Linn wants to take? Wilfred is fine, and strong, Linn has noticed.'

There were tuts from around the circle – Sara and Gwennan especially pretended not to be interested in taming horses that weren't theirs. Elin and Anwen, on the other hand, hung on her words.

'Perhaps she just likes the way Synne has her hair,' Sara said.

But there was no silence in Viola. 'Who would want such scarecrow hair? She must be doing it for his attention.'

I saw nothing of Horse or Rowan in those early days. I was wrapped up in the warmth of the women while I mended from the sores of the camp. I would think about leaving soon, I told myself. Soon. I ate and worked and slept in the meantime, with thoughts of Tad never too far away. In the night, when dreams came, Viola was there, stroking my hair and whispering nonsense and kindness until I was soothed.

I almost forgot I was captive.

36

BY THE TIME ten days had passed, the hazel catkins were forming, butter yellow on the stream banks, and the pain in my ribs was all but gone. I had worked in the workroom most days, but Rowan had called me twice, once to help thread her loom and another to wring out and hang lighter clothes, ready for the promised spring, though we still woke to frosts.

I could run, now, if I chose.

I eyed the paths out of the village as I went about my work.

Sara noticed my restlessness. 'Your strength has come back,' she said as we swept the workroom one late afternoon.

'I feel better, yes,' I said.

'You're as skittish as tethered cats. Don't we work you hard enough?'

I pulled the broom across the floor, chasing the rolling grains. 'People are contented to stay here, aren't they?' I asked carefully, watching her brow. 'The Welsh, I mean?'

'Contented?' She was frowning, troubled by the question. Had I used the wrong word?

'Yes,' I said. 'Happy? I mean, there's food and warmth. Much more than there was in the British camp I was at. And there are no walls or ditches to keep people in. They stay because they want to.'

'I'm not one for spreading tales . . .' she said.

'No, Viola does enough of that for all of us.'

'She hasn't the sense she was born with, that one. She'll find herself in trouble one of these days. Still,' Sara became more serious, 'she hasn't seen what I've seen.'

The broom slowed in my hand. 'What do you mean?'

Sara twisted her mouth sourly. 'You think you aren't watched? Don't be so foolish. Half the women in the workroom would share your secrets with the Saxons for one roast chicken before you could say *onedayonenight*.'

'Really?'

'Sure certain,' Sara said. 'They don't need walls when everyone is watching everyone else. And you haven't seen what they do to runaways, have you? Fair, to tell the truth neither have those girls. It's just tales told to frighten them. But I've seen it. And heard it. And it's something I never want to witness again.'

She turned away, bending heavily to lift the quern-stones. She toed the few hidden grains into view.

'What happens to runaways?' I asked. My eyes flashed

to the door and the tidy, quiet homes of the Saxons beyond.

'They send out the dogs. And when they catch you, the men take you to the tree in the woods. Once, it was the tallest oak standing, hard by their temple. It fell in one terrible night of storms. Struck by Woden, they believe. When it fell, its roots were ripped up from the earth. The roots are still there, spreading up into the air like burned house posts.'

I knew about burned house posts, the smell of ash in the air. The fear.

'What's that got to do with runaways?' I asked.

'They tie you to those roots and whip you until the ground is red. Then you're left. Just left. And no one is allowed to help you down or give you water.'

'For how long?' I whispered.

'Until you make no more noise. Not even when you're cut with your own short knife, as if you were meat.'

'The people . . . the runaways, they die?' I pulled the broom closer, using it to hold myself up.

'In the end. After three or four days, I dare say you'd welcome it.'

'Like Iesu.'

Sara cackled then. 'You think we're like the Blessed Baby? You're more full of tales than Viola. Listen, Mai, whatever you do, don't find yourself near the tree of traitors. I've never seen cruelty like it. It would frighten demons. Do you hear me?'

I nodded. I heard. Even if I had somewhere to run to, the image of those blackened tree roots was enough to kill all thoughts of escape.

I didn't walk back to the Welsh barn with Sara after that. My mind was too full.

I paced the village. I walked the paths and sidewynds between halls, the open garden, the hide-acre they called it, now full of shadows, on the slope of the hill. I went to the edge of the field where small sheep and their newborn lambs grazed shoots that looked black in the twilight.

The village looked as if it were part of the land beyond, paths and streams leading out of it. But, if Sara was right, then I had just walked the edges of the whole world entire. To step beyond was to step into horror.

My heart beat with the walk, with the fear.

My days here were cradled by the women I worked alongside, but I was trapped as sure as the spider trapped the fly.

The fast walk brought me full circle, to the stream. It was there that I heard voices. One of them familiar: Welsh.

Anger leaped in my chest. He had helped them catch me. He had trained me as though I were their dog. He had forced the Saxon words into my mouth.

I followed the sound of his voice. Firelight glowed near the stream bank. Two men sat close to the heat of its flames, to keep out the cold. Something dark and humped lay between them.

My footsteps disturbed them.

'Mai!' Welsh said, when I was close enough to be seen. 'How is it with you? You look better. Less bruised.'

I said nothing. I glowered at his easy smile, the cup in his hand that, no doubt, held cider or mead, given his smiles. I glowered too at the man who sat beside him. He was big, dark, younger than Welsh, he had no grey in his hair. He wore his fat comfortably on his belly and his beard stretched to his chest. He held what looked like leather strips in his hands and more of these lay at his feet.

'Oak, this is Mai. We found her on the road like one of the fair folk. Mai, this is Oak, the best sawyer in the village. Though he is busy at fishing tonight. If the coracle floats.'

Oak growled amiably at Welsh and folded one of the leather strips around the dark shape between them. It was bowl-shaped, but big enough to hold Oak – his fishing coracle.

I didn't care about their plans.

'Why did you bring me here?' I asked Welsh. I tried to push the question, slap-strong, but it sounded weak and tearful.

Welsh sighed. He put his cup on the ground and pushed himself to standing. 'Oh, Mai,' he said. 'What are you asking me?'

'You helped them. You're British, but you helped them bring me here.'

'Yes. And you look stronger and plumper than you did when we found you.'

'So you were helping me?' I couldn't look at him. I stared instead at the flames.

'You're alive. You're fed. It could be worse.' He stepped closer. He took my wrists too tightly. He was bigger than me. My eyes were level with his chest. The muscle of his shoulders unyielding as rock.

'Grow up, Mai,' Welsh said, leaning in close. 'You are without family, without protection. This is the best you could hope for. Horse is strong and getting stronger. West Saxons from all around flock to him. If Rowan marries well, he might unite the East Saxons too. The Britons, such as they are, are scared of his shadow. They hide like goats on hilltops. He won't let them hide for long. There's war coming. You've found yourself on the right side, because of me.'

War?

I turned my face away from his words. He held my body still.

'Make yourself useful, as I've done. As Oak and Sara have done. In time you might buy back your freedom. Until then, be valuable.'

Haf had said the same thing. Be of use. Everyone was

full of the same words – behave, belong. But it led to betrayal.

All the fight left me.

Welsh let go of my wrists.

'You've frightened her,' Oak said, with the ease of someone talking of the weather.

'Good. She needs to find some sense, and quickly,' Welsh said. 'Now. Is that thing ready to go near the water?' He stepped away from me, his mind back on the coracle and the flowing stream and fish for his own stomach. I was forgotten.

The spring night sent cold to the tips of my fingers and toes. I hurried away from the men, shivering. As I passed the goat pens where the sour-smelling animals bleated, someone whispered, '*Isht*. Mai.'

'Viola?' I tried to see her, but the wicker fence was draped in shadow.

'*Isht*. They'll hear you.'

'What are you doing?'

'Fresh milk. Still warm. Want some?'

She clambered from the pen, her eyes star-twinkled, and her top lip was half-moon white with stolen milk. She wiped it on the back of her sleeve and held her wooden beaker out to me.

I glanced back to the river, to the path.

'What are you afraid of, little mouse?' she asked me softly.

'Everything.'

She waited. I wanted to say more, to tell her about my nightmares. But the words wouldn't come.

Still she held out her beaker. 'I try not to worry my thoughts.'

I took it, listening with every hair of my head for the shout of 'Thief!'

No shout came. I drank. The milk was sweet and sour and fat.

'Better?' she asked.

Somehow it was, for the moment.

37

I WORKED. MY body healed and the blisters on my hands became calluses. Days passed. Weeks, even. But I barely noticed. The world was tinged grey, as though the winter clouds still lay heavy on the spring land. War was coming, Welsh had said. There was nowhere to go, even if I risked the dogs and the tree of traitors and ran.

This was all there was, everywhere. The camp, the village, the woods beyond. It was all the same. Be of use, grow up, or be hurt by the people you thought were kin. I stayed small and quiet and I did as I was told.

The warmth of the farm and the joy of the stories Tad told seemed very far away. He was gone, and Haf, in choosing the camp over me, was gone too.

I dragged myself to the lean-to byres where the Saxons kept their goats and I milked the thin-tempered beasts, or I went to the stream to wash the underclothes the Saxon women wore, or to the workroom to grind grain, without feeling that I was even really there. Blossom bloomed on the orchard trees; the leeks of St Peter sent up dark green shoots around the trunks.

I was sinking and I didn't care.

Viola was the only one who stopped me slipping under the tide of sadness. She'd wink at me from her place at her quern-stone then sneak something tasty into my palm. She walked the paths with me, keeping up her cheery chatter. At night, she held my hand if I woke, sweating with terror.

Sometimes, sometimes, when there was no one else near, not Welsh or Saxon and only the martins swirled above our heads, she would whisper to me just in British. Hearing those words made my heart beat as nothing else did. I heard Tad in every love-loss sound.

Her walk was like dancing, hips swaying to some sound only she could hear. When the workroom was shut up for the day, but the night hadn't yet fallen, she strolled the village as though, in the space between two lights when everyone else settled into their homes, it belonged to her. I walked with her, sometimes. Following her, as I'd followed Haf.

'You've got to come back to the world,' she told me. 'The grass and the hills and the trees don't care what men do. You shouldn't either.'

'You think I should be like the grass?'

'Waving about in sunshine with no work to do? Yes, I do!' She laughed then, and her laughter was balm for my bruises.

One day, when the sun was warmer, though the shadows

still held their chill, we found dappled sun pools under the white blossom. The air smelled sweet and she sighed with the taste of it. We lay on our backs with the bare skin of our arms touching. As I glanced at her I could see the curves of her, chest, belly, thighs, like honeycakes herself.

'What do you dream of, when you sleep?' she asked.

'Dream?'

'Yes. When you thrash around giving blue bruises to your bedfellows, what do you dream of?'

'Nothing. I don't know.'

'Yes, you do.' She raised herself up on her elbow and peered at me. 'Tell me.'

Her eyes were full of life, dancing always, but they were kind too. I found I wanted to tell her everything.

So I did.

The fire at the farm, Tad, the camp and Gwrtheyrn. I told her about the tomb when I thought I would die in the company of dry bones. The terror of it. The words were difficult to find, in Saxon or British, to explain that the Mai who came out was not the same Mai who had gone in.

She was silent for two heartbeats. Then her hand cupped my face and she looked me in the life of my eye. 'And you think it was your sister who told them you planned to leave?'

'They said it was her. I don't think they had reason to lie.'

'I hate that they did that to you. But you're so brave,' she said. 'Braver than anyone. Grown men did that to you and you got out, all by yourself.'

I wiped my face. Tears had fallen somewhere along the tale. 'Why are you so kind to me?'

Viola smiled, as she did at most things. 'I'm nice to everyone,' she said. 'Why do you think I get so many honeycakes to share?'

'But why share with me, though? Why not Anwen, or Sara?' I tried again.

'Sara and Gwennan are old, and they don't like me. They think I delight in my own voice. And Elin and Anwen have each other.'

She dropped onto her back and we lay side by side watching clouds scud far beyond the blossomed branches above us.

'You've been happy here,' I said. She recognised what I was asking.

'I've made my life. Some days it's worse, some days it's better. But I won't always be Welsh, you know.'

'What do you mean?'

She stretched, enjoying the pull and push of her body. She sat up. 'I'll have my own hall on the hill, one day.' Viola picked one blade of grass and began peeling its sides away, fraying it into fine strands. 'I'll have my own servants and I'll sit on comfortable stools and embroider my own tunics. And all my little children will tumble and play in front of my own hearth.' She fanned herself with the flowing grass. 'I'll have sheep and oxen and fresh bread every day. And I won't even get out of bed unless I want to.'

I laughed then, at her dream. As if we could change who we are just by deciding. As if the world and the people in it didn't choose for us.

'I'm serious,' she said.

'How are you serious?'

She tossed her grass fan at me. 'I'll get it all, you'll see. And soon.'

'How?' I pressed her. I had sudden, frightened thoughts of her running into the woods. Dogs. The tree of traitors.

'I'm old enough to wed,' she said, her face dreaming again.

'Who would you wed?' She didn't answer. I thought of the hairiest, fattest man I knew. 'Is it Oak?' I teased.

Viola gosling-gasped with horror. She poked me, too hard, in the chest.

'Hey! That hurt,' I pushed her hand away. She prodded me again, and tickled, and I fought back, and dreams were forgotten as we giggled in the grass.

Viola wasn't the only one thinking of marriage, as spring burst out in earnest and waxy new leaves unfurled. One of my tasks was to take the fine wools and linen tunics of the Saxon women to the stream to air them and to scrub clean the plain underclothes they wore next to their skin. The outer fabrics were dyed and trimmed with woven patterns as complex as the patterns of butterflies. But the clothes under the finery were coarse and hard-stained and stinking after the winter. It was arm-and-elbow work to get them even part-way clean. Often I worked with one or two of the other women, but one day, as the blossom dropped in snow-tide flurries, I did the work alone. And that day, strange as it was, Rowan came to watch me.

I was at one of the big wooden tubs that grew up on the banks of the stream like mushrooms. It was more full than not of cold water and the rendered tallow that slithered the grime from the surface of the wool – eventually. The cold stream-water froze my fingers blue. But the scrape back and forth kept the rest of me warm.

'You'll wear yourself away,' Rowan said. She appeared between two birch saplings. They were fat with rising sap. She rested her hand on the taut trunk of the nearest tree. Her pale skin matched its silver eerily.

I kept my eyes on the washing. It seemed safest. I was being useful.

She came and sat on one of the wide rocks that marked the edge of the stream in full flood. She tucked her ankles under the hem of her tunic. What was she doing here? I listened carefully for the sound of footsteps behind her. Was she meeting someone away from the prying eyes of the village? I shook myself. That was the kind of half-sensed idea that fuelled tales for Viola. Rowan was just walking and had stumbled across me. That was all.

I worked the fabric twice as hard, sloshing water up the sides of the tub.

'I was born here, you know,' she said.

My scrubbing slowed. What was she talking about? She didn't seem in her right sense. I glanced at her, but her eyes were on the stream, not on me. She might have been talking to one of her water gods. Or the spirit of the trees, or clouds, or whatever power these Saxon pagans mistook Iesu for. I kept my mouth closed tight as harp strings.

'My mother was pregnant when she sailed west. The boats landed on the coast of this island and two months later, I landed here too. I've known nowhere else.'

She picked up loose stones and tossed them, one by one, into the pooling water of the shallows. *Ploop.* Ripples spread in urgent circles, reeds rustled with rodent scurries.

I wished she would go away. I had no want to hear her woes. I couldn't imagine she had any.

'The men walk the world whenever they want,' she said. 'Or they get sent, I suppose. They expect to see beyond the borders of the village. But I won't see anything of the world until I leave with my husband.'

Her husband? This tale was one Viola hadn't shared yet. The cloth I was scrubbing sank into the dark water and I had to fish for it with both hands. Would Rowan say more? I told myself I didn't care; these weeds were in her

247

garden. But I found I wanted to know, I wanted to have something to take back and share with Viola. I scrubbed harder, pounding fabric against the wooden block inside the tub.

'My father will see me married to someone who can help him with his ambitions. I'll bind the man and his people to my father. It will be someone who will bring strong, good men to fight and build. Or I'll leave with him to go to his village. Will it be like this, do you think? Or is this the only good place in the world?'

Good place? Not with the tree of traitors and the hunting dogs. I willed her to leave. To shut up and go.

'You've been beyond these woods, haven't you?'

I rested back on my heels. My back ached and the water had shrivelled my hands.

'What's it like, out there?' she asked.

I looked at her then. Curled up on the rock as if she was some water sprite hauled from the wet. Her clothes clean by my hands. Her belly full by my hands. Asking me for more. I thought of Tad and our neat farm, the fields ploughed at the right times, and sown carefully. I thought of Haf running across the swept yard, her hair free in the sunlight. No. This was not the only good place.

I said nothing.

'Tell me,' she said. Her fingers plucked at the folds of her skirt. 'Please,' she added.

I thought of the camp, and the aching hunger, and

the cracked tombs of long-dead Romans robbed by desperate men.

'It's not safe,' I said finally. I turned back to the tub and hauled the wet wool out, like landing heavy fish. I carried it, sopping, to the edge of the stream and let it twist and billow in the clear water. I held it fast so it wasn't whipped away. It moved, female and full, under the surface. Drowning or dancing. When it was rinsed, I pulled it out and wrung it tight.

Rowan hadn't moved, or spoken. She'd watched me, huntress keen.

I dropped the dark cloth into my basket. There were three more underskirts to wash.

'You lived, though? You flourished out there?' she asked, needling me.

'I lived. My tad didn't. And my sister was lost.'

'That's bad,' she said.

She believed Haf dead. I let her. I didn't want to share any more with Rowan than I had to. The air we breathed, the soil we walked on. That was all we had in common. I was just her Welsh. I plunged another skirt into the tub, watching the blue turn black as it soaked up the water. Rowan rose. Taking her leave, I hoped.

She walked into the woods as quietly as she'd come. Had she really asked me for my thoughts? I spat deliberately into the tub and carried on scrubbing.

38

I HAD SPREAD the damp underclothes to dry on the branches around the stream when Viola found me. She should have been working, but she was skilled at living on her tail, not by her fingernails.

'How long till this one is aired?' she asked. Her hands rested on one of the lesser tunics that Rowan owned. It was pale green and hemmed with red wool. Not the finest work, but better than our own dun dresses. It fluttered in buttercup sunshine, the light and heat would go some way to killing the smell.

'Not for hours, I only hung it this morning.'

'Good. Sit with me while I wait. Then I need to borrow it for the evening. I'll put it back without Rowan seeing.' Viola settled down on one of the mossy stumps beside the stream.

She wanted to take one of the fine tunics? And wear it herself? Why? What could she want it for? The thought of it made my heart beat faster.

'You can't take it. If they catch you . . .'

'It will be the tree of traitors for me,' she laughed as she said it.

'How can you joke about it?'

'It's no joke. I know that. Have you heard Sara talk? She's seen them use it. When she was young. She says the screams of the slave were so loud that the Welsh barn trembled.'

I pointed to the tunic that swung lazy in the breeze. 'Why risk it for that?'

'Because it's the worst punishment the Saxons can think of, it's for great crimes. And borrowing one tunic, for one afternoon, and putting it back afterwards is no great crime, is it?'

'What would they do instead?'

'That's for me to worry over. Sit!' she said. 'What have you been about?' she asked once I'd dropped onto the springy green beside her.

I told her about the visit Rowan had made. In the telling, and watching Viola be stunned, the misery of it became funny. Viola could do that. She leaned in to listen, her eyes wide, her mouth set open, laughing away sorrow. She took troubles and turned them into gifts.

'She asked you to pity her?' Viola clasped her own palms in excitement. 'With her soft hands and hair she's never combed herself? Oh, Iesu, that's perfect. And did you dry her eyes for her and tell her it would be all right?'

I smiled, despite myself. 'No. Not exactly.'

'Good girl! That woman needs to be dunked in the real world quick as wicks.' Viola leaned in close and whispered, 'Imagine her washing her own monthlies from her skirts!'

I blushed, and laughed, and blushed again.

The strands of her hair were close to my eyes. Her shoulders felt warm against my arms. Like Haf had been once. Tad. Haf. Home. I shivered despite the sun.

'What is it?' Viola asked.

'Nothing,' I said. 'Where did you come from, Viola? Before you were here?' Curiosity didn't come naturally to me any more. I watched from the edges, afraid of the answers my questions might bring. But I wanted to know how she had stayed so cheerful. Was there some secret to it?

She wrapped her arm around me in heavy comfort. 'Why do you want to know, Mai love?'

I shrugged. I hoped she would feel what was in my heart.

'I was Roman and Briton, like you,' she said. 'I lived in Aquae Sulis. You know it? We call it Caerfaddon too, after the Roman baths there?'

The old Roman city at the end of the road. 'It has red roofs, and white walls,' I said softly, remembering Tad and his stories of it.

'Once. In some places,' she said. Her fingertips trailed across my forehead, pushing back loose strands. Somewhere close, I heard wood-doves cooing. 'It was beautiful once, people say. The big houses had tended gardens. Now they're overgrown. Most are empty. When one falls, its stones are used to patch up another. It's as though the city is eating itself. But the springs are still there. They run hot! Some people say the water's warmed by the white flame of the Holy Ghost. I don't know. It doesn't smell very holy, I wouldn't wash my dog in it.'

'Did you have to leave?' I asked. I wasn't sure how to ask what I really meant – were you taken? Stolen from your people?

She breathed, her mouth open and I felt the warm air on my cheek. 'I had to leave, you could say. My tad wanted me to marry one of the old men of the city. He was powerful, as rich as anyone could be in that tumbledown place. But he wasn't kind. He beat his servants. He would beat his wife too, I knew. So I ran. And I didn't run far before I found the travellers that brought me here. I had nowhere else to go. So I stayed and made the best of it.'

She'd been prized by her family. Wanted. And yet she'd chosen to be here? Why would anyone choose to be captive? I pulled away, but her arm held me tight.

'You don't know what it is to be with someone who can't see you,' she said.

I had no idea what she meant. How could anyone not be seen?

'People see what they want to see, what they expect.

So, my father looked at me and saw Viola, his dutiful daughter. The old man looked at me and saw Viola, his pliant wife. Neither of them knew the real Viola. Now I might be Welsh Viola, but as long as I work, I'm left alone.'

'Is Welsh what you want to be?'

She moved away from me. I breathed in the scent of flour and summer fruit that seemed to be always on her.

'It is,' she whispered. 'It is for now. It's not bad here. I've got you.'

'Me?' The word dropped, stupid, between us.

She laced her fingers through mine, her palms rough, but warm and solid. 'Yes, you. Of course you.'

'But I'm . . .' I wanted to say *useless, frightened, lost.*

'You're my sister,' she said. 'Like my sister, anyway. I never had one. The other girls, in the barn, they think I'm low. Lazy and low.'

'They don't.' I knew they did.

'Liar,' she smiled at me. 'I don't mind. They don't know how to live when everything is trying to throttle the life right out of you. You do.'

Did I? I wished I could see what Viola saw.

'I'd like to be your sister,' I said.

'Good. Then we'll swear to it.'

She let go of my hand and reached for thin reed stems, seedheads bobbing at their top like elfen trees. She took two and twisted them quickly. She'd made two dark green bands.

Her hand took my wrist. She eased the green band over my fingers, careful not to tear it.

'You're hand-bound to me now,' she said.

I looked at the thin, twisted reed on my skin.

Viola was asking to be my new sister. If I wanted one.

It was hard to breathe, suddenly. I wanted one. I wanted one so badly, I thought the heat of it might burn the reed stem. But I had one sister already, somewhere. One that had betrayed me, abandoned me. One sister who saw no use for me and threw me aside like heel-worn shoes when something better came along.

Would Viola do that too?

My fingers clenched. The band threatened to snap against the muscles of my wrist.

Viola rested her cool fingertips on my fist. Her laughing eyes had turned serious. 'I can be your sister. I can, if you want it.'

She held out her own wrist, pulled back the cuff of her tunic.

I slipped the second band over her fingers with no twice-thoughts.

'For life!' she said, smiling again. 'For this life, and the next and the one after that.'

'Do you mean after we die?'

'No! I mean our lives won't always be this. We won't

255

always be Welsh, there's more coming to us. I can feel it. Don't worry, I'll take you with me when I go.'

'Where will you go?'

Her fingers rested on her reed band. She was weighing her answer. 'The man who found me on the road. He saved me. He saved me then, and he'll save me again.'

I felt my skin prickle. 'He didn't save you. He brought you here to work.'

'I might have died on the road. Wolves. Bears. Men. I might have been killed. But instead I came here. Where there's food, and warm beds and people like you to be my family. He says we must be secret for now, but one day, he says, when the time is right, I'll have my own home with him.'

I felt as though she had pushed me plunging into the stream. 'Who is he? Where is he?' I hadn't seen her give her smiles to any one person in particular – she scattered them like spring rain.

'He comes and goes. He likes the road.'

Who could like the danger out there? In my mind, I saw our farm burning.

Viola felt my body stiffen. Her fingers brushed my face again, soft as catkins, despite all the work they did. Not that Viola did half the work of the rest of us.

'Don't worry,' she said, pulling me back into the swaddle of her arms. 'I'll take you with me. I won't leave behind my Mai. My sister.' She leaned in as close as my own skin, and whispered in my ear. 'He's on his way here now. I heard it from Oak. He'll be here before sunset.'

I let her take the green tunic. But I said no more than five words to her when she went. The thought of the witch-dream she was imagining for herself with her Saxon man shut my mouth tight. She barely noticed my misery.

At the end of the long afternoon, I folded the dry clothes and walked back along the path alone, up the hill to the hall where Rowan lived. This was the kind of hall that Viola wanted. The door made thick from solid wood, with iron hinges and its own latch. Two fires, kept stoked, warmed either end of the room. Skins and woven fabrics decorated the floors and walls. Carved hunting scenes loomed from the timber beams above. The air smelled of woodsmoke and drying rosemary. I thought of the ruined city Viola had left, of the British camp I'd tried to call home, where people were kept straight through fear and hunger. I thought of the woman in the wood with her dead baby.

Yet here, Rowan had plenty and pickings to spare. Viola just wanted the same. Could I really be angry with her for that?

The hall was empty of people, which was strange for this time of day. I moved to the dark wood cist beside the bed. Balancing the clothes in one hand, I opened the lid to the scent of rosemary. Sprigs of herbs were folded between the layers of wool and linen fabric. I smoothed the tunics that were already in the cist. My fingertips ran over something bumpy. I pulled back the cloth to see metal glinting. Jewellery. Rowan kept her jewellery in the cist too. I glanced about. No one was watching. I could take out the heavy gold bangle, or the silver pin and try them on.

But, twin terrors stopped me: the tree of traitors and the memory of the Roman tomb that still haunted my sleeping.

I wouldn't touch one single thing that I wasn't meant to. I wasn't Viola.

I dropped the clothes I carried into the cist in igam-ogam order and left the hall as quickly as I could.

The sun headed towards the treetops as I stepped back into the village. It should have been quiet outside as tasks came to their end and meals were cooked in homes. But there was crowd-sound. People laughing and cheering.

I couldn't help myself, I hurried down to see who was causing the noise – I wanted to see the man who mattered to Viola.

The scene reminded me of my own arrival back in the grip of winter. Women, men, children, flanking the path. Noise. The babble of Saxon. But this time, I knew enough to understand the cross-flung greetings.

'Nyle, you old fool, you're back!'

'We never thought to see you so hale, Ware!'

I stood on the edge of the crowd. Bodies blocked my view. Backs and broad shoulders brought shadows between us, but the names I heard pinned me still. Nyle. Ware.

I knew those names. Spoken by Algar as he lazed beside our hearth. The mud men who had rolled into my farm.

It couldn't be.

But Horse had been calling Saxons to him for months. I knew that. This village was important. These coblyn-look creatures would come slithering here sometime. I should have expected it. My skin felt on fire with hatred.

Were there only two, or was the third here with them?

Algar.

I pushed forward into the stink of people, elbows like oars, shoving at arms and waists and the heads of the younger ones.

I was through.

Two men stood grinning like fools. It was them, Nyle and Ware. But there was no third. Was he dead on the road? It was too good to even dream. He wasn't with them, but he would be here somewhere, like foul floodwater spilling from gutter to grate.

He was here. I knew it.

My stomach shifted, sick with misery. Where was Viola? I scanned the crowd. I could see almost every smiling face. Ruddy, nut brown, pale. But none belonged to her. The green dress with red hemming was nowhere in the press of bodies.

Demon thoughts flared in my mind. Why had she wanted that green tunic?

No. It couldn't be.

I pushed out of the pack and headed for the darkening halls. Would she be at the Welsh barn? Perhaps she was just working.

Ha. Viola working past the end of the day? No.

She wouldn't be working now. She should be here, watching the arrivals, full of smiles at the excitement of it. Here was her proper place.

I pushed the answer away. I didn't want to know it.

But it pressed back: where was Algar; where was Viola?

If I was right, then there would be too many eyes watching here. I had to get to the guts of this, no matter what I found. Where was quiet? Sheltered? Hidden?

The workroom. It would be swept and shut up for the evening.

I broke into running. My breath caught in my chest as though some giant had wrapped his hands around me.

The hut looked to be in darkness as I approached. No movement, no light. I sighed. I'd been wrong. Should I go back?

Then, I heard Viola laugh. Bewitched and beguiled. I strained to hear the reply. The words were muddled, but the tone was low-voiced and soothing. I was hearing two lovers.

I crept to the workroom wall. The planks were laid carelessly, some touching, others jammed with loose wool or dried heather to plug the holes. I pulled some wool free and peered inside.

There was just enough daylight left to see as the couple moved into view. The woman in green, her tunic trimmed in red. The man, taller, dark and road-rough. The last time I'd seen him had been with the taste of smoke on the wind and fear in every inch of my heart. Algar. The Saxon who had burned our farm. He was here, in this room, with Viola in his arms. His hands on her back. Those hands that had struck at Haf. She held his neck between her forearms, her fingers entwined behind his head. She was content to be there, resting her weight against him like mistletoe around oak.

Fire raced rancid in my limbs.

My heartbeat battered with whips.

My skin scourged red in the winds.

He was here. He had lived, when Tad had died. He was smiling.

I wanted to yell out, to tell her to step away. I wanted to grab the nearest log and run at his head with it. To beat him with it until his breath was still and his eyes glassy. I wanted to hear his bones break.

But I crouched, mouse-meek. All the bile that swilled inside me only burned myself. I had once wanted to fight him, to run him through with my sword. I had hoped

Gwrtheyrn would train me to do it. The memory came dirt-dark.

In the workroom, Algar swept Viola in circles as though dancing to music only they could hear. Then he leaned down and kissed her. When they finally parted, Viola kept her eyes on his. It was clear that she breathed with him. Her face shone with it. Her honey limbs melted into his. His road-dirty hands were firm on the small of her back.

I felt black.

Tad.

Haf.

Home.

Viola.

He'd taken them all from me.

39

ROWAN STANDS ON the path that leads out of the village. She watches me.

And I watch her back. I choose to look her full in the face.

Her skin is tallow-yellow, with sweat shinning on her forehead. She looks as ill as broken-tailed dogs. Her tunic, one of her finest, of course, is mud-streaked and torn. The fine weaving at the hem is loose. I had taken hen-steps towards liking her. That seems very long ago now.

'Mai,' she says, her voice cracked.

'Did you know?' I ask. I hadn't meant to ask, to speak to her even, but the words tear themselves free, salmon-leap from my mouth.

'Know?'

'Did you know what your father had planned?'

'No!' she shouts. Then her eyes dart swift, to the path, to the halls about us, to every shadowy space where someone might be listening. The village is quiet but for birds, and the bark of dogs. None of the usual sounds of morning. No one comes.

263

'No,' she says, more quietly. 'I would have stopped it.'

'Would you?'

'If I could have.'

We are both silent. I notice her arms are gooseflesh, her hands shake. I look at my mistress and see the frightened girl under the finery. I feel for her, though she is Saxon. She has seen horrors tonight too. I step closer, I take her wrist and press the hard pads of my fingers against her skin.

'If I'd known, I would have tried,' she says again, almost to herself.

'The men aren't back,' I say. 'You could go. If you wanted you could go right now.'

'Go where?'

'I don't know. Is there anywhere safe for us?'

I realise that I said 'us', not 'you' and wish I could snap the words back into my mouth. We hold our eyes locked, for one moment. Willing each other to say more, but not daring to speak. Not trusting each other.

She takes her arm back. Then risks speaking. 'You know how to slip through the world without being noticed,' she says. 'Your clothes are the brown of the earth, your hair and eyes too, you shade into the trees.'

'Like mice,' I whisper.

'Yes. Yes, exactly. You blend into the background where others would stand out. There's freedom in that, you know.'

Is there?

It has felt more like running and hiding than freedom.

I got out of the tomb, but for months its walls have still been all about me, keeping me small and silent and watchful. I've been trapped by more than just the will of the Saxons, alive but not living.

'I don't want to be that mouse any more,' I tell Rowan, 'I wanted to be Buddug once.'

'Buddug?'

'The Romans called her Boudicca.'

'Was she one of their gods?'

'She was one of mine.' I glance at the sky and hope Iesu didn't hear me say that.

'Well, we're in strange days indeed if mice become gods.' She wraps her arms around her waist, holding herself tight.

Are we in those days?

The thought makes me fearful, but there is hope in it too.

'They wouldn't look for you,' Rowan says suddenly. 'If you went, they wouldn't look for you. They won't notice you've gone, if I don't tell them.'

I feel the heat rosing my face. 'Where would I go?' I repeat her question back to her. Where is there for either of us in this world built by men?

'Some Welsh cross the sea to the south,' she says.

'The Welsh . . . the Britons . . . are settling there in such numbers, it's being called Brittany.'

Across the sea? In my mind, I see boats whipped on waves in shades of blue-green. Wood warped and wet with salt stains. Sails wind-full. Is this the way out?

Perhaps it is possible. 'Why are you telling me?' I ask.

Rowan just looks tired. She presses the tips of her fingers to her eyes. 'It might not be true,' she says. 'It might be nothing but stories. But we all need stories sometimes.'

We both lift our heads as horns sound in the woods. Dogs bark in answer.

'They're hunting,' she says. 'If you go, keep away from the paths, the open spaces.' She moves suddenly, reaching her arm across herself. She pulls hard at one of the brooches that pin her tunic at the shoulders. It tears free; wool snags and curls. She holds it out to me. I notice the dirt crusted under her fingernails.

The jewellery in her hand is slight, made of gold strands wound, coiled and plaited, with red garnet pooling like blood between the coils.

'My mother gave me this,' she says. 'My grandmother gave it to her. Take it. You can cut up the gold. It's soft. It will buy you some favours.'

'You could come with us?' I ask. My sister will never forgive me if Rowan says yes. But I can't help but ask. She is as trapped as we are; the fine tunic she wears is the net she is tangled in. 'I can teach you British. We can find poorer clothes.'

She laughs without joy. 'I'm not brave enough. You might be stepping from the griddle to the flames. You might reach the harbour and find safe sailing, but you might run straight into the hands of Saxon traders and be sold on tomorrow. I'll stay with my father.'

'After what he did?'

'He's my kin.'

'You can choose your own kin.' I can too, I realise.

She laughs again, hard and bitter as crab apples. 'You should run while their eyes are busy elsewhere.'

She is right. It is time to go. I don't say goodbye, but I hold her in the life of her eye, looking at her for longer than I have ever dared before. She looks back, seeing me clearly.

Then I leave her for the final time.

I cradle the brooch Rowan has given me in the palm of my hand as I walk back to the barn where the baby sleeps. The family I am choosing.

It seems to me now that we can't choose who we love. But we can choose what we want to do with that love. I will choose to do my best for the boy, whoever his father and mother. This gift will help me do that. I will be Buddug for him. The days of the mouse are done.

Then, I think that if anyone sees me with the brooch, they will think it stolen.

I slip it up my sleeve and break into running.

40

I WAITED IN the Welsh barn, curled up on the sleeping sacks. People came and went, hurrying about their tasks now that the village was slipping into evening celebration at the arrival of Ware and Nyle, and the third one. But I didn't move. Breathing hurt. I kept seeing Viola with her arms on the shoulders of that dunman – my new sister, as false as the old.

In the trees around the barn owls cried *goodie-hoo*. Mice ran for cover the world entire. The reed band Viola had given me had dried and shrivelled on my wrist. I pulled it off, snapping it. It dropped to the floor, lost in the cut reeds.

It was with early light that Viola slipped in to sleep beside me. Her hair smelled of brewed beer and sweat. I thought to close my eyes and fake slumber, but anger burned in me.

'Viola,' I whispered, 'I saw you tonight. I saw you with him.'

She rolled to face me. Her eyes sparkled with captured starlight. 'Did you? Where?'

'Does it matter? I saw you kiss him.'

She giggled. 'You were watching me?'

'I know him. I know what he is.'

Her brow creased. 'What?'

'It was him. He came to my home, my old home, before the camp.' I saw the flames of that night again. Haf thrown to the farmyard floor. Tad ashen pale. 'I told you Saxons ruined it. It was him, your Saxon.' My words stabbed at the air.

Her fingers pressed against her lips. Her eyes were so wide I could see their whites pearl-shining in the darkness. 'He hurt you?' she whispered.

I nodded. He hurt me more than words in any language could say. 'He's filled with badness,' I said. 'He's rotten like maggoty apples.'

She shook her head. 'I can't believe it.'

'I don't lie!' My voice was too loud. Anwen, or Gwennan maybe, moaned at me to be still.

'I didn't mean to say you did,' Viola said. 'But perhaps it isn't the same man. Perhaps he just looks like the man you know. Cousins, maybe?'

She was trying to lie to herself. I grabbed her wrist in anger. 'I know his name. Algar! It is the same man. You have to stop this. You have to get away from him.'

'I can't,' she gasped.

'You have to. He'll hurt you. It's his nature.'

'You don't know him, you can't.'

'I know enough.'

I dropped her wrist. Her arms wrapped about herself, cradling herself carefully.

I pushed down my anger. Viola needed me to help her, not judge her. 'Viola, it's all right. You have me, and your friends here. You've been happy while he was out on the road, and you'll be happy again. But you won't be happy with him, I know it.'

'I can't send him away. What will people think of me?'

'They'll think you have wisdom.'

She shook her head, then whispered. 'I've my baby to think of.'

'Baby? What baby?'

'His baby.' Her hands folded across the round of her stomach. Sara had hinted at it more than once, but I had thought that snide sniping. Viola was plump and like soft pillows, but I'd thought that was from the extra food she charmed from the Saxons.

But there was his baby curled inside her.

'How long have you known?' I ask.

'Four moons, maybe.'

'And you didn't tell me?'

How could she keep this from me? She was my friend, my sister.

'I didn't want anyone to know. Not until I was married. Even when that happens, people will know and laugh on my head over it. People are cruel, Mai.'

I knew that. The baby would have one of the cruellest as his father. I felt sick. I turned my back to her. She reached out for me, but I flinched from her touch as though it burned.

I heard her sob into the sweat-soaked sack.

We didn't speak again that night.

41

SUMMER SOLSTICE, AD455,
EARLY MORNING.

Run.

My feet stumble. I right myself in the moment.

I must get back to my sister and her baby boy with the brooch Rowan has given to us. It can deliver us from here. We can choose new lives, if we want.

My honey-sweet girl hen sits
In our nest.
Am I cruel to crave leaving?

The sun is rising fast now, the bright disk clearing the lower branches of the farthest trees. If we are to go, it must be now, before the villagers crawl back. I tear towards the Welsh barn hoping that my sister and her baby are well enough to walk.

I throw back the leather door and fall inside. It feels like safety. But I know it isn't. Elin gasps, then moans as she sees it's just me. I ignore her and the huddle of sleeping souls that have found their way back.

Sara is rabbit-curled on the floor beside the fire. I go to walk past, but her eyes open. 'Where have you been?' she chides. 'You were told to rest.'

'I needed air,' I say. 'How is my sister? Has she woken?'

'She sleeps, thanks to Iesu.' Sara pushes herself to sitting. She winces as the bones of her spine click and crunch. It's clear that the night has aged her. Years have fallen onto her bones in hours. She prods the embers and teases out one or two weak flames. 'We need something warm in our bellies and three days of sleep,' she sighs. 'We can have the first easily enough. Fetch water.'

I push my treasure further into my sleeve and do as I'm told.

Soon the fresh bite of mint drifts from the clay pot beside the embers. I breathe it in and feel the knot of tension in my shoulders give and drop. It would be nice to sit with Sara, sip mint-brew, wait for the day to come and let the horrors wash past us both, huddled around the hearth.

But I can't.

'I don't have time to waste,' I tell her.

She raises her eyebrow and hen-clucks at me.

'I mean it. I want to get away. And I want to take Viola and the baby with me.' I pause, looking at her bare feet. 'You can come too, if you'd like.'

'And go where?' she says, scornful.

'I don't know. Across the water, maybe. South.'

Sara cackles gently. She pours the brew for both of us and I sip, grateful for the heat. 'I can't go south. Nor north, or west or east either. I'm too old, girl. It's too late for me. I'll stay here and live with whatever it is that comes next.'

The mint is bright and clean on my tongue. It runs down the red road of my throat bringing warmth and hope to my body. I am young, I realise, looking at the worried wrinkles on the face beside mine.

'I'll be leaving with her today,' I say. 'This morning. This moment.'

'Are you sure?' Sara catches my eye. There's pain in her look, and love too. She wants us to be safe.

'I'm sure.' It isn't me who replies. It's my sister, Viola. She's standing behind us. She has pushed aside the sack curtain that has shielded her all night. The baby is in her arms. She looks weak and pale. Only her will is keeping her upright.

My heart breaks. It's too late. She's too weak and I've left leaving too late.

We'll be caught on the trail within hours.

Viola sees all this and more on my face. And she smiles.

'What?' I ask. 'What is there to be happy about?'

'Him to start with,' she says. 'Look at him. Look. Paradise has sent him to me.' She drops eager kisses on his head. I see something of the honey girl in her face.

She walks towards us, slow-stepped but certain, and settles beside me. 'Hold him,' she says.

She places the boy on my lap and takes the cup from my hands. He's so light and small. His skin is blotchy, but clean. His tiny eyes seem glued shut with sleep, but his mouth moves as if he's singing to himself. I let his fairy fingers grip around my thumb. He holds tight.

'He's strong,' Viola says softly. 'And so are we.'

Sara snorts.

'I am!' Viola insists. She finishes the brew and pours herself more. 'I want to go. Mai is right.'

'You can barely walk,' Sara says.

'We don't need to walk to leave. Oak has his coracle. He uses it to fish. We can take it, he won't mind. The stream floats south, doesn't it? Towards the sea?'

She's right. Of course, she's right.

I feel excitement pulse through me again. 'Rowan has given me her gold and garnet brooch,' I say. 'If we go by stream, and travel light, we won't be caught. The dogs won't be able to follow. We can buy safe passage at the coast.'

'We'll go?' Viola asks. 'Together?'

'Sure certain,' I tell her.

She flushes then, pink with pleasure.

She's going to come with me. We're leaving.

42

AFTER VIOLA TOLD me about the baby she was going
to have, I barely slept. I could feel that she didn't either,
but we didn't comfort each other as we might have done
before. There was no comfort. She had tied herself to the
man who had taken my home.

With the arc of the day, I rose, and dressed and ate
without speaking to her. I headed to the workroom
without looking back to see how she fared.

She didn't join us.

I sat beside Sara and worked my bones short that
morning. I didn't pause, didn't stop. I pulled the quern-
stone back and forth as though breathing depended on it.

'What's the matter, child?' Sara asked. 'You'll wear the
stone away.'

Her kindness was unlooked for, unwanted. I had lived
through fire and death and betrayal. I could live without
one more thing. I could lose Viola too. It was nothing
compared to what I'd seen.

Nothing.

I felt tears burn my eyes.

'Mai?' Sara rubbed my back. Firm strokes up and down my spine.

My tears splashed onto the flour, ruining it.

'*Cariad bach*,' she whispered soft as catkins. She hoisted me up and steered me out of the open wall. We stepped onto the grass. She walked me, as children walk straw dolls, until we reached one of the thick tree trunks that lay on their side waiting for the blade. 'Sit,' she said.

I sat, pup-obedient.

She settled down and wrapped her arms around me. I rested against her shoulder and wept. For Viola, for Haf, for Tad, for myself. She rocked me, sea-shifting side to side. She let me weep without words until there was nothing left to fall.

'There, there,' she said, finally. 'The world has fallen on you with heavy hands, has it?'

I nodded.

'What worries you?'

I couldn't tell her. It wasn't my tale to tell. But Sara kept her eyes open and her mouth shut, for the most part, and she had noticed the coldness between us that morning. 'Viola been breeding thrashings, has she? Making trouble for you?'

I said nothing.

'She's wilful-wild,' Sara said. 'There's no pretending she isn't. But she'll always choose kindness where she can. If you can forgive her, you should. We need friends like we need family.'

Forgive her?

The idea made my skin shrink. She'd called herself my sister. But then she'd chosen to love Algar. Her head was mopped with him.

'What has she done that's so cruel? Hmm? Why did she bare her teeth?' Sara asked.

'She's not who I thought she was,' I said.

'She's thoughtless as beans and full of gossip, but her heart is good.'   .

'Her heart is foolish.'

'All hearts are foolish. We don't choose what's in them or when they fill,' Sara said sternly.

Viola had met Algar many moons before she met me.

The thought leaped to my mind unbidden.

I tried to squish it like bedbugs. But it swelled and grew. She had loved him first. He'd been the sun in her sky. She hadn't even known I lived back when the baby was made.

'She won't have meant it.' Sara kept her hand heavy on my back. 'Whatever it was.'

What had Viola said? That Algar had been her rescue when she had need? He'd found her on the road and given her shelter. She was wrong, but it was what she thought. Viola was only half-sensed when it came to him.

She loved him and was going to have his baby. She was foolish. But she wasn't cruel.

I could never be happy for her. Never. But could I really hate her?

Sara ran her thumbs across my cheeks, wiping away the tear tracks. 'That's better,' she said. 'Now. Come. The wheat won't grind itself.'

I didn't see Viola as the sun crossed the blue. She didn't come to the workroom and I stayed away from the Welsh barn. I didn't want to see her. But I did want to see him.

My mind itched, wondering where he was in the village. Did he have his own hall? Who would he stay with? I didn't know the Saxon families well. I kept apart. It was easy to do. The Welsh worked in the orchards and hide-acre and fields, at grinding or washing, not in the halls of the Saxons. We liked our own company. I didn't know the people, and I hadn't wanted to. Until now.

Where was Algar?

I asked, quietly, as the day drew to its close. Sara tutted. 'Not another one of you making goat-eyes at him?'

'No!' I said sharply. 'It isn't that. I just want to know.'

She looked at me, her eyes drawn suspicious, but she answered anyway. 'He comes and goes. Mostly goes. He has one brother here. They don't get on. The brother has his hall near the big blackthorn tree.'

I went there to watch. I couldn't help it. I found the thickest slice of darkness to hide in, in the shade of the blackthorn. I didn't want him to see me. Autumn had become spring, and inside I was not the girl he had met at our farm – but outside I didn't look so very different.

The hall was not the grandest, nor the poorest in the village. The planked walls were mellow and faded, it had stood for ten or fifteen winters, maybe. There were windows, their shutters still open and smoke rose through the hole in the roof. In the firelight, I could see inside.

He was there.

Sitting alongside someone who was enough alike to be his brother, while the woman of the house served their meal. The men weren't smiling. There was no warmth in that home, despite the fire.

I was glad. I was glad that his family held no comfort. He had burned my home to the ground as though it were the stubble of autumn wheat. He had caused the hurt to Tad and Haf. I hated him. I watched until the air grew cold and stars appeared above me. I only left once they had closed the shutters and Algar was gone from view.

Viola didn't come back to the Welsh barn that night, nor for two nights after that. I didn't see much of her in the daytimes either. She worked hardly at all. Sara warned about people who sowed thorns then walked barefoot. I just worked, and tried not to think about where she was.

When I did see her, I watched her from the corner of my eye. How had I missed the swell of her belly before? It was slight, but clear to those who looked, the folds of her tunic couldn't hide it. I wondered when it would come. Did she know herself? No doubt she was hoping for her own hall, with Algar, before it did.

43

WE BARELY SPOKE to each for seven or eight days. I was trying to forgive. I was. But the words were trapped in my chest as though they had been put inside their own tomb.

I worked hard. My anger turned grain to flour, took dirt from cloth, swept the workroom floor clean as lamplight.

In the evenings, I walked the paths of the village, or along the stream bank, pacing out the small edges of my world.

Oak saw me at the stream one evening. The sound of the water was soothing. His hands worked, smoothing what I thought must be another oar for his coracle.

'Mai, is it?' he said. His voice was gruff, but kind enough. He was nothing like Tad to look at – Oak was big, thick-necked and thick-armed, where Tad had been tall and thin – but there was something about the kindness in his voice that made me think of Tad.

So, I answered him. 'It is.'

'Nice night.'

It was. I had hardly noticed, but the air was warmer than it had been for many months. It felt soft against my face.

'Spring,' I said.

'Be summer soon.'

I didn't reply. I hardly knew him. He kept working at the wood, moving with the grain, rubbing sand in tight circles. It showered to the ground and was lost in the gloaming.

'Longer days coming,' Oak said.

'It just means more hours to work,' I replied.

'There's pleasure in work, in making. This oar is here because I wanted it to be and I made it so. You see?' He held it up. It was pale as moonlight.

'I make flour,' I said. 'It doesn't last.'

'Where would we be without bread?'

'Hungry.'

He chuckled. The oar and his stomach both fought for space on his lap. 'We all do the best with what we're given. Life isn't smooth, but you can choose not to make it rougher.' He dropped another handful of sand onto the oar.

I wondered if he had heard about my fight with Viola. It was likely he had. All gossip was quickly in the mouth of the world here. It didn't make him wrong though. Like Tad, he wanted me to see the world in the best of its light.

I trudged back to the barn. I missed Viola. I wanted to be her sister again.

My chance came the next day. Rowan had found more underclothes from somewhere for me to wash. I took them to the stream and fought the folds of fabric, struggling to hold them under, and got as wet as water rats, when Viola came upon me.

I could see straight away that something had gone ill with her. Her eyes were puffed as mushrooms, her nose red. All thought of our fight was gone in one breath. I stood and hurried to her. 'Viola, what is it? What's wrong?'

She looked heart-gone at me. 'He's left,' she whispered.

'What? Who?'

'Algar. He's gone. I told him about the baby. He was angry.'

'Where has he gone?' My hand reached for hers, unthinking.

'I don't know.'

'Is he coming back?'

'I don't know.'

She burst into fresh tears. I held her tight. I felt her shiver in my arms like willow in the wind. The sound of the stream and the leaves and the birds and small creatures and all the insects gnawing away in their holes swam around us. I was holding her up. The land was holding me up. Here we both were, on the edge of everything –

not British any more, not Saxon ever, whatever dreams Viola had. We would never be able to choose for ourselves.

The stream sounded like river torrents. It was my own heartbeat in my ears, I realised.

'He doesn't want bawling brats about. That's what he said.'

I held her, as Sara had held me days before. I soothed and shushed. But I didn't talk of forgiveness.

There was no forgiveness.

Only burning, flame-hot anger.

44

THE FURY DIDN'T leave me, not that day, or the next, or the next. Algar had left Viola the moment she needed him. He wasn't her saviour. He was another sickness we had to suffer. He, and men like him, took and took and took with no thought for what remained. I wished I could be the warrior I'd wanted to be, Buddug in her chariot.

I worked at the quern-stone. I spoke and smiled with the women. But inside, I imagined him falling into water and sinking, struggling all the way to the bottom; or catching some plague and weakening away with warts and boils on his face. The idle thought gave me comfort.

Viola didn't seem angry, once the tears dried. To speak plain truth, she seemed happier than ever. As though the baby wasn't growing inside her every day, clear for all to see. Laughter, and treats given to her by boys with red faces and tangled tongues, were enough to make her smile again. Though I tried to talk to her about what was to come, she turned her face away and talked of other things. It was as though there was no baby.

Soon bluebells were making patches of sky in the wood

and the bean plants twisted and twined in the hide-acre. Gwennan asked Viola what she would name her baby, and Anwen offered to cut down old tunics to make swaddling. Viola just smiled: if anything, more butterfly-light than before.

And I kept my anger close. I thought, narrow-eyed, that if he dared to return, I would burn the hut he slept in. Or I'd mix ground foxglove in with his flour.

When the press of anger got too strong, I walked. Not beyond the bounds of the village. I believed what Sara had told me about the cruelty of the Saxons if I tried to run. And, anyway, I couldn't leave Viola while she needed me. But my feet paced and paced, wearing new rabbit paths across the village.

More often than not, my steps would take me towards Oak, the Briton who had found his place in the world of the Saxons. He didn't mind me. He liked to explain things to anyone who would listen; the weight any beam would bear, the best way to mix clay and straw for the finest finish when it dried, the right time of year to cut and store timber. He enjoyed talking, and didn't care whether it was the bravest warrior or the lowliest Welsh girl who listened. He had the same gentle tale-telling heart as Tad.

It soothed me to listen.

'Rub the sand across the grain,' he said, one early evening. We were sitting outside his workroom, where fresh planks were carefully stacked, smelling of pine needles and resin. I took one handful of sand and tried again, moving it sideways across the surface.

'That's it,' he said. 'It will take the skin off your fingers too, mind you,' he laughed.

I held up my palms, yellow with calluses. 'The quernstone has given me leather skin already.'

'Aye, we've all hands older than our faces, that's true enough.'

'Where will you use these boards?' I asked. 'When they're done?'

'Horse has big ideas. Ten new halls by winter. We're digging out the floors now, making good dry pits to lay these boards over. The walls will go up soon enough. Horse is welcoming new arrivals from over the sea.'

'More Saxons?'

Oak nodded. 'He sent messengers east. It's not just Saxons either. Angles. Jutes. Even Britons from the north who see strength and are drawn to it. Rowan might marry soon and Horse will want strong allies. He wants to clear the land hereabout and repair the road to the eastern harbours. The track will become Roman-sturdy.'

We could just about see the path that led out of the village from where we sat. I doubted the mud would ever be stone-capped. But then, the village was doing better than the British camp. There they were squabbling over scraps. Here Horse had his eyes on the lands beyond ours.

'And we aren't just building new homes. We're building new feasting halls too!' Oak slapped his thigh. 'And when the Saxons feast, there's food to spare. One too many hogs on the fire, one too many barrels of beer brewed. It has to go somewhere!' His belly hung over his own lap. He'd not been hungry for months, maybe not ever.

'Everything changes, doesn't it?' I asked him.

'Nothing can stay the same and you wouldn't want it to, not really. Time only stops for the dead. But these boards will see many winters, they'll last years, don't you worry.'

I liked the idea of work that I'd done lasting ten or twenty years, standing tall and telling the world that I was once here.

Algar didn't return.

Viola waxed like the moon, her belly growing round and full.

The bluebells withered, their petals turned brown.

I was sweeping the empty workroom when Viola whipped aside the leather door and stood full-fool grinning at the threshold. My heart sank. Was he back? My knuckles gripped white around the neck of the broom.

'The Saxons are celebrating,' Viola squeaked.

'What do they celebrate?' I asked, not sure that I cared much for their parties.

'Rowan is to marry.'

I pulled the broom back and forth, not troubling to watch it. I remembered the strange conversation we had had by the stream, when Rowan had wondered about the world she would see beyond the village.

'Who is she to marry?' I asked.

Viola jigged on light feet, delighted with her news. 'That's the best part. He's British!'

What? British? That made no sense. Why was Rowan to marry someone her whole kin thought of as slaves? 'You're wrong,' I told Viola. 'You must be.'

She stuck out her lip, mule-mouthed. 'Don't believe me, then. Suit yourself,' she said and turned on her heel.

'Wait!' I rested the broom against the wall and hurried after her out of the workroom, banging the leather aside. 'Wait.'

Viola wanted to stay angry. There was drama in every hair on her head. But she was also bursting to tell me the tale. She let me trip after her for twenty paces, then she turned back, smiling. 'The blessing is happening tonight. At the temple.'

'Is the groom here already?'

Viola shook her head. 'No, it's just the first blessing. We won't see him until the betrothing. They'll be married before autumn comes. Tonight is just for the women, to start Rowan on her journey to being wife-bound. Isn't it exciting? There'll be dancing.' Viola grabbed my wrists and turned me spinning about. Her hair flew free of the loose scarf she wore, curls bouncing like sunbeams. I worried for her humour, but I laughed with her. We spun and spun until the village blurred and my toes tied themselves in knots. I fell to the floor. She came to sit beside me, lowering herself frog-like and squat. Her belly in the way.

'Why would Horse choose someone British, though?' I asked again. I checked the weather of her face; had my question angered her? Her moods were unpredictable lately.

But, no. She stayed sunny. 'I don't know. Perhaps he wants his grandchildren to be the lords of east and west, and north and south too.'

'Rowan told me her marriage would be to someone strong, who could bring men.'

'Well, no doubt he will, whoever he is. You'll come with me to the temple tonight?' Viola asked, breathless.

I let my head fall back on the grass. The sky above scudded with white clouds. I wanted to go. I was curious. But I had never been near it, not in all my moons here. The pagan gods were devils, as far as I could see. To worship them would be to invite the bad man in. I imagined myself on his horns. Gored and burning.

'I don't know,' I said. 'I don't know if I should come.'

'Of course you will,' Viola said simply. 'You'll come with me.'

'What happens there?' I asked. In my mind I saw hens

and goats with their throats cut, dripping blood on the faces of worshippers below.

'The priest or priestess goes on and on and on, while everyone else feeds wooden faces. There are masks, and gnarled old tree trunks. It's very strange. But there's no harm in it, and some fun. You'll come.' She wasn't asking.

My heart pounded. What if Iesu saw? What if He struck me down with fire? I vowed then and there that I wouldn't speak, or raise my eyes, or do anything that might look like worshipping. And never in the days of the Earth would you catch me feeding wooden faces. I had no idea what that even meant. Could the wood really eat? My skin shivered. The grass against my back was suddenly itchy and spiky.

'Rowan will want you today, I daresay.'

Rowan did. Her hall that late afternoon was boiling with women. They were to decorate Rowan like some blessed well, tied with ribbons and shells and brooches and tassels.

Was it really true her husband was British? I couldn't understand it. Had it made her angry with her father? She was to be wife of some mountain lord whose tongue was foreign and whose customs were unknown.

For the first time, I pitied her. The men about her made all her choices.

But, if she was angry, I saw no sign of it. There was no doubt in her. Her eyes were clear and the line of her jaw was tilted up. In the glow from the fire her skin looked like beaten gold, so hard were the planes of her face.

Maybe what Oak said was right, about choosing how to feel when the road was rough.

We dressed her as though it were her wedding. Her under-tunic was wool so finely spun that it looked like cobweb. Then two more tunics, one died bright red, the second palest blue. Where they overlapped, purple shimmered. She wore jewellery too, at her wrists, shoulders, and to hold her veil in place. Yellow and red, bright garnet wolves chasing golden deer, as the Saxons chased the Britons.

I tried not to wonder what this wedding might mean. Peace with the Britons? No coming war? Would Rowan still keep Britons as slaves?

'You look as beautiful as the day,' one of the Saxon women said to Rowan. 'May the gods bless you.'

She was still pagan, still Saxon. No wedding would change that.

We didn't eat our meal as we usually would, in our own halls, instead bread and cheese and fruit were passed about and we cut our own slices. The Saxon women first, of course, but then the Welsh too. There was sweetened ale and cider. By the time night fell, the ground felt soft and pliant under my feet.

Rowan was finally ready. She walked ahead, with duckling women in her wake. The rest of us followed behind. Viola slipped in beside me. She had washed her hair, somehow. I could smell the fresh rosemary as she walked. 'This is exciting,' she whispered, bobbing like rafts in rapids at my side. 'Look at her jewels. You could eat for years on those.'

It was true, they glistened in flamelight like stars sewn to cloth.

The Saxon temple was deep in the woods, beyond the stream. We walked in the darkness for long enough to make sweat prickle my back. The evening air was chilly, but the soft chatter of the women flowed like river water.

Before the temple was in sight, Viola caught my arm. 'Look,' she whispered, 'the tree of traitors.'

She pointed to something set off the path. In the light from the burning torches, I saw the huge fallen oak. It had crashed to the ground in storm-winds, as Sara had said, tearing the earth with it. The canopy was scarred by the hole it left, one dark eye looking down at us as though Woden himself leered at the earth.

But the tree wasn't dead, despite the violence of its fall. Its clawed roots had been ripped from the earth, yet somehow new growth had uncurled from the fallen trunk. It was something monstrous, half-living, half-dead. The new growth was gnarled and twisted, knotted around itself, too weak to stand straight, too wilful to die.

At the end of the trunk, the roots were ripped up clean. They spread, looking for all the world like the thick twitching legs of spiders grown big enough to prey on men. I swear I saw the roots move, shivering with hunger.

It should have died when it fell, rotted back into the good earth, but something had kept it alive. Slaves dripped their blood in sacrifice. Their screams kept the tree from slipping into its final sleep. The Saxons gave us as offerings to keep this demon tree strong.

'It's . . .' I couldn't think of any words in British or Saxon to say what it was.

'Keep walking,' Viola said. 'Don't let them see you looking.'

I moved faster, striding to escape the shadow of the tree. I didn't want its roots creeping towards me.

The crowd of women reached the temple. It was deliberately left dark, as though wanting to tempt their devils in with secrets. Leather walls flapped in the breeze, like broken-winged crows. I feared it. Trees crowded above, branches twining tight together. Trees, then temple, then the tattered Welsh and Saxons in their finery. It was sure strange.

Viola tugged me. 'Come on, we'll miss it.'

Stepping inside was like dropping into one of the cold pools beside the stream, or crawling under moss. The air was wet with breath and sweat. Two or three dozen women crowded together. I saw, part by part, that the tent had been built around one of the ancient oaks of the wood, its thick trunk rose in the centre. Perhaps the acorn-brother of the tree of traitors, and just as dark and demonic as its brother.

I caught my breath. What was I doing here?

Chanting began from somewhere in the tent.

'Viola?' I whispered.

Somehow, she heard and turned to me. Her eyes shone. 'Isn't it exciting?'

The voices of the women took up the chant. They called for the blessings of their gods. What blessings could slither from this dank place?

The women cleaved apart as something approached. Three people in masks. Wooden faces. Black gashes and gored eyes on one, skull-carved shapes on another, red swirls on the third.

The chant grew louder like high bird-chirrup. Patchwork voices filled the air, picking up the chant, twisting it. Someone barged into my shoulder. I staggered. Bodies swayed. Stepped. Swayed. Suddenly they danced. As though the chant had ignited something inside them. Hips, arms, breasts moved in the semi-dark with the sound of carrion crows coming from their mouths. I backed away from the pack. My spine pressed against one of the poles that held up the roof.

I couldn't see Viola, or Rowan, or any other one woman. They were one body now, like worms twisting, endless. How was this any kind of blessing?

Hands grabbed my elbows. The wooden mask of the

one-eyed god towered above me. The wearer pulled me forward. I wondered who it was. Which of the women with their brood of children and their neat hall had become this monster? I couldn't tell. Her eyes were shaded by the mask. I tried to dig my heels into the earth, but she had unnatural strength.

I was pulled into the dark moving heap of women. Their flesh welcomed me, soft under fabric. I was pressed into them, swallowed up. They surged with sour wine in their bellies and thunder in their heads. I tried to ride it as I might the swell of the river. The whoop and cry of the women beat in my blood.

I was chanting too. When had that happened?

I shook my head. But there was no clearing out the heat and the draw of the beat pulling me on. I was held up by the bodies of the women around me.

Viola swam into view, her face red but smiling. She pulled me into her arms and held me. 'These women are mis-minded,' she said. 'But I think I might be too!' She flung herself away from me and was lost in the *bwr-lwm* of the crowd.

Mis-minded. That was how it felt. In the middle of these dancing demons. Iesu would see me here, no doubt. Tad said he was always watching. This was wrong, this wasn't me. This was wrong!

'I have to get out!' I shouted.

I pushed against the bodies. The smell of sweat and rosemary mingled in my nose.

The wet air pressed against my skin, womb-warm.

I had to get out. I'd been sleepwalking with demons and I hadn't even noticed. I'd let myself think that having work and companions and somewhere warm to sleep at night was all that mattered. That having somewhere to heal after Haf had betrayed me was enough. I'd become mouse both head and heart.

And I disgusted myself.

'Let me out!' I cried. Dancing women smiled at me. 'Let me out! Let me out!'

I ripped myself from them, lunging for the cold air of the night.

Out of the temple, I pressed my side against the nearest tree and pushed my hands against the tiny, dusty valleys of the bark. My heartbeat was quick as sparrow notes. I gasped and pulled freezing air deep into my belly. I'd woken from my dream. Tad was dead. He was dead and not coming back, and Mam, and Haf too, or might as well have been.

They had all left me.

And I'd found myself slave-bound to the demon Saxons.

45

I RAN BACK, alone, through the wood. Should I keep going? Right up the path and into the woods beyond? Was this my chance? While the other women demon-danced for their strange gods?

I tripped over roots, fell hands first into moss and pine needles. The dark pressed in all around.

No. There was nowhere to go. Nowhere I belonged. I had run from the British camp right into the jaws of the Saxons. I was still the mouse who had scurried from the Roman tomb. I was still the mouse who had had Saxon words dropped into her open mouth.

The path took me past the tree of traitors. I didn't look.

Inside the Welsh barn, the men were sleeping. I slid onto the sack I shared with Viola. The dip where she rested her growing belly was clear to see. She was pretending that all was well, ignoring the coming baby. I'd been pretending too, when I was really full, full to the brim and spilling, with fear.

Even if I could run, could I really leave Viola? Could I leave my sister when she needed me?

Sleep was long to come.

I began to hoard food. Squirrelling it away in every hole and corner I could think of. I didn't know if I meant to run or not, or when I might do it. All paths seemed as dark as each other. I wrapped roots in leaves and left them in the dark space between sleeping sacks. I took the grain that should have been swept away and gathered it in twists of cloth trimmings. It was thin hope, but it was something.

Viola noticed my burden. 'You're so quiet lately, it's like walking with two shadows,' she said one day while I worked at the quern-stone, and she watched.

I didn't know how to answer. How could I say I wanted to run?

'Are you ill?' she asked. She pressed the back of her hand to my forehead. It felt rough with flour.

'Not ill.'

'Then what?'

I had no time to answer. Elin rushed into the workroom at that moment, the door flapping like her tongue. 'I've news! I've news!' She swirled into the space the way Viola would have done before her belly got too big.

'What news might you have?' Viola asked.

Elin twirled again before answering. 'Rowan is to be

married on the longest day, on the solstice!' Elin beamed. 'Rowan will see sun on her wedding band!'

Sara rose slowly to her feet and dusted down the floury front of her tunic. 'Are you sure?' she asked.

'It's decided! Horse sent men and they brought back word that the British lord is impatient. I heard it in the cook-house.'

'What were you doing there?' Viola asked.

'When does solstice fall?' Sara spoke over her.

Most of us turned to the open wall and looked at the grass and woods beyond. We had many more moments of sunshine than we had of darkness now. The bluebells had given way to tangled dog-roses and the bramble and elderflower were in bloom, scenting the paths with sweetness.

'Twenty or thirty days,' Viola guessed. Elin squealed, as though all the fairs were come at once.

I smiled at her mirth. But my smile slowly drained away. Weddings meant guests, and feasting and drinking. The more important the wife and husband, the more free-flowing the ale. The less anyone would notice what one small, mousy Welsh girl was up to in the middle of the *bwr-lwm*. It might be her chance to run.

Viola scowled at me. Cross, no doubt that Elin had been first to the mill with the story. Then she leaned close, putting her lips to my ear. 'Do you think *he* will come back?'

She was thinking of Algar. Of course she was. And of course he would. He wouldn't miss the chance to feast.

It felt as though another stone dropped into my belly, crag-hard lumps of worry building inside me. How could she still want him after everything?

'Right,' Sara said, 'if Elin has got the story with its head the right way up, then there's work to do, and lots of it. I don't want to see one single empty quern-stone for the next fortnight. Viola, that includes you too. Work.'

Before she turned back to work, Viola spoke to Elin. 'Who is Rowan to marry? Do you know?'

Elin shrugged. 'His name is Gwrtheyrn.'

I had known.

Somehow I had known it would be him.

I felt burning acid rise in my throat. My hands flew away from the stone. I was up, jumping from the raised floor, through the open wall onto the grass.

'Mai!' I heard Sara call behind me.

But I didn't look back. I rushed to the shade of the trees and leaned against them. Blood rushed in my ears. I felt the solid trunk behind me, the only thing keeping me upright. Was Iesu laughing at me? Perhaps the Roman dead had cursed me after all.

No. It was done deliberate. Horse knew that Gwrtheyrn was the strongest British lord for days of marching. Of course he had chosen Gwrtheyrn as his son-in-law – if he was to spread west, it was the simplest way. This was no cruel joke, or spite against me. It was just the way of the world: girls were caught up in the tales and dreams of men. I folded over, head down.

'Mai?' Viola spoke, close by. 'What ails you? Are you sick? Mai, you're frightening me.'

I felt her hand on my back, rubbing from neck to tail. 'I'm well,' I whispered. I righted myself but still needed one hand on the tree. Viola peered at me, her face storm-troubled. Behind her, I could see the other women watching from the workroom. I was the newest spectacle.

'You don't look well. Was it something you ate?'

'No. It isn't that.'

'Then what?'

'Oh, Viola,' I leaned into her then, over her belly. She soothed me as my own Mam might have done, with soft strokes and whispers.

'What is it, my love?' she said.

'Gwrtheyrn. I was at his camp.'

She gasped. 'The one Rowan is to marry?'

'Yes.'

'Oh, poor Rowan.'

I sob-laughed. I hadn't thought for one moment about her. It was myself I was frightened for. I didn't want to see Gwrtheyrn, or Rhodri, or March again. I didn't want to share the same air as them, ever. If Rowan kept her own slaves with her, I would be going back to the camp.

Would I see Haf again?

Viola wiped my cheeks dry with her thumbs. 'My poor chick. I'll tell Sara you're sick.'

'But the work!'

'I'll do yours too today. You need to rest.'

'You're offering to do more than your share?'

She smiled, indignant. 'For you and only you. Yes. Now go, go to the Welsh barn. Rest.'

She gave me her cheerful, honey grin, then walked back to the workroom. She swayed, loose at the hips as she went.

I stood.

Was this my time to flee?

46

SUMMER SOLSTICE, AD455,
EARLY MORNING.

SARA HOLDS THE baby boy while I help Viola eat
and wash. We hear Sara singing to him. The lullaby is
both British and Saxon, words Sara remembers from
her own childhood, words she has sung over Saxon
cradles. The sounds make no sense, but they mix in the
air like sunshine and birdsong.

I forget, while she sings, the horrors of the world.

47

LATE SPRING, AD455

I PRAYED TO Iesu.

For the strength to stay, or the strength to go, whichever He saw fittest for me. As soon as I reached the Welsh barn, I took sticks from the store beside the fire and bound them, crosswise, hurriedly. I set it on my bed and kneeled on the wooden floor. The altar I'd made was rough, but I hoped He wouldn't mind. My head sank over my clasped hands and I prayed harder than I had ever before. It wasn't the cross that Mam had loved so much, but it was enough to make me feel that she and Tad weren't so far away.

What was the right thing to do?

The room was dark, despite the daylight. Small stones and grit pressed into my knees. Was He listening? I had to believe He was.

'Our Father in Heaven,' I whispered, 'please let me know what to do. I can't be here when Gwrtheyrn and Rhodri come. Nor Algar either. But I can't leave Viola. Can I? Please help me. If you see fit. Amen.'

The words rushed like the stream in winter flood. Would He listen?

I let go my hands and sank onto the floor. Were there signs?

I scanned the dust and dirt, looking for patterns, for clues. I listened to the birdsong, the soft hum of insects, the growing lambs beyond the village calling like new babies.

Did that mean I should stay and wait for Viola to have her baby?

The leather door was pushed aside. Gwennan hobbled in, out of breath. 'Sara says she doesn't care if you're dead as horn, you're to come back to work.'

I tucked my cross between two sacks, pin-quick.

'Viola was going to do my share.'

'It's arm and elbow work needed from everyone,' Gwennan said. 'Workroom. Now. The wedding will make this the hardest stretch of your life.'

I doubted it. Days watching Tad die, days shut in the dark were the worst days.

But it was hard, nonetheless. Over those days following, the Welsh of the village had to prepare food, drinks, feasting gifts and sleeping space for the guests. The women took on most of it, working at snake-killing pace to get everything ready.

But there was one job that fell to the men. They set about finishing the great hall that Oak had started. Like the rest of the Saxon halls, it was framed in wood, with panelled walls, but the scale of it was beyond anything the village or the camp on the hill had seen. It was Roman in its dreaming. Trees were felled at the edge of the village to make way for it. Dried planks were brought from the stores. Smaller huts were dismantled, to reuse the wood. Upwards of twenty men toiled daily to give it shape and heft, Welsh and Saxon both.

Horse, at the head of the Saxon men, was at the heart of the plans. He swaggered around the site growling at his sawyers. It seemed he urged the building up out of the ground with his voice. The world seemed to be built by men trying to out-frighten each other. Where was the place for mice like me in all that?

With the men wolf-scavenging the countryside or labouring over the hall, the women were left alone. We worked from the arc of dawn until night. My body moved as one with the others, grinding, stewing, salting, steaming, pickling, peeling, brewing. Making, making, making all the time. Turning want into abundance somehow. Nothing was elegant, or spiced with flavours from traders beyond the sea, but it was wholesome and fresh and full of sunshine.

I took what little I could and tucked it away in my hiding places. Roots, hard biscuits, anything that would last.

I still didn't know whether I was going to run or stay with Viola. So I waited.

*

With spring finally giving way to summer, and five days left until the wedding, the chores of the day were mostly done. I went to the new hall to watch it take form. The shingled roof was on. Decorations, carved and painted, would be next. Wooden deer brought down by wooden hounds, boar against bear, hunters and prey, would run all over the fresh doorframe.

I found Oak washing his face and neck in barrel-water.

'Rowan will be pleased. It's fit for her wedding feast,' I told him.

His face and beard were dripping as he looked down at me, but his mouth was set with his warm smile to match the warm evening air. 'It is that,' he said. 'Sixty men can sit with as much room for their elbows as they'd have in their own bed. We still have to make the last of the tables for the warriors to sit at, but it will be done, girl, it will be done.'

'Is there enough time?'

He laughed. 'You'd be my master if you could, is that it? It'll be ready, don't you worry. The yearling lambs will be fit for eating and there will be such revelry that you will wish you'd been born Saxon.'

I couldn't imagine wishing for any such thing. Though being born Briton wasn't anything to be proud of either. I thought of the tomb that still haunted my dreams. I thought of the hunger and the distrust at camp. Would

Rowan take me with her after the wedding? Would I be Welsh or British if she did?

What would I say to Haf if I did see her at the camp? She had thrown me to the wolves when she told Rhodri that I needed watching. She would see how much farther I had fallen since then. I burned at the thought.

'Let me show you,' Oak brought me back from my wondering. He waved me towards the door of the hall. As he led me inside he dropped his right hand onto the doorframe, as though dropping it onto the shoulder of his beloved child. This hall was more to him than wood and wattle.

The scale of the hall was monstrous, with walls so far apart that the weight of the roof must surely make them topple. Thick ceiling posts were ranged in two rows. It was only these that stopped us being crushed by falling beams. I rested my hand on the first one, its splinters still unsmoothed. It felt too thin for the task. Oak must have read my face. 'Don't fret,' he said, 'this place is going nowhere. It will still be standing in three generations. Your granddaughter will see the inside of this hall.'

Would she? Was my whole life going to be spent here? Oak seemed so certain.

Viola needed me. She needed her sister when the baby came. But the chance to slip away from the village, in the middle of the revels might not come again. It might be days before anyone even noticed I'd gone.

'There will be three tables, set along three sides,' Oak said. He waved at the walls, clearly seeing the feasting before him. 'Horse and his men will sit at the best table,' Oak continued. 'Rowan too, of course.'

Of course; Rowan was the afterthought at her own betrothal feast.

'Horse plans for the Britons and the Saxons to sit, not separately, on either side of the hall, but together, as companions.' Oak waved again.

'But how will they talk to one another?' I asked.

Oak chuckled. 'When men drink and eat together and are served by fine women in great halls, the sparks of friendship are sure to spurt.'

'The language, though?' I insisted. Didn't Oak remember learning Saxon? Didn't he remember how hard it had been to use the Saxon we had in our mouths; it was like chewing stones to get the sense out at the beginning.

Oak crossed the hall and rested his thick hands on the window frame. Beyond I could see women gathering children to their skirts and hurrying about their tasks. Smoke rose from thatch and shingled roofs. The life of the village went on, despite the coming celebration.

'There are men here,' Oak said, 'who have seen the life the Britons lead, have spoken with them and shared their food. Those men know some of the tongue. They will help make this hearth feel familiar to the Britons.'

Men like Algar. I felt heat rise within me. If he came,

310

Algar would be one of the important men here, the cockerel on the heap. As the beer flowed and the women brought meat, and Rowan sat with her eyes wide open and her mouth shut, Algar would preen. Welsh too, he'd be another, scuttling between Horse and Gwrtheyrn, translating their tales, fawning on them both.

Men who took, thankless. Mindless
Of women put in harness
Or babies raised in ruins;
Sowing thorns regardless.

They were terrible men, all of them. I saw them, in my mind, calling and pawing at the serving girls. At Viola. She was too full now to push them away. My hand gripped one of the hall posts and my fingers tightened around it. I wished I had the strength to snap it in two.

Oak slapped the window frame and turned back to me. 'In less than five days it will be done. And it will be something to see.'

I smiled tightly. He had no idea of the storm that blew within me. My fingers were white as they squeezed tighter and tighter. But the post held. Of course – I was tiny beside it, my arm had no strength.

But I would find strength. I knew now what I was going to do. I was going to stay. For Viola, and Sara and all the other women who had been kind to me. Even for Rowan, who was scared of the world beyond her village.

I wouldn't run while the feast raged. I had to stay.

I would stay beside Viola for as long as I could. For as long as I had any choice at all in it. I couldn't leave Viola to the wolves. That was the bravest thing. It was the right thing.

Before I went to bed that night, I took my small hoard of food from the holes and corners I'd found, and I shared it with all the girls in the Welsh hut.

48

I WOULD STAY for as long as Viola needed me. Even if that meant I ended my days here. I was choosing her and that was that.

Still, those days as solstice approached were hard to bear. Full of work and toil and worry about the men who were on their way.

Viola brought the news when it came, of course. She waddled into the workroom, one hand at the small of her back. 'They're here,' she told the gathered women. 'The Britons are here!'

We stilled our quern-stones.

All but Sara. 'No!' she said, 'No. Keep to the task. What if we run out of flour? If there's no bread on the tables, Horse'll have us all on the tree of traitors!'

No one minded her words. There was too much excitement. The women rushed, strim-stram, out of the workroom. Bodies crushed together at the door, spilled onto the path. I followed on reluctant soles, I didn't want to see any of the British men again. Voices around the village shouted – men mostly, barking instructions.

But women too called to each other, *Come see, come see.* I realised, from the keening excitement, that some might be hoping to see brothers, or cousins, long-lost.

At the point where the forest path became the village path, they gathered. My view was poor. I stayed at the back. Gwrtheyrn was close, nearly here.

I sensed, rather than saw them come. The crowds whispered names, remarks, idle thoughts, all in Saxon so that the visitors wouldn't understand. They could say whatever they liked and the Britons would have no stunted clue what they meant. I caught fragments. The whispers called the men handsome or ugly, brave or ungainly, they were darker than expected, or more blond. The crowd was all rumour. Who were these Britons who had been welcomed as equals in the Saxon village? Who stayed Briton and didn't become Welsh?

I had to see for myself, finally. The temptation was too great. I wriggled past one mother and her baby. Onto the path. In front of the visitors. And I stopped stone-still.

Gwrtheyrn.

He led his horse, the animal thin-looking and weakened even to my unskilled eye. But in other regards he was what the Saxons expected in their warriors – his breast was strapped tight inside his leather breastplate; gold circles twisted at his wrists, arms, neck. His hair had been stiffened to add extra height.

He led two dozen or more men.

There was Rhodri. My throat burned with acid heat. He was here then, my tormentor. I wondered if Bryn was one of the foot soldiers.

But it wasn't Bryn I saw next in that crowd. Amid the throng of men there was one woman. Haf. My sister was here, walking alongside the men.

I had to step back. My heart pounded sickly-bird quick. Water in my limbs. Noise where my mind should be.

I bumped the woman with the baby. She tutted. I didn't plead pity. I had no breath in me for words.

Haf was here.

Was I sure certain?

I looked again. It was her. No doubt.

She was smiling. Her lips full and wide. It was the same smile Tad had had. It sent ice through me. She was so like him, and yet not like him at all. What was she doing here? Had she known where to find me?

She walked beside Rhodri. Did that mean anything? Was she part of his household? Rhodri had been the worst of them all. He had shut me in with the dead. After Haf had told him my plan. The poison had come from her. I turned away and pushed back through the crowd to the edge of the path.

The procession passed on. The Saxon men mingled with the British. They were leading them to their sleeping hall. Would Haf go with them? Did she belong to one of them?

Sara stood at the very edge of the crowd, her face saying that she had seen enough in her lifetime for this to pass as just another day. Her arms were folded tight. Welsh stood beside her, talking in her ear.

Once he had moved on, I stepped to her. 'Sara,' I asked, 'do you know where the woman with the Britons is to sleep?'

Did I want to know so that I could to run straight to the place? Or to make sure to keep away? I didn't know.

Sara rolled her eyes to Heaven. 'Aye, that's strange to see. As if I haven't enough to do today. It seems she gives him counsel, would you believe? Perhaps he wants her opinion of Horse and the rest of us? Who ever heard of such things?' Sara clearly believed that the Britons had wandered off the path of right-thinking.

'Will she stay with the men?'

Sara tutted. 'No. She's not as brazen as that. Though did you see her tunic? I've never seen one so fine on any British back. She looks like someone who wants their nest neat and doesn't mind who builds it.'

Did she? Had her heart turned so cold? It was possible. I hadn't seen her in six moons, and so much had changed in that time.

'She'll be sleeping in the hall with Rowan. Welsh says we are to carry one extra bed in. Oak has one, I'm told. Here,' Sara clapped her hands together suddenly. 'You can help. Come. Let's leave Viola to this foolishness. There's work we should be doing.'

Sara turned, sure certain I would follow. And I did. I had no interest in seeing the rest of the procession. The Britons were pretending at wealth and the Saxons were pretending at hospitality. It all churned my stomach. I would rather work. At least that was honest.

Oak picked out one of the smaller box-beds for us. It was simple, but well-made, with neat joins. Someone had rubbed it hard with sand so it was smooth for sleeping.

'It's nice,' I said. She was lucky to get it.

'It should be,' Oak agreed, his hands protective on its side. 'My son made it. With me watching his every move, of course.'

'She likes nice things,' I told him.

His eyebrows scrunched like bristling thornhogs, but I didn't explain. How could I say what Haf was to me when I didn't know myself? Sister. Snake. Both at once.

'Lift the head end,' Sara snapped.

I did as I was told.

We carried the bed balanced between us, through the village. We could still hear the sound of the welcome, but we avoided it.

The hall where Haf was to sleep was deserted.

'Where shall we put it?' I asked.

Sara looked about. Rowan had her sleeping area screened from the other women. The two hearths at either end gave warmth through the night, though none of the beds and sleeping mats were near the doorway or windows, for the draught.

'They won't want her too close. Guest or not, she's still British and the warmth of this welcome might go as sour as sheep feet. We'll put it under the window. She can run away in the night if she needs to.'

'Why would she need to?' I asked.

'They won't know how to treat her. She's the old corn of the country. Her family has grown in these lands for ever. The Saxons? They're new stock, with weak roots. They'll be jealous of what she is. She'll not sleep easy in here tonight.'

We shuffled the bed into place beneath the window. The wicker shutter was thrown open for fresh air.

'There are furs in the cist,' Sara said, waving me to fetch them.

As I crossed the hall, I heard the sound of women approaching. High birdsong chatter and dancing steps on the path. I froze. She was coming.

49

THE DOOR PUSHED open, smooth on oiled hinges, and four women entered, surrounding the fifth. Their talk didn't stop. I watched her face, my sister, I watched her at their centre. She was smiling, but her eyes were cold. She couldn't understand the words the women spoke, I realised. I knew something she didn't.

There were small changes to her. She was thinner, maybe taller too. She held her head higher. Her clothes were fine and well-made. I saw one shoulder was pinned with Roman jewellery. I knew where that would have been found.

But I could see her as she had been too. The girl lying beside me in meadows, with daisies, clover, buttercups between me and her smile. She was still Haf.

I couldn't move. Being in the same room had pinned me as traps snare rabbits.

'Mai,' Sara hissed. 'The furs, girl.'

I barely heard her, and the order wasn't powerful enough to move me.

Haf glanced about the hall, taking in the height of the

319

roof, the fresh straw on the floor, the well-made furniture. And me.

I felt, rather than heard her gasp. She knew me. I hadn't changed on the outside, however different I felt inside.

For more moments than I could bear, it was only the two of us in the hall. In the world. All other sounds and senses, but the sight of each other, died.

She walked towards me slowly, melting through the village women. She reached out and placed the lightest of hands on my cheek. I could see Tad in the line of her jaw, the curve of her mouth. It sent splinters through me.

Her press became heavier. Both hands on my face. Thumbs under my eyes. Her hands slipped to my neck, my shoulders. Then, she pulled me towards her, hard. I could feel the press of her breast, her jutting, too-thin hips. She held me tight.

The hall was silenced.

I stiffened. I let her hold me. But I made no move to hold her in return. Over her shoulder, I could see that Sara and the Saxon women were staring at us, their jaws open, catching flies.

Haf didn't care about the sudden hush. She sank her face into my shoulder and I could feel the wet of tears.

'I thought you were dead,' she whispered.

'Or hoped it?' I said, soft as duck down. The British sounds came so easy, though they brought pain.

'What?' She pulled back, holding me still but with wariness written on her.

I said nothing. I turned to the cist, raised the lid and lifted out the top fur, wolf. It was heavy and already warm to the touch. The hair at the hackles was coarse, but the belly was soft.

'You're not pleased to see me?' she asked.

I was. I was. More than anything.

My heart was full. My sister was alive.

But she had betrayed me to Rhodri. He'd said so. There was no forgetting or forgiving that.

I said nothing. I held the pelt to me as my shield.

Sara stepped between us and the Saxon women. She addressed Haf, in our own tongue. 'My dear, it seems you aren't strange to us, after all. Not, at least, to one of us?' I could tell that Sara was burning with questions, though she kept her eyes modest.

Haf shaped her face as hard as the wooden masks I'd seen in the Saxon temple. Playing at being the lady again, no doubt. 'I'm grateful to the women here for their welcome,' she said to Sara, 'but I'm tired from the journey. Might I have some moments alone, do you think?'

Sara carried the words into Saxon for the village women. They looked cross. Perhaps because they'd been told to keep their eyes on Haf, or because they wanted to know why the lady of the Britons should greet the Welsh girl with such warmth.

They would have to be kept in ignorance. Haf got her way. They bustled out, whispering rude guesses to each other. Haf caught my eye and gestured. She didn't want me to leave.

We stood in the centre of the hall, like twin saplings, wondering which would be the first to bend.

Part of me wanted to run into her arms and sob. Be held by her the way I had been when I grazed my knees or felt frightened by the dark. But the greater part of me was angry. I'd been frightened by more than the dark, because of her. I'd been shut up to die with the Roman dead. Her words had put me there.

I moved to the empty box-bed below the window and dropped the wolf pelt onto it.

'Is that for me?' she asked.

I nodded.

'It's nice. Nicer than the one I have at home. Nicer than the one I shared with you.'

She had her own bed somewhere. She slept at night. My rage came in black waves.

'Why aren't you pleased to see me?' she asked.

'How can you ask that after what you did?'

'And what was it I did?'

'You know! You know full certain. You told Rhodri to watch me. Do you know what he did to me when he caught me trying to leave?'

Haf sat. She stretched her legs before her. There was

dust on the hem of her skirt. I wondered who would be tasked with cleaning it. Her hands were balled in tight fists in her lap. 'Here's what I know,' she said carefully. 'I know that you left. When I needed you, you weren't there. Tad had been dead only two days before I lost my sister too. You left me, Mai.'

'I was taken! Rhodri picked me up with his own hands and shut me in one of the Roman tombs.'

She looked at me sharply, shocked. 'He did what?'

'You didn't know?' I asked. How could she not know? It felt as though the floor was crumbling beneath me.

She shook her head. 'I looked for you, for weeks. I sneaked out of the camp and called your name in the woods. I watched the grave we made for Tad, to see if you brought flowers. I couldn't ask anyone for help. I was alone, Mai.' Her voice was full of pain. She paused, sighed, then smoothed the fur on her bed, neatening it, putting it in its place.

'It wasn't done deliberate,' I said.

'You *told* me you were leaving. Wasn't that done deliberate?'

My mouth felt dry as summer creeks. I turned my back to her and strode to the cist. I pressed my hands against the lid, to hold myself up. The carved animals with their bared teeth twisted across the wood.

'I wouldn't have left without saying goodbye,' I said.

'But you did,' she spat.

How was this going her way? How was she making me

feel small and stupid as though I hadn't lived for two seasons without any help from her?

I slapped the wooden lid. 'Rhodri took me, I didn't leave. He didn't tell you?'

'I couldn't talk of you to anyone. I couldn't be sad, or frightened. I had to keep smiling to stay safe. You never understood that.'

'You did talk of me!' I was furious now. 'Rhodri only found out what I planned because you warned him. You betrayed me.'

'I did not.'

'You used me to impress the big men. You use people to get what you want, Haf.'

She stood and stepped towards me. There was anger in every inch of her. 'The night you left, I was wild-minded. Tad was gone, you were threatening to leave. I found Bryn at the great hall. I asked him to help me watch you. I was frightened you'd leave me. I didn't say one word to Rhodri.'

'It was Bryn, you're saying?' My mind flew, seizing upon any answer. Was it Bryn who had betrayed me? He had seen me that night on my way to the store.

'Maybe. It was busy at the hall, I wasn't as careful as I might have been. Maybe someone heard me tell him. I don't know.'

'Is Bryn here? I can ask him.'

She shook her head. 'He's not here.'

That was good for her. It was just her word that it had happened as she said.

We were both silent. The sounds of the village drifted in, children shouting, men calling to each other. But it felt as though we two were cut off from the rest of the world, on our own raft, adrift. Could we ever be sisters again?

'When I got out of the Roman tomb,' I said, 'I wasn't me any more. I was more animal than girl. It's taken many moons to come back to myself.'

She walked to me slowly and rested her hand on my shoulder, ran it down my back, soothing, stroking. I felt myself lean towards her. I wanted to melt against her, hear her sing childish songs again.

'I'm sorry that happened to you,' she said.

'I'm sorry you were alone for so long,' I said.

I was close to reaching for her, holding her as one sister should hold another. But then she said, 'You look well for being here though, better than some of the women at the camp. Perhaps what put you here doesn't matter.'

'What?'

'Your cheeks are round. You've grown nearly as tall as me. Perhaps it suits you to be here and not at the camp.'

How could she say that? I scampered from her, rustling the fresh straw. 'What happened to me *does* matter. It will always matter. What they did, Rhodri and Gwrtheyrn and Algar—'

'Don't put their names with his. He's worse than they could ever be.' She held her hand up to stop me speaking, palm up, fingers firm.

She had held her hand in just the same way when I'd found her in our yard, when she was sprawled in the dirt, where Algar had thrown her.

'Rhodri hurt me worse than Algar hurt you,' I said.

'I didn't know we were in competition,' she snapped.

'It was one clout about your face. You'd had worse falling out of trees.'

'One clout from the man who had just set light to the farm. Who had hurt Tad. You sound like you're six years old, Mai. Can't you hear yourself? Rhodri was cruel, but he did what he did to protect his people. What was Algar protecting?'

She was siding with him.

She was siding with Rhodri against me.

Him

Over

Me.

The weight of her being here, saying what she was saying, slammed into me. My knees buckled. The floor hit me hard. My blood pounded in my head. I felt straw pressing patterns in my face. Then, Haf was beside me. Her hands on me, stroking, mewling, soothing me.

'Mai? Mai?' she said.

I pushed her off. I rolled away from her and sat, my

back against the side wall, my knees bent, bank and ditch, defending against her.

'Mai.' She reached for me again, her hands on my knees. Her fingers so familiar. But the hem of her sleeve was not, the fabric stolen or traded from the back of some poor wretch.

'Listen to me, Mai. We're together again now. I've found you. And this wedding means you'll come back to the camp. Gwrtheyrn can ask for you.'

'Ask for me? And I'll be handed over like livestock – is that what you want?'

'Don't you want to come with me?' Haf tightened her grip, but I batted her hands away.

'I can't go back to the camp. I can't forget what Rhodri did. I have nightmares about it still.'

'Nightmares? You're alive. You're healthy. That's more than many can say.' Her face stormed with feeling. 'What do you want me to do? The whole world is turned on its forehead, do you expect me to put it the right way up?'

'You're my sister,' I hissed.

'I'm your sister, not Iesu himself. Mai . . . what would you have me do? There are no avenging angels for girls like us. There's no justice coming. Not in this world, at least.'

I raised my head enough to spit my words at her. 'You're as bad as Rhodri and Algar. I wish I'd never seen any of you again.'

She winced at my words. But it wasn't my hate that she wanted to speak of. 'You saw Algar again? Where? Here?'

I nodded slowly. With my arms around my knees, I was curled as tight as ash-bugs prodded by sticks.

'Is he here now?' She moved to her bed and looked out of the window at the wooden walls of the Saxon village.

'He's not here,' I said. I didn't want to answer her. Who was she now? I didn't know her at all. While I'd been busy becoming mouse-Mai, it seemed Haf had been growing into something much more ferocious, she had teeth and wasn't afraid of her own bite.

I pushed myself up. Stood, shaking. I needed air. I moved to the door. I was out. Gasping fish-gulps.

'Mai?' Haf called behind me. 'Where are you going?'

'Stay away from me,' I said. 'You're not heel-nor-thumb better than they are.'

I left her there, at the window. I was willow-weak and trembling. The Welsh barn wasn't far, but I felt that I'd walked half my lifetime in getting there. There was no one inside when I pulled back the leather. Was the welcoming party still taking place? It seemed impossible.

I fell on my sleeping sack.

I listened. Had she followed me? I listened hard for her steps.

The sounds of the village were louder than usual: babies, dogs, laughter and shouts; no footsteps.

The sun still moved across the sky, but in my heart

nothing was the same. Haf had changed. The moment Algar had stepped onto our land it had begun. He was the first stone thrown down the mountainside that bounced and rattled the rest loose until I was caught in the landslide.

50

THE WELCOME PARTY continued into the night. I heard the Welsh returning to the barn in driffs and draffs, letting in cold air and the smell of the night. My sleep was restless, I dreamed of dark walls and thin bones and packs of dogs racing through trees.

But I must have slept. For the next thing I knew, Viola had her hand on my shoulder and was shaking me.

'Mai, wake up, wake up. You're something sorry this morning!' She laughed at my groggy movements as I swam up to greet her.

'Is it late? Have I missed it?' I asked.

Her hair was free of any covering and her curls waved like meadow flowers as she shook her head. 'You haven't missed it, neither the fun nor the work. I came to find you. We have to go to the cook-house to help them prepare. The feast begins at nightfall, with the wedding itself tomorrow on the longest day.'

I looked at the window. The light was blossom pink, the dawn new. There would be hours of daylight today. Long enough to work our bones short. I wiped sleep from my eyes. They felt full of stones and grit. Had I cried in my sleep? Cried for Haf who had chosen Gwrtheyrn and the camp over me? I lay on my back staring up at the roof beams and the untrimmed thatch that crawled with insects.

'Get up!' Viola scooped me up with the weight of her shoulder. 'I heard news about you,' she said.

I didn't reply. I tried to pull my woollen blanket back over my eyes, but Viola tugged it off.

'I heard you know the woman who came with the Britons.'

She waited. But not for long.

'Is it true?' she asked.

'I know her. I used to know her. Now I'm not so sure.'

'Who is she?'

'She used to be my sister.'

Viola flopped down, heavy, beside me on the bed. 'Your sister? From the camp? Did you fight like dogs and pigs when you saw each other?'

I smiled despite myself. 'The past is the past,' I said.

Viola rested her free hand on her stomach. 'Sometimes. Did she tell you why she did it?'

'She said it wasn't her.'

'Do you believe her?'

The anger I'd felt yesterday had drained like the tide. Did I believe her? 'I don't know. She said she's on the side of the camp, even after the men shut me up with the dead Roman.'

'Would you prefer she became Welsh here and passed the next thirty years grinding grain with you?'

'Is that really all the choice we have?'

Viola shrugged, no doubt bored of thinking of the future. 'Oh, don't be gloomy. Today is for feasting,' she said.

'And working. There's plenty of that about, sure as being.'

Viola laughed as she wrestled my body upright. 'What's wrong with you?'

I couldn't start to make Viola understand. My mind was under the whip of ill winds. Haf was here with the men from the camp, and she was standing by them, even after she learned what they had done to me.

'Everyone's coming to feast!' Viola said.

Everyone.

She was thinking of Algar, sure certain. She hoped he would come back, and love her again, her and the baby. She hadn't learned that dead bees make no honey. I wasn't going to be the one to tell her.

'Get up, get up!' she insisted.

I would. I would get up, and work by her side and do my best to keep her safe, whatever happened, as if I really were her sister. The sister I had chosen, not the one I was born with.

Soon after, Viola waded into the thick air of the cook-house, with me dragging myself behind into the heavy wall of heat. The ovens were stoked so high I could hardly breathe. The place was busy already and every forehead glistened wet, women wiped their faces on aprons to stop sweat dripping into the food.

'Here, girl, bake these.' The woman who spoke was someone I had seen around the village. Bee-sting bitter with the world, she barked her orders. I took the wooden board she held. It was piled high with raw pats of dough, ready to be griddled. The fire was open and the iron skillet too hot to touch. I dropped them on three at once, and sniffed the air for any hint of burning.

Viola slid past and swiped one from the cooked pile. 'You should try one,' she said, 'they taste of Heaven.' There was nothing that could dent her spirits today.

I thought, as I pressed water into the barley flour, of my other sister. Had Haf slept well with the Saxon ladies? Or was she still waiting at the window for me to come back?

Of course not. She was dressing for the feast. Perhaps with Welsh girls combing her hair and washing her hands and feet. She wouldn't risk losing that for anything; her tongue wouldn't cut her own throat. I thumped at the dough, sweat running rivers between my shoulder blades. Over the morning, the pile of fresh bread grew, but my misery shrank not one bit. I felt midden-wet and just as dirty. I looked about for Viola.

There was no sign of her.

'Is Viola taking her rest?' I asked the sour-faced baker.

'That one barely started work before sliding off somewhere,' she told me. 'Go. You're dripping sweat onto my loaves.'

I was grateful. My mouth was dry and my skin slick.

'Come back soon though,' she warned.

Outside, the ground about the new feasting hall was churned, despite the lack of rain. Too many busy feet. The benches and tables that Oak and his son had made were being carried in. Some men worked on the makeshift tent that would serve as the place to prepare the platters.

Was that where Viola had gone?

I stepped into the hall, careful to wipe my shoes on the reed mats at the door. Two children swept the floor, trying hard to push out the mud just as quickly as everyone else walked it in, the task as pointless as ploughing sand. Someone had sprigged the walls with green. Full leaves, like teardrops, dripped from the rafters. Wild roses filled the hall with their scent, though the petals would fall long before the feast was over. I was struck again by how strange this wedding was. Horse could have married Rowan to his own kinsmen. He could have united his village with the strong Saxons to the east. And yet, he had chosen Gwrtheyrn. King of his dung-heap on the hill. And now the Britons were guests. The whims and worries of men threw us all about.

It was sure strange. Unsettling.

Oak and his son were moving the last benches into place.

'Has Viola been here?' I asked Oak.

'No, not that I've seen,' he said.

'Do you know Algar?'

'I know him.'

'Has he been here?'

'I heard he was back with his brother. I've not seen him. Why do you want him?'

'I don't,' I said. 'But I know someone who does.'

I went back outside. Not sure where to look. I had no want to see Algar, or Haf, and if I wandered the village I might find them. But I did want to know Viola was safe and not staring goat-eyed at Algar.

I sat, stupid with doubt, on the only bit of grass that wasn't mud. The sun was warm on my skin. The sweat drying to itchy flakes. I would have liked to wash in the cold stream, with only willow and reeds for company. The wedding could go and scratch for all I cared.

'Here you are!' Viola rolled herself to the ground beside me.

'Where have you been? I baked all the bread in the world while you were gone.'

'Don't be grumpy,' she said, leaning her shoulder against mine. 'I've got news.'

'It will be sad the day when you have no news,' I replied.

She giggled and reached for her feet and tried to pull off

her leather shoes. But it was hard for her to reach past her belly. I watched her struggle, then leaned over and did the task for her. She wiggled her toes in delight.

'What's your news?' I asked, kinder.

'We are to be serving girls at the feast. I asked the cook if we could. He said that the Saxons wanted to show off their finest in everything so naturally we could.'

'That explains why you could, not me.' I was speaking for the sake of it, to give my mind time to catch my thoughts. I would be in the hall with Rhodri and Haf and Algar.

'No it doesn't. We're both the finest.' She dropped her voice to whispers, 'It's Sara and Gwennan who are to be left out.' She carried on, saying something about old women and witches.

I was to serve Haf while she sat beside the man who had hurt me? I was to pour beer for the man who killed Tad and betrayed Viola?

'You're not listening!' Viola said.

'I am. I heard.'

'You're not smiling. It will be the stuff of tales. I've seen the food. We'll be there together to enjoy our share of the loaf.'

Her eyes were hare-bright. She could imagine nothing more wonderful in the world than to trail at the hem of fine-dressed ladies like Rowan, or catch the smile of men like Algar. She would be in the Promised Land.

I would be in the underworld. There was no other word for it.

But I couldn't let her do it alone. She couldn't take off her own shoes, let alone push off men who would want to paw her.

'That's not the end of the tale,' she said. 'I got us something special to wear. Come with me.'

She pushed herself to standing, but carried her shoes. We walked to the Welsh barn, which was empty and quiet. On her sleeping sack there was something bundled. She unrolled the cloth. Two aprons. Dyed bright rose madder. It took work to get that colour.

'Where did you get them?' I asked.

'Don't ask questions, don't hear lies,' she said gaily.

'Does the person who owns them know you have them?' They would be recognised, I was sure. I wanted no one to pay attention to me. I wanted to be unseen, unnoticed. I wanted to be like the night air itself in that hall.

'Don't worry,' she said. 'They're gifts.'

'Gifts from who?'

'I get you something nice and you pout at the world. Shut up and put it on,' Viola snapped.

'Are they from Algar? Is he here? Did you see him?'

Viola threw down the aprons. 'They are not. I haven't seen him. Not yet. But when I do I want to look the best I can, despite this –' she rested her hands on her belly – 'so stick your harp in the roof and stop complaining.'

We stared at each other. Her eyes were angry. I had made her that way. I picked up one of the aprons and pulled it over the bird-brown tunic I wore. I smoothed it flat with my palms. As I looked down I realised the dye hadn't taken evenly, there were darker streaks of red in patches.

Viola picked hers up too. 'We all have to belong to someone Mai. This baby belongs to Algar.'

I said nothing. There was nothing to say. Viola needed me, whether she knew it or not.

51

THE SUN HAD dropped into the branches of the trees and sounds had quietened. There were few voices on the wind. Perhaps the village had gone to paint and primp themselves for the feast. They would be out soon enough in high voice and high spirits.

Viola slipped her arm through mine as we walked to the bakehouse beside the feasting hall. I wondered if Haf might see me with the sister I'd chosen. Part of me hoped so, part of me never wanted to see her again.

But there was no sign of Haf or Rowan as we walked.

Viola was caught up in dreams of the evening ahead. 'There might be dancing later,' she said. 'Do you think I can dance still?'

We took the back routes through the village, rabbit paths that would get us there quicker. Soon, we weren't alone. I was surprised to see Saxon women and children, in small groups of three or four, walking against us, away from the hall. Their heads were down, the children pulled close as cloaks about them. They didn't look or speak to me as they passed. It was sure strange. Where were they going? Didn't they want to eat the food that we'd been preparing?

Perhaps they were heading to their temple. I whispered quickly to Iesu, so he would know I wasn't joining them in their pagan place.

I asked him to give me strength to stand in the hall with my enemies all about me. Viola wanted me there. Needed me. I could do this. I had lived through worse, I told myself, straightening my spine to it.

The air smelled of roasting meat, banks of hot fires, and fermented apples. There was the faint smell of men too, sweat and hair and restlessness.

'Follow me,' Viola said. Of course I did. I had spent the last six moons following her. We went into the small tent that had been thrown up beside the feast hall. The cooks and serving women were gathered like sheep in their pen.

'Viola!' It was Sara. 'You two, take ale and bread. More bread than ale if these lollin men aren't to lose their heads.'

Viola songbird-laughed, and scooped up the nearest pitcher. I grabbed one of the platters of bread – loaves I'd griddled myself that morning. Then, we headed for the gaping mouth of the hall. In the tallow light and torches, Viola had skin like soft honey and her body was round with pleasure. The roar of voices made my skin feel raw.

I wasn't ready.

At the threshold of the door, swords and axes were

lined against the wall. Some in fine scabbards, carved and painted, others bare in shades of fish-scale grey. Each was thrust down, biting into the earth.

Viola saw me looking. 'No weapons at the feast,' she said. 'Britons are the guests. The world is turned on its forehead.' Her curls shook in wonder.

She led the way inside. Rumbling notes of song and laughter filled the hall, as though the rocks of the earth had joined the chorus. Mountains of men making music. I gripped the hard edges of my platter tight. My body floated away from me, I was walking on wool, breathing cloud. Only the hard edge biting into palms kept me tied to the earth.

Were they here?

My eyes hunted for Haf, Rhodri, Gwrtheyrn, Algar.

Three tables, one for the important guests, two wings coming off it. Men sitting everywhere. Saxon and British men, side by side, one then the other. Their dress different, plaid then plain, trimmed then hemmed. Their jewellery was different, broad bands of silver at the necks of the Britons, gold and red clasps at the shoulders of the Saxons. But they made the same noise, roaring in their cups, stabbing food with their short knives, slapping greasy palms on the tables. The only women here were Welsh, here to serve.

I searched the table at the head of the hall.

I saw Horse, his face ruddy with drink. Beside him, Gwrtheyrn, silent, watching the room. Then Algar. Then

Rhodri. Then someone who looked so like Horse, he had to be his brother. The last two were talking in the way pigeons fight, with puffed-out chests and stabs of noise.

I froze. There was no sign of Haf.

Viola, clutching her pitcher close to her chest, leaned close. 'Don't be frightened,' she said, 'if it helps, remember their mams wiped their arses when they were babies.' She winked fox-sly, then moved towards the nearest table to cheers from the men who sat there.

They might have been babies once, or knee-scabbed boys, but they were men now. I forced myself to offer bread to the grabbing hands closest to me. Anwen, one of the only other girls in the hall, rushed to me, hissing, 'Horse first, Horse first. Take the bread to his table.'

I dragged my feet towards them.

What would Rhodri say when he saw me? Ghost-risen girl that I was.

Welsh was there, standing between Gwrtheyrn and Horse, carrying their words between them. The platter of bread shook in my hands. Horse took up the black, heavy-bellied bottle from the table in front of him and poured into his horn cup. Beer sloshed as his drunken hand filled too quickly. There was beer on the ground too, I could feel it seeping sticky into my soles. The table was wet with meat juice. Carved haunches of deer and boar formed small hillocks, with roast roots oozing into the blood and hot fat. Dogs scavenged the ground hungrily.

I offered my bread. My mouth too dry to speak one word, but the platter held out before me. I waited for their eyes to flash with recognition. For their mouths to fall open to see the girl Rhodri had shut away to rot, the girl with no tad, the girl who had refused to belong.

But there was nothing.

They didn't even glance my way.

Gwrtheyrn took the bread in his thick fingers, tore at it, and rushed into his next tale. Through awful Saxon he spoke of dead heroes and battles long grassed over. Pointless prattle. Horse leaned in to listen, his eyes hard, his teeth bared. Two men, still thinking of war, even as they broke bread. None looked at the girl serving them.

I left the bread platter beside the meat. They could serve themselves.

They didn't look at me. Not one of them. Was my life so little that they couldn't even see it? I was nothing more than the fly they swatted while drinking in sunshine, the vole who dived for its hole as they splashed in the river.

I stared Algar full in the face, but he didn't notice. He was watching something else. I followed his eyes. His gaze was on Viola. She moved, smiling, between the men, thick arms reaching for her and her pitcher. The feast rolled around Algar: the other men were like sailors lurching with the tide, while he stayed steady. He sipped from his horn cup, but it was Viola he was really drinking.

My heartbeat galloped in my ears. My wild breaths

tasted meat on the air. He wanted her. I could see it post-plain.

No. No. No. My heart beat the word, again and again. He

    would not

        hurt her

           again.

In that moment, Horse clapped loudly. He stood, scraping back his chair, the metal on his body glinting in the torchlight.

The whole hall hushed.

'Honoured guests!' Horse called out, 'Beloved kinsmen.' Welsh repeated the words for the Britons. Hearing British spoken aloud in that feast hall stilled the beating of my heart. It was like cool water in summer days, like soft blankets and warm food. I held back my sob.

'Welcome to my home,' Horse boomed. His dark beard made his face rock-round and massive. He spread his arms, beer spilled from his cup, but he didn't notice. 'Some of you are friends I have known for years. Others were strangers yesterday, but today we step closer together than ever before. Today we see new bonds forged between us. Our actions here tonight will become the stuff of legend. Rowan! Rowan! Where are you, girl? Bring wine.' He laughed, not able to imagine that wherever she was in the world she wouldn't come at his call.

And come she did. The door opened, letting in some

welcome cool, clear air. Then she stepped into the frame. She wasn't alone. Haf stood at her side. Between them they carried the wine cup. It was silver, and it took both pairs of hands to hold its ears.

Rowan held her head high, trying to claim her place. Haf was too busy watching her step and the cup to make sure it didn't drop. I suddenly saw her, as she used to be, carrying eggs in her folded skirts across the farmyard. They walked, side by side, like sisters. Equals. Why was she doing this?

'Come!' Horse bellowed.

He was thirty or so steps away from the door. The two girls looked so young as they walked up through the centre of the hall, avoiding the hearth and the fire, towards the top table. One slip on the greasy ground, or trip over the tail of some pork-bellied hound and the feast cup would go flying. Spilled wine would omen spilled blood. The men around them were bears and wolves. Their bodies tense, despite the celebration.

The poor girls, my heart suddenly sang.

Those poor girls who had to do as they were told just as much as I did. Even though they claimed to rule their own halls, they were as bound as any Welsh. I saw something of the danger Haf was in. Danger, I realised, she had always seen so clearly.

'My daughter!' Horse yelled. The dogs beneath his chair stirred and circled. Gwrtheyrn leaned back on the bench and smiled.

The girls made it to the top table and together, their eyes locked on each other for one scant moment; they lowered the cup onto the wood.

Horse laughed. 'Rowan!' The hall cheered. Her cheeks blushed dark rose. Horse took her forearm in his grip and pulled her close. He said something small and sly that slithered into her ear. All around, the hall toasted her, loud and loose. But I kept watching.

Rowan snatched her arm back. Her mouth hung open, fish-stupid. She reached for Haf, but Horse struck her hands. He spoke to her, spittle hitting her face. In the *bwr-lwm* I couldn't hear what he said. But she was frightened now, sure certain.

What had Horse said?

Rowan turned and walked quickly from the hall, skirts lifted so she could move faster.

Viola stepped aside to let Rowan through.

What had he said?

Haf was still in the centre of the tables, near Viola. She turned to watch Rowan go. Saw me. Stopped still. We looked at each other, surrounded by the beast-bellows of men. I tried to send her my pity, I thought it hard, over and over.

Horse kicked back his stool, sending it skittering clear. 'Now!' he yelled. His voice brought hate and war.

The reaction was in the moment.

All around the room, the Saxon men reached down to

their calves, under benches, threw aside reed mats, revealing the sax blades that had been hidden there. I heard the sound of knives unsheathed in biting bright metal. Swords. Swords where they shouldn't be. Swords in the hands of hosts. And the Britons were armed with nothing more than the tiny knives they used for eating, their swords stashed beyond the door. Before the Britons could move, the Saxons lunged.

'Haf!' I yelled. 'Viola!'

I saw Haf look wildly around at the top table. The cup fell. Wine splashed the front of her dress.

No. Not wine.

Rhodri fell forward, clutching his neck. Red ran through his fingers. He was bibbed in blood. His beard dripped with it. Algar stood beside him, his sword red. Horse punched metal into men. Gwrtheyrn hit back with his short knife, the wooden boards, the bench, anything he could reach. He landed blows, bruises and gashes, but it was nothing to the savagery of the Saxons. They yelled battle cries.

Flashes of blades in fire flame. Meat chopped from bone. Screams and screams as unarmed men fell.

'Viola! Haf!'

I couldn't see them now. They were lost behind the wall of writhing bodies.

I crouched down, at the level of the dogs. I saw one black hound lick at bloody puddles. I covered my face, but my ears were still open. This room of men was full of slaughter.

Haf.

Viola.

They were both in here somewhere.

Men wanting blood didn't care who supplied it. I forced my hands down. I had to find my sisters. One of the Britons was inches from me, his eyes open. The wound on his side had almost cut him in two. But he wasn't dead, not yet. His eyes screamed at me, to help, to stop the pain. His lips tried to form words.

There was nothing I could do. Death was his only help now.

My back scraped up the wall.

'Sax-on! Sax-on!' The cry began with one voice, but others joined in, and quickly. It was the beat of war drums, the weight of hammers on anvils, it was the sound of men at their worst.

Betrayal.

They were traitors. I saw clearly what had been done. Horse had gathered the best and brightest of the Britons and slaughtered them in their cups. It had been done so swiftly, there was little time to fight back. Horse and his men were barely scratched. He would be devilled to the clouds for this.

My feet were wet. I looked down. The Briton was dead, his blood pooling around my shoes, dark and sticky.

The cheers were louder. 'Sax-on, Sax-on, Sax-on!' Blades clashed in celebration. War music. The smell of hot blood, like iron newly forged, filled the air.

At the high table, Horse yelled for rope. Gwrtheyrn lived! And was struggling to free himself. It was Algar that handed the rope to Horse. Gwrtheyrn swore and cursed, his lips spitting blood. But he was soon bound.

Then, Horse leaped up onto the table at the head of the hall. 'Saxons!' he yelled.

The clamouring quieted. Every face was demonic. Red with effort, red with blood, red with hate. They were men no longer.

Where was Haf? Where was Viola? I tried to see past the demons.

'Saxons!' Horse went on. 'Tonight has changed everything. When we woke this morning we were mice nibbling at the edges of this land. Tonight we sleep as lions. The boldest Britons for one hundred miles at all points are no more.'

The room rang with cheers.

I keened. Whimpering.

Where was Viola?

'Tonight has brought the end of our petty skirmishes, the end of our humiliations at the hands of the hill folk. We will rule from the western beaches to the eastern shore. This land is Saxon!'

The cheers were deafening.

I forced my feet to move. Edged along the side wall, back pressed against the fresh wood. I looked wildly. Men robed in red stood to honour Horse, red swords held high. At their feet, or tossed across the table, or slumped in their seats, were the corn-doll bodies of dead Britons. Wounds dripped. Folds of flesh flapped from bone. Would the Saxons turn on their slaves too? Where were the Welsh men? Were they safe?

I had to push worry for Oak aside.

Haf.

Viola.

They were what mattered. They were here, somewhere, in this carnage.

Then I saw them. Both still living. Arms around each other, heads pressed tight together, crouched low to the ground with the dogs under the far table.

Viola must have grabbed for Haf in the *bwr-lwm*. Or Haf grabbed for Viola. They had found each other. Thank Iesu and the Father. They clung limpet-tight to each other, their dark and mouse hair tumbled loose, hiding their faces. They looked so small. My sisters.

I wanted to reach them, to sweep them both from this place, but I dared not move. How had this happened?

Horse clapped his hands. 'Algar, take this one and the girl. Keep them safe.'

The leader of the Britons stood all alone now. His men, dead. Rhodri, dead.

Other hands pulled bodies aside, searching for Haf. She was found in moments. She clung to Viola, but was wrenched up.

No.

No.

Not my sister.

Haf and Gwrtheyrn were dragged from the room and led out into the night.

52

SUMMER SOLSTICE, AD455,
MORNING.

VIOLA SITS WITH her baby while I find all the things she has squirrelled away in every hole and corner of the Welsh barn.

'Check the woodpile for dried fruit,' she says. 'And I sewed lengths of linen and wool into the seam of the bed Gwennan sleeps on. Oh, and don't forget my comb. It's in the gap between that wall plank there.' She points while I winkle out the comb.

'Isn't this one that Rowan threw out last month?' I ask, I recognise the shape of the snapped teeth where the bone was trimmed too thin.

Viola winks. 'She threw it, but it didn't land far.'

I smile. Viola could find fish in grey water. We will be all right on the road together.

It's hard to say goodbye to Sara. After our days and nights of sorrows, this is one more too many. I almost change my mind as I hold her tight.

'Don't cry.' Sara wipes her own tears. 'The day is long, but night will come and we will all rest.'

Viola holds her too, the baby cradled gently between them.

Then, we leave. The leather door flaps closed and we blink in the early morning light. The poorer Saxon halls and the workroom are close to us. Mist rises with the sun, softening their edges.

But there is the smell of burning that floats nearby too, it will stain the walls for moons to come. I feel Viola stiffen.

'Don't look,' I tell her. 'Don't let the baby see.'

'Where are the funeral pyres? Do you know?'

'At the head of the village, before the path. We don't need to go that way.'

She pulls the baby close, so his head is held at her neck, warm and soft. I hope it's enough to keep him quiet too. I have no doubt that bloodlust still walks through these woods, men drunk on ale and knife-work.

53

IN MOMENTS ALL signs of the wedding feast were gone from the hall. The tables and benches had been heaved aside. Haf had been taken. Viola was curled on the floor, her hands around her head. The bodies of the men who had sung and drank there were dragged outside. Someone pushed me to help, but my hands felt as though they had become part of the wall, I couldn't move.

Around me, I heard Welsh women crying, gasping for breath. The food they'd been serving had been dropped for the dogs, who fought with snarling teeth for the morsels.

The Britons, who had been guests just moments before, were corpses.

My mind raged to understand.

Some of the younger Saxon men clapped each other on the back. Proud of the job they'd done. Proud of the slaughter. Some older men looked grim-faced and angry. One or two patted down the bodies of the dead, looking for trinkets or silver.

Where was Haf? Where had they taken her? I was sure that the horrors of the night weren't over.

The hall emptied fast. The shouts of the Saxon men came from outside now, spreading like plague in the night.

Oak crept into the hall. He looked old, struck bent with grief. He saw me and staggered closer.

'You should leave here,' he said. 'It's no place for you.'

'Where were you?' I whispered.

'They shut the Welsh men in the barn. But I heard screams and pushed my way out. What did they do? What did they do?' His bright new hall smelled of blood and shit and vomit.

'Viola!' he said, spotting her shivering on the ground, her tunic and apron wet with beer or blood or piss. Black on red, I couldn't tell. Oak slipped his hands under her and hoisted her to her feet. She clung to him.

'Take her and get away from here,' he told me.

'To the Welsh barn?'

'No. Listen to those men.' Outside, the full-throated cheers of the young Saxons carried like wolf-baying on the wind. Bloodlust. 'It isn't safe for anyone out there, British, or Welsh, they'll see no difference. Go to the woods. Hide like deer do in the short months.'

I shouldered Viola, let her lean on me. She kept looking back at the place where Algar had been sitting. At the blood splattered all around the spot.

'What about you?' I asked Oak.

'I'll see there's none of ours left in the village, then I'll hide too. It will take days for this Saxon heat to cool.'

What about Haf? What of her? But Viola could hardly stand. I had to get her safe and then I'd worry about my other sister.

I tugged and pulled at Viola. We had to hide. Oak was right, there was only safety in silence and stillness. Viola took one step, then another, then we were both moving. Away from the feast hall, following the path we had come down earlier that night when we had seen Saxon women heading away from the hall.

'They must have known,' I said softly to Viola.

'Who?'

'The Saxon women. They were taking their children away from the feast. They let us walk right in like calves to slaughter.'

Viola didn't answer. Walking took all the strength she had. She kept her free arm wrapped around her stomach.

How could they let us walk into danger like that? Even if we were Welsh – slaves – we were just girls. Just girls! As we passed the Saxon halls, closed-up and dark, I wished that embers would roll from the hearths and burn every last one to the ground.

'Let's make for the trees. Hurry.' In the wood, the trunks and branches were solid black, blocking starlight. Leaves rustled all about. Were people there, hiding? Or the scare-bod ghosts of the slaughtered Britons?

'It hurts,' Viola said.

'I know.'

Where could we go? We might find somewhere to hide amongst the roots or brambles. But Haf was still missing, and I was walking away from her.

'I need to get you to Anwen or Sara,' I told Viola.

'What about you?'

'Let's just find them,' I told her.

How could I find them in the dark? Branches cracked and beasts yowled and I couldn't see where nightmares stopped and the real world began.

'The temple,' Viola said. 'The women will be at the temple.'

Of course. Where their demon gods would watch over them.

'Come,' the word fell rock-heavy from my mouth. My feet remembered the path. I was barely thinking. I kept seeing Rhodri fall facedown, his neck torn, the blood dripping from his beard.

And Haf. She'd left the hall alive, I'd seen it. But what then? Where was she now? I couldn't imagine that they'd let her live.

I cared. I cared despite her cruelty in choosing the camp over me. She was my sister, and she was just trying to live in this world that wasn't made for her.

The temple was close now. I heard the murmur of voices, and someone hushed their crying baby. We weren't the only ones seeking safety, it seemed.

The black shapes in the darkness were huddled like

cattle under the hanging leather walls of the temple. The storm had hit and they were taking shelter wherever they could. The wives, the children, the lovers, the chattels of the men who had massacred their guests.

The horror of it hit me in another wave. Who would break the guest-bonds so wantonly? It was evil.

Viola stepped out of my grip now we were within the temple bounds. There were other Welsh here, I could see familiar faces in the starlight. Each one marked with fear and horror. We had thought to see Rowan married, but instead it had been slaughter. Was she with her father now? Were they gloating?

'Viola.' I spoke her name the way I might speak to injured animals. 'Viola, you can rest here.'

Her eyes sparkled, wet. 'It hurts,' she said again.

'I'm going to find someone for you to sit with. Someone safe.'

'Where are you going?' she asked, her voice frail as spring frost.

'I want to see what's happening in the village.'

'Why? It isn't safe. It can't be.'

'Haf,' I said. 'I want to know, if I'm . . . alone now.'

Viola wrapped her arms around me, pulling me against the warmth of her full body. 'You're not alone,' she said fiercely.

We searched the temple ground. The huddled people all looked the same, Saxon or Welsh, it made no difference – they were women, children and old men all broken with fear. We looked long and late before we found Sara. Her grey hair hung free, she had lost her shawl somewhere and was shivering without it. She sat on the bare earth of the temple ground. This earth that men fought over.

'Sara?' I whispered.

She looked up. Her face shone with tears, streaked against black smears of smoke and fire.

'Are you hurt?' I asked her.

She didn't reply, but shrugged as though she knew nought about it.

'Viola's here. Will you watch her?' I lowered Viola down to sit beside Sara. She felt so frail in my arms. It was as though the smallest breeze would float her to the green isle. Sara wrapped her arms around Viola and *hushed* into her hair.

'Just watch her for me, please?' I asked Sara. It wasn't clear which of the two needed the most caring for, so I hoped they would serve as strength for each other. I had none left to give. Not while Haf might be dead.

I left them under the loose folds of the temple ceiling, taking refuge beneath its bat-wings. More people had come, like floodwater, into the clearing. I beat through bramble, avoiding others on my way back to the village.

As I neared the place in the woods where the tree of traitors stood, I heard male voices, shouting at each other, barking wolf-hungry. What were Saxon men doing near the tree of traitors? I felt fear drip down the bones of my back. Were they hunting for any Welsh, not just the men who had come with Gwrtheyrn? Had someone tried to run away in the chaos and been caught?

I had to know. I had to run and warn Sara and Viola if the men were coming for the Welsh.

I shrank down into my shoulders, bent low, and followed the sound of the voices. Roots, thick as thighs, tried to trip me. Rough bark, black with lichen, grazed my hands as I scrambled through the trees. The voices grew louder, but they weren't the victory-filled war cries I'd heard earlier. These were barked orders, someone had his mind fixed on his task and was whipping the others along.

I could see the open space between the trees, though I kept to the shadows.

Flames lit the scene, bright as beacon fires. Ten or more burning branches hissed and spat sparks. I could smell the tallow fat they'd been dipped in. The branches had been set in the ground around the edges of the space. Within the circle of flames, the men were at work. Their bodies were black against the yellow light, but I could tell that the man in charge was Horse. The bulging muscles at his neck and shoulders were more beast than man.

I was right at the edge of the light now, kept in shadows by the trees, but close enough to be seen if anyone happened to look my way. No one did, they were all focused on the task Horse had given them.

They were preparing the tree.

Its unnatural trunk stretched along the ground then twisted up into the black canopy. Its roots were disc-spread, like the moon rising over the night horizon. In the torchlight the roots glowed, polished to sheen by years of touching. They stood as tall as any man.

Ropes had been tied to four of the thickest roots. Blocks of thick wood had been placed to be the stage on which the victim would stand. Two men cleared the old leaf litter.

Someone would die on the tree tonight.

Gwrtheyrn.

And Haf? What of her? I had to know. I dropped to all fours. My knees pressed through the fabric of my apron into the damp earth. My fingers and palms too. I kept myself small and secret, and edged as close as I dared to the fallen tree.

Horse yelled instructions in his booming voice. 'More rope. We need two lengths.'

'Yes, Horse,' his men leaped to it.

I shrank low, so my chest was on the ground, cold against my heart.

'The Lord of the Britons is to watch,' Horse shouted. 'The woman, the fool they called wise, she is to die first.'

They were past me and onto the forest path before I dared move. Haf. He was talking about Haf.

I'd not thought there was anything worse to feel, I believed that I was numb to pain. But I was wrong. Blackness opened up inside me like night filling my chest. Haf was in terrible, terrible danger. The tree of traitors was pain and fear and death. It would come slow, so slow.

I couldn't let that happen. Whatever else I did, I would not let Haf die like that.

54

How could it be stopped?

I had to start by moving. I was more rock than girl by now, the cold earth beneath my chest and the fear within it had me frozen. But there was something within me stronger than both of those things – love for Haf. It hit me like charging cattle. It was hot and raw and couldn't be ignored.

I staggered to my knees. The blood in my veins beat her name, over and over, *my Haf, my Haf.*

Where was she?

Horse had told the men to fetch her. So she wasn't here, near the tree, watching. She must be back in the village, held under the eyes and blades of the Saxon men. But where? There were so many halls in the village, many and more of them. She could be shut up in the home of any of the Saxon families.

Though, would they take her? The shame of the thing was strong. They had murdered their guests. Their crime was terrible. Even their pagan gods would be angry. Would they take Haf into their homes with their one-eyed god watching?

Where else was there?

The halls that Oak had built over the summer.

They were new and strong but had no hearths to make them homes yet.

I plunged back into the cover of the trees to the village. I stopped behind the Welsh barn, and watched. There were no women or children, or even animals to be seen. The few people on the paths were all thick-muscled, square, with hair and beards covering their faces and dark splashes on their clothes.

I moved from doorway to eaves to chicken coop and byre, pressing myself into the dark spaces of the night. I watched, hunting for any clue that would lead me to her.

The men I saw were in pairs, I realised. They strode like fighters, elbows out, with spears, swords, even clubs and sickles clutched tight. Their torches held up to the sky, watchful. The whole village had had orders and were keeping to them.

The new halls were to the north on the hill. Just yesterday I would have run to them, with my heart clear. But not now. Now I crept up like the mouse who fears owls above, my spine curved low, my head down, hoping to stay hidden. I peered around the edge of one of the old halls.

I saw pin-straightaway that my guess was right. In front of one of the new halls, four men stood. Four men. On this night, when the bonds of trust had been broken so badly, Horse would only spare so many men for the most important of reasons. Haf, or Gwrtheyrn, or both, were in that hall. Its door and windows were shut tight, with wooden planks hastily nailed across them. The dawn was still far from breaking, but the moon was full. In the silver light I could see dark stains on their clothes and hands. Blood drying to copper flakes.

Killers. Killers all.

My body burst with hate. And fear. It wanted to run, my feet felt hare-nimble and eager to flee. But I breathed, once, twice, three times, until I was sure my feet wouldn't betray me.

I had to get past the guards. If I were Viola, I would saunter up with light words of gossip or handfuls of honeyed fruit. If I were Haf I might weave cunning tales to convince them. If I were Rowan, I could use my family name and have them stand aside.

But I was Mai. Farm girl, runaway, slave, mouse. What could I do?

It seemed so hopeless.

I'd lost Mam and Tad and the only real home I'd known. Haf was all that was left of that life. I had to save her.

How?

I crouched in the grass and clung to the edge of the building. I stared at the ground, where the wall met the dark earth.

It was built so stout and strong. I'd seen Oak do it with

my own eyes. From digging the shallow pit below the floor to nailing the shingles to the roof, I'd watched it all.

The pit!

The space beneath the floor in all the halls. Perhaps I could get inside by going under the wall and crawling under the floor.

If I had something to dig with.

I had broken into guarded buildings before. At the camp on the hill, all those months ago, I'd got into the store. Bryn had shown me. It had been easier that time, there had been just one guard, and he had no trouble in mind. And Bryn had prepared the way.

But here I would be the mouse making its nest in the cat-fur.

It was much more risky.

Oak kept his tools in his workroom. It wasn't far and it only took moments to run there and find something I could use – I didn't know its name, but it was part axe, part shovel. It might be noisy.

The guards would hear. Unless their ears were filled with something else.

I stopped by the byre nearest to the new hall. Two or three goats were bleating sadly inside. They had missed their last milking, no doubt. Unhappy goats wore their mood on their foreheads. I worked at the gate clasp quickly. The wicker was woven in neat patterns by someone with nimble fingers and was tight enough to keep out draughts and rain, but the catch was simple; it opened easily. I ducked behind the open gate. The miserable goats mewed and hawed their way towards the first people they could see – the guards.

'Hey, get back.'

'You grab it.'

'Get off my tunic.'

'Hold it. Hold it!'

Their eyes were on the beasts. So, I raced with my digging tool to the back, where the new hall faced the hill. The ground was damp in the shade. My work was frantic, more scraping than digging. But the noise was gentle compared to the goats. Earth shifted enough for me to scrabble space for me on my worm belly. I tore the gap wider with my fingers. Then the ground gave way and dirt fell into the pit. I was in, below the floor. The drop into the crawl space was short. I landed on dry, musty dirt, with floorboards above my head. I had to stay on my hands and knees, there wasn't room to walk any way other than dog-like.

There was little light, maybe from one torch in the room above, not more. It glowed, hair-weak, between the boards. My eyes sucked up the yellow glimmer thirstily, until I could see enough to move. I heard the creak of someone walking above me, shadows passed over the cracks.

Was it them? I paused, waited. Then I heard Haf speak! Her words were muffled, but the voice was definitely hers.

I had to reach her before the Saxons saw me and we all ended up on the tree of traitors.

I lay with my back firm on the ground and my knees bent enough to get my shoes against one of the floorboards. I pushed with my thighs. The board creaked. I pushed again. I felt it give. Then I heard scrabbling above me. Fingernails on wood. Someone helping me. I doubled my efforts. Pushed again. With the groan of wood shifting against wood, the board lifted.

I looked up, mole-wary. Two pairs of eyes looked down at me – Haf and Gwrtheyrn. Their faces were streaked with blood and pain, but they were alive. I was in time.

'Mai!' There was such love in that word that my breath jammed in my throat. I forced the lump down. There was no time for feeling.

The gap I had made was wide enough for my head and shoulders, with wriggling.

Haf hurried to pull me up. Her arms were open, reaching for me. I took her hand. She pulled me close and breathed against my cheek, her heart beat against my chest, her sinews pulled me tight as rope knots.

'You're alive,' she whispered. 'I couldn't see you. In all that death I thought I'd lost you.'

'I'm here,' I said. The lump had come back. 'We have to go. Now.'

'Forgive me for what I said. I have to say it now in case there's no time later. Forgive me.'

'*Isht*, there will be time,' I said. 'Keep quiet. The guards.'

Gwrtheyrn stood by the weak torch. He was as dark and hollowed as charcoaled wood. There were blue-black bruises beneath his eyes. His shoulders were round, like boulders in the riverbed, worn down by care. The man who had laughed in his camp on the hill was gone. His eyes flitted from me to Haf and back again. 'My men?' Gwrtheyrn asked. 'Have you seen any of my men?'

'Dead,' I said. 'Quiet.' I didn't want to even look at him more than I had to. It was Haf I was here to save.

His head dropped to his chest. Turned away from us both.

Haf glanced past me, at the hole in the floor where I'd appeared. I kept tight hold of her hand as I urged her to the gap. She took two or three faltering steps. Then stopped and looked back at Gwrtheyrn.

'Mai,' Haf said, 'him too.'

'Leave him, it's him they want really, not you.'

Haf half-smiled. 'Mai. Please. For the people of the camp, if not for me. The British have lost so much tonight.'

I looked her in the life of her eye. I sighed, 'He can come. If he can fit. But you go first. I mean it. Go!'

Haf nodded. She lowered herself silently into the black pit I'd made in the floor. Her skirts caught around her hips, but she forced her way. I followed. It seemed darker than before, with her body blocking the moonlight. I could hear, but not see, Gwrtheyrn struggle behind me.

The space was too small for him. He worked and worried the wood that wedged him still. I could hear it crack and warp. I hoped the guards outside had poor hearing.

Finally the wood gave way. The crack was loud. Gwrtheyrn was through, but only guards horn-deaf wouldn't have heard. *Great fat lump of man*, I cursed him to the clouds and back.

'Haf, move!' I whispered.

On all fours, I rushed to the heel of the wall and the hole, where we were delivered from the darkness into the silver grey of night. Haf was beside me, Gwrtheyrn struggled behind.

From inside the hall, I heard wood squealing against wood, heavy thumps, curses. They'd opened the door.

'They're coming!'

I looked down the hill, towards the wood. There were Saxon halls between us and the safety of cover. Could we all three run across and bury ourselves amongst the branches?

'You go first,' I said. The first person across would have the best chance of escape. Even if they were spotted, they would have the head-start. Gwrtheyrn could go last.

She sim-sammed on the spot, unable to decide. I knew she had counted the same sum. But there was no time to argue. I pushed her hard. 'Run!' Haf took aim with her eyes, and ran.

She crossed the open space lightly and soundlessly.

I waited one breath, then followed. I ran like the hare before the hounds. Head down. Feet pounding. Arms beating out the pace. *Run. Run. Run little mouse. The dogs are coming.* I didn't look left or right. The sounds of shouting were faint but furious.

The trees opened their arms to me. I plunged into the brush, rattling twigs and bough. I dropped, under canopy and shadow. Somewhere birds shrieked in alarm. Haf found me, pulling me close as though she wished to never part.

We both peeked between brambles at the hall on the hill. I couldn't see Gwrtheyrn at all.

Then there was movement across the open space. Lumbering, heavy, crashing into the trees. Damn Gwrtheyrn. He was too big, too loud. He would get us killed.

'I'm here,' he said, reaching us.

'Good,' Haf replied. 'Now we better run.' Haf grabbed my hand, tore through the bushes, with that great clobyn smashing his way behind us. Away from the hall. Dragging, dropping, twisting from even the rabbit paths that cut the forest floor. I felt sharp rips, slashes to my face, hair, clothes.

Wood snapped, branches shook behind us.

I glanced over my shoulder.

They were following us. Our trail was clear, even in the dark – Haf was making us easier to hunt, not harder.

Any fool with eyes could see the path we were tearing. Gwrtheyrn made it worse: breaking it wider with his great hulking body.

We were all going to be strapped to the tree.

We had to be Welsh, not Britons. Mice, not wolves.

We had to hide in plain sight. The forest couldn't hide us, but the crowd could.

Hope came unwelcome, dangerous. If we could get to the temple, then we could sit still and quiet with the others and not be discovered. The Saxons were looking for warriors. We had to be weasels.

'Stop,' I told Haf.

I watched the trees; I listened. The cries of the Saxon men were the boldest noises in the air, but they weren't the only ones; the earliest birds sang and other animals crept through the dry leaves and scrub. And, to our right, the song of water. The stream. It would lead us to the temple.

'This way!' I told her.

Her glance lasted no time, but in it I saw irritation with me and joy that I was there at all, the sort of glance that only sisters share. My heart twisted again.

Haf followed my wake, crashing through the tangle of ivy and briar that bound the route. Gwrtheyrn was behind us too.

If he lived and Haf died, so help me I would flay his bones clean.

The stream was louder. We slithered down the bank, thick with wild garlic and dead bluebells, into the freezing water. It sloshed over my ankles and knees, my tunic sucked it up, weighing me down. My hands splashed to catch me. Rocks night-green under fingers. More splashing as the others slid in beside me. I followed the flow of the water, pulled with it, as though it wanted us to find our way. *Go on, go on*, it said as it gurgled over stones.

Gwrtheyrn slithered and slid in the water, splashing on all fours. He fell, gasped in pain. 'My ankle,' he said.

Haf stopped, looking back. 'You're hurt?'

'It's nothing,' he said. He stood and took two steps. But his knee gave way and he landed, hard, in the water.

Gwrtheyrn looked Haf full in the eye. She was pinned still, shaking like pine in the wind.

'Go,' he told her. 'Go, now!'

'I can't leave you,' Haf told him. 'Who will lead the camp?'

'You can and you will. Find Bryn. Stay safe.'

'I won't leave you. Mai, help me.' She splashed to his side.

Gwrtheyrn struggled to standing and pushed Haf away. 'You'll go because I'm your lord and I order you to. Tell the Britons the story of what happened here. Then you lead them, keep them safe.'

The shouts of Saxon men were louder now. We had to

get to the temple and Haf had to sit amongst the Welsh with her eyes meek and her hands folded. Now.

I grabbed her arm and stumble-pulled her into the stream-water. She mewled. But let herself move.

The stream turned and twisted through the trees and in no time, Gwrtheyrn was finally left behind.

55

SUMMER SOLSTICE, AD455,
MORNING.

'OAK KEEPS HIS coracle on the near bank, downstream from the washing spot,' I say.

Viola nods. Her skin is grey. She walks slow and uncertain, with the baby swaddled in her arms. I must remember how weak she is.

Behind us, the village is horrible-quiet, save for the crack and drop of embers. I imagine bones burning, collapsing down on themselves.

We step softly. The sun gallops into the sky. Viola has left her red-stained shoes behind. We're both barefoot. I'm glad of it. The morning earth is warm on my toes. The trees seem to welcome us. We can hide and creep from each trunk to the next, like shrews under the *goodie-hoo* call of the owl.

'Will we survive?' Viola asks me uncertainly.

'Me and you? Of course we will. This isn't the end for us. And the baby is only just beginning.'

She steps onto ground wet with stream-water. Her feet sink into the mud. I reach out to steady her. She hugs the baby tight.

'We can't call him the baby. He needs to know his name.'

'What will you call him?' I ask.

She doesn't answer straight away. Instead she picks her way carefully over

Tree-root troughs of rain run-off

Puddles. Mud brown but for

Glint-lights, golden with sun spots.

I squelch my way through the dank forest floor behind her. The sounds sooth me. The *hip-hip-hip* of jays and low ground-rustle of late-sleeping thornhogs are fondly familiar.

What can she call the baby, I wonder. He is Saxon, Welsh, Roman – and none of those.

He's his own child now.

'Durwyn,' she says. 'His name is Durwyn.'

It is good. The word is Saxon, 'dear one', but Welsh too, 'pure metal'.

She sees my smile and knows my thoughts. 'It has another meaning. Latin, the tongue of the Romans. I don't know much, just words my grandmother shared. "Durven" means "hard arrival".'

The edge of the stream is in sight and I help Viola and Durwyn, the strong, beloved child who arrived to hardship, step into the cold water. He can choose what his name means. That is our gift to him.

The coracle Oak uses to fish is tied to one of the thick curling roots of his namesake. We will be on our way soon.

56

SUMMER SOLSTICE-EVE, AD455, LATE NIGHT

'QUICKLY.' MY LEGS were heavy with stream-water, but I forced them on. Willows maiden-trailed their branches in the water, hiding us from view. We might get to the temple to hide. We might.

Haf stumbled, splashing hard onto the stream-bed.

'Get up,' I told her.

She sobbed. Crying for Gwrtheyrn, I guessed.

'They'll find him, won't they?' she asked. I was right.

'They might. Get up. We have to keep moving, Haf.'

'What will they do to him?'

'Get up,' I said, more softly this time. I put my hands about her waist. Her ribs were like sticks under my fingers. She was straw-doll light. She kept walking along the stream, watching over her shoulder.

'He can't die,' she said. 'What will happen to all the people at the camp? Their best men gone. No leader.'

'He said you were to lead,' I reminded her. 'Why are you so worried about them anyway?' I burned again. Angry at the choice she had made.

'After you left they were all I had. Don't you understand that?'

I stumbled in the water. Of course I understood. I felt the same way about Viola. Even about Sara and Oak. They felt like family after all these months of taking care of each other. I said nothing.

I heard fires now, and smelled smoke on the air. We were close to the temple, and the tree of traitors further into the woods. We'd be damp and dirty, but I hoped there were still cattle herds of women and children and Welsh men we might join. Hiding in plain sight. It was the only way to stay alive.

'This way.' I led her up the bank. Her face was mud-splattered. I took off my apron and tied it about her, hiding her feast clothes. She looked half-way Welsh.

As we trailed into the temple grove, my skin shivered with cold. I could taste mud in my mouth. I would never be warm or rested again. Groups of people sat like weeds on the ground.

'We need to find Viola and Sara,' I said.

Haf gazed about her in horror at the black strips of tent, the carved roots and painted signs. 'What is this place?' she whispered. 'The bad man walks here.'

She went to cross herself. I caught her hand before she did. 'We'll be safe, as long as they don't look too hard at you. Don't talk. They expect us to speak Saxon. No British. Understand?'

I kept hold of her hand. It was cold; corpse-flesh walking.

Few about us talked. The night and its events were still too raw. Babies cried here and there and mothers hushed them. I led the way to where I'd left Viola with Sara.

They were still there.

And something was wrong.

Viola was pale as the setting moon. Her face was slick with sweat, despite the chill.

Sara looked up at our approach. 'Grief has come to greet us. The baby is coming,' she said. 'It's coming too soon.' Her eyes rested on Haf. 'What in the name of the Father is she doing here? Are you trying to hunt trouble?'

Viola gasped. 'I don't want the baby to die. Is it dying?'

My heart twisted like storm-birds. My poor Viola.

'*Isht*,' Sara said. 'You're not dying.'

Haf leaned in close to my ear. 'Is her baby coming? She needs to be somewhere safe.'

Sara tutted again. She said in Saxon, 'Of course she needs to be somewhere safe. Mai, tell that girl to keep quiet. As if there isn't enough to think about without her drawing unwanted eyes. She has to go.'

Go? Where would Haf go? My plan had got no further than just hiding here.

Haf looked from Sara and Viola to me and back again. 'She thinks I'm putting you in danger, doesn't she?' Haf asked, feather-soft. 'She's right. I am. I should leave.'

'No!' The British word came out of my mouth too loud. Sara threw up her hands. 'No,' I said, more quietly. 'Haf, I've only just got you back.'

'I can't stay, but you could come with me,' Haf said.

Leave?

Viola moaned and drew her knees in to her chest.

'Help me get her up,' Sara said. 'She can't stay outdoors in the dark. We'll take her to the Welsh barn.'

'Is it safe?' I asked.

'Nowhere's safe,' Sara said. 'Not while that one's with us.'

Sara shepherded us, whispering beguiling words to Viola, telling her she would be well. The unhappy crowd shuffled aside, letting us pass.

Viola spread her weight between us, but even so, it was hard for her to walk. The pain made her stop every few moments and gasp as though gales whipped her breath away.

We were on the path that ran beside the stream, on our way to the Welsh barn by the quickest route, when we heard the sound of struggling and cursing. One thump of male fist on flesh.

Haf stopped. Even Sara looked for the source of the sounds in the starlight.

Then the branches nearest the stream parted. Gwrtheyrn limped through. His arms held, tied, behind him. New blood on his cheeks and chin. His captor walked behind. Algar.

I felt tethered to the ground, unable to walk in any direction.

Algar too stopped, and stared at our sorry little group. In the starlight, I wasn't sure certain that he knew me, or Haf. But he recognised one of us. 'Viola?' he said.

Her head rose slowly, her breath still came in painful gasps. I felt her stiffen against my hands. Did she still want him? Did she still love him?

Viola spat on the ground, the white glob splattering the leaf fall at his feet. 'Stay away from me, oath-breaker,' Viola said. 'Guest-killer!'

She was crying, I realised.

'I know you,' Haf said. Her voice came from well-bottom depths. Terrible slow anger in each sound.

'I know you too,' he said, replying in British.

'You killed Rhodri. You killed my father,' Haf said, her voice flint-hard with hate.

Algar pushed Gwrtheyrn forward. His bound hands and hurt ankle made him stagger and fall to his knees. He cursed angrily. But Algar grinned. 'You'll lose this one too. He'll be tied limb to limb, his tongue cut from his mouth. And you too. You'll die in this village. So will your little sister for helping you escape.'

He looked all ready to shout for aid, to call Saxons to come running to the spot to capture us all.

But Viola stepped right up close to him, her belly between them. '*Hündin*,' she called him. '*Bradwr*.'

Dark anger storm-scudded across his face. He raised his hand, knuckles outwards, and struck. The crack of his hand hitting her cheek drew gasps from us all. Viola mewed with pain.

Haf moved first. She reached to my waist and the short knife that hung there, small but fine edged, fury laden.

She drew it.

And lunged at him in one motion.

Algar cried out.

The sound was cut short.

The knife in his neck.

Redbeard raw.

All in the space of

one

breath.

In the moonlight and starlight, silver through the trees, I saw Algar fall, face forward.

Haf wiped the short knife on the skirt of her apron. It joined the other smears of mud and dirt.

Viola screamed. It was wild and wolf-like. More animal howl than woman. Somewhere, deep in the woods, wolves howled in reply.

And Algar drained blood into the good, good earth.

57

WE STOOD FOR only one or two heartbeats, with Algar on the ground between us. But it felt as though acorns dropped and grew into oaks and died while we watched the corpse with the knife wound in his neck. Gwrtheyrn, Viola, Sara, Haf and me, watching his blood run into the ground. There were no signs of Saxons or Welsh in the trees around us, but they can't have been far away.

It was Viola who made us move. She cried and doubled over in pain.

'We have to get her inside,' Sara said.

'Take her,' I said. 'Go on. It isn't far now. I'll join you.'

'Where are you going?' Viola asked.

'The Saxons can't find this –' I waved at the body on the ground – 'they'll blame us all.'

'Come.' Sara took Viola around her waist and arm-slung swayed her back towards the village. They held each other up, it seemed to me as I watched them go.

Then, all my mind was on Haf. 'People will pass this way. We need to hide him. And you.'

Gwrtheyrn turned so Haf could untie him.

I pulled at the tunic Algar wore. 'Help me get this off.'

'Why?' Haf bent to help.

'If Gwrtheyrn looks Saxon you might get out of here alive. Take his undershirt too. Stuff it under your apron. From afar you might pass for Viola. Cover your hair.'

She cut her underskirt and tied her hair beneath the torn fabric. In moments, Algar wore nothing but loose trews, and Gwrtheyrn and Haf might pass for Saxon and Welsh, if no one looked too closely.

'Roll him into the briar,' Gwrtheyrn said.

We three put our arms and shoulders into shifting him. Algar was heavy, and stank of ale and piss and dried blood. He was rotten already. And he had brought this on himself. I saw no question there. Any guilt at his death should be light-worn, and floating. We pushed him so that the tangle of thorns hid him from glancing eyes.

'It's well-done,' Gwrtheyrn said.

'Come. Quickly,' I said. 'The path out of the village rises beside the stream.'

They moved ahead of me. Gwrtheyrn hobbling on his injured foot. I wondered how far he could run before being caught again.

'We don't have to go far,' Haf said, reading my thoughts like the sister she was. 'Bryn should be to the south, not even one morning of walking away.'

'Bryn?'

'Aye,' Gwrtheyrn replied. 'It was Rhodri who suggested

it. He didn't trust the Saxons.' I heard his voice waver. Tears in his throat too. 'Rhodri told his boy to wait, with his horse close by, for news. Just in case anything was to happen.'

'So you can escape? If you make it to Bryn?' I asked.

But Haf slowed. Turned. 'What do you mean, *you*? *You* can escape? *We* can escape. You're coming with us.'

The trees overhead whispered in the wind and I feared it was the voice of the Saxons closing in. I hurried her along the rabbit paths that cut the grass beside the stream. 'Don't stop walking.'

She let Gwrtheyrn walk ahead, almost out of hearing. 'Mai,' my sister said, 'tell me what you mean.'

The lump in my throat was solid and painful.

'The girl back there, Viola, she's your friend?' Haf asked.

I didn't reply. She was more than my friend, and always would be.

'You'll miss her when you come with us, is that it?' Haf asked.

'No. I'm not coming.' I had made my decision, though I wasn't sure when, or how. 'I'm going back.'

'Back there? To those monsters?'

'Yes. To them. Viola has no one now. You have Gwrtheyrn and Bryn. Viola needs me. If the baby lives. If she lives when it's born.'

I couldn't leave Viola. I'd seen, over the last two days,

that Haf was grown. She was so strong, so brave. She would be grieved without me, but she would flourish in the end.

'But what about us? Me and you?' Haf had tears on her cheeks.

'I'll know you're alive. That has to be enough. It's more than I expected to have. And the camp needs you.'

The sound of the water and woods seemed so ordinary. Small birds sang. The moon moved towards setting. All so ordinary, as I said goodbye to my sister.

'You really mean to stay?'

I nodded.

'And I really have to go.'

'I know. What will you do if Horse follows you? Attacks the camp?' I asked.

Haf laughed sadly. 'I hadn't expected to live to see the sunrise. I have no plans. Gwrtheyrn thought we could head west, into Gwent or Powys, maybe. We can take the people from the camp with us. Its women and children and old men. But the boys will grow. The old men will teach them. The Saxons are strong, but their time will come.'

I leaned against her, feeling the warmth of her shoulder, the strength in her heart. I was glad to know that there would be part of this island that my people could call home, even if it was far from me. Even if I never lived to see it.

'What about you?' she asked.

'Tonight I'll be Welsh and take care of Viola. Tomorrow, I don't know.'

'You can come and find us.'

I shook my head. 'They aren't my people, they're yours.'

'Who are your people?'

'You and Viola.'

'Is that enough?'

'It will be.'

Haf reached for her collar bone and pulled free the necklace she wore. I recognised the cross. The one that had belonged to Mam.

'You got it back?' I asked.

'I did. Now you must have it.'

'No. No.' I took her hands and wrapped them in my own. 'No, I can't take it. Keep it with you. Take it west. Remember me, when you look it at. Remember me and Mam and Tad and all that we were. Sing the lullaby Mam sang.'

She pulled me close. I could feel her heart bird-beating against her ribs. 'I'm glad I saw you one last time,' I said.

'Don't say that. It might not be the last.'

I felt that it was, though.

I had no idea what would face me once I went back to the village. The tree of traitors was still hung with ropes.

I said, 'I love you.'

'I love you,' she says.

She kisses me, once, on the lips, my soft, sweet sister. And she is gone, running after Gwrtheyrn. I watch them until they are lost in the dark.

I walk back down the rabbit path alone. The stars and pale moon show the way. And there is bonfire light from the village. I don't think about what's burning. My feet are grey on the rocks. I might be the only person left in the whole world. It might belong to me. Foolish thoughts. Childish thoughts. The hills are full of hunters, even if I can't see them in the dark. My walk quickens.

The village at the bottom is nearing empty. Still, as I get closer to our barn, and hear moans, I wish Viola would suffer with less noise. She is too loud. I want to gag her mouth and push the sounds back down where they come from. Safer that way. Safe is all that matters.

As I pull open the flapping leather door, I stop and look back at the hill. The path is bone white in the black before dawn. I see no people, no movement. I stand on the threshold. It isn't too late to turn back. To follow the path, if that's what I choose.

'Close that, Mai!' Sara snaps. 'Where have you been? Get in here and help.'

58

THE LONGEST DAY of summer is here. Viola clambers into the coracle, her dress wet, her baby splashed, but her face smiling in sunshine. '*Bore da*,' she whispers to the trailing willows.

The stream sings as we bob *ling-di-long* in its waves.
Green boughs bow, grown heavy, bent
Towards the water, trail their
Summer scent of leaf and bark.
'Do you know how to steer?' I ask.

She just laughs. 'No. But we don't know where we're going, do we? So we don't need to steer.'

It's true. The stream is our unknown road. We don't know where it leads, but we know what we leave behind.

I wonder if Haf reached Bryn.

I wonder if Rowan has dried her tears.

I want to believe they have.

'Watch out!' Viola says.

We are floating too close to the bank, tangled roots will trap us, if we don't mind ourselves. I push at them

and the small coracle bobs clear. It's hard to manage, round and seemingly with its own will. But Viola is keeping me on course.

'Will we float for ever, do you think? Or will they notice we're gone?' she asks, lulling the baby in her arms.

'We'll float from here to some small island in the middle of the sea, where bread grows warm on the branches of trees every day of the year,' I tell her.

'Your dreams are sweet,' she says. 'But, I'm sure there will be quern-stones in our future. Wherever we land. It's what happens to girls like us.'

'I don't mind hard work,' I say. I trail my hand in the cool water. Midsummer streams run shallow and I can see the brown and grey pebbles beneath our ripples. The colour of mice. The colour of our clothes. The warm earth-brown of good soil and strong wood and good food roasting.

'You are more foolish than you need to be,' she says.

'And you love me for it.'

'I do.'

I've seen what slaughter looks like. Killing, pain, the depths of cruelty. But the stream is taking us from it. Taking us south.

And, somewhere to the west, I have another sister watching the sun rise over the valley. I imagine her, for one instant, atop her hill with the eagles calling on the wind and the people looking to her to remember their stories.

I know I might never see her again. Hours ago, we said goodbye. But she is alive and free. That is enough.

The world is changing. I can feel it. The stomp of soldiers will shake the land. Britons or Saxons. It hardly matters. Horse won't stop until he has the whole island. Gwrtheyrn will never give it to him. They will lock horns like bulls. We will have to be the mice that scamper between their hooves.

My sisters and I, and the baby boy.

Viola kisses Durwyn softly and begins to sing to him as the stream sweeps us along.

Leabharlanna Poiblí Chathair Baile Átha Cliath
Dublin City Public Libraries

 ACKNOWLEDGEMENTS

This novel would not exist if it weren't for the help of all these wonderful humans, to whom I owe a huge debt of gratitude: Rose, Chantelle and John at SWW-DTP for all their practical support; Lucy Christopher, Bambo Soyinka and Simon Rodway for wisdom and encouragement; everyone who came to PhD Forum or hung out on The Sofa, for listening to me moan; Vanessa Harbour, Wendy Meddour and David Almond for pushing me further; Anna Wilson for knowing about Nouns; Jodie Hodges for everything always; Charlie Sheppard, Kate Grove, Chloe Sackur, Jack Noel and everyone at Andersen for making sure the book was fit to be seen in public, and to my family – *caru chi gyd* – for love and snacks when they were needed.